Amanda McCabe wrote her first romance at sixteen—a vast historical epic starring all her friends as the characters, written secretly during algebra class! She's never since used algebra, but her books have been nominated for many awards, including a RITA® Award, Booksellers' Best Award, National Readers' Choice Award and the HOLT Medallion. In her spare time she loves taking dance classes and collecting travel souvenirs. Amanda lives in New Mexico. Visit her at ammandamccabe.com.

Also by Amanda McCabe

The Queen's Christmas Summons
Tudor Christmas Tidings
'His Mistletoe Lady'

Bancrofts of Barton Park miniseries

The Runaway Countess
Running from Scandal
Running into Temptation
The Wallflower's Mistletoe Wedding

Debutantes in Paris miniseries

Secrets of a Wallflower
The Governess's Convenient Marriage
Miss Fortescue's Protector in Paris

Dollar Duchesses miniseries

His Unlikely Duchess
Playing the Duke's Fiancée

Look out for the next book,
coming soon!

Discover more at millsandboon.co.uk.

PLAYING THE DUKE'S FIANCÉE

Amanda McCabe

MILLS & BOON

First published in Great Britain 2021
by Mills & Boon, an imprint of HarperCollins*Publishers* Ltd,
1 London Bridge Street, London, SE1 9GF

www.harpercollins.co.uk

HarperCollins*Publishers*
1st Floor, Watermarque Building,
Ringsend Road, Dublin 4, Ireland

Large Print edition 2021

Playing the Duke's Fiancée © 2021 Ammanda McCabe

ISBN: 978-0-263-28970-1

11/21

Chapter One

1873

'I wish it would either rain or shine,' Violet Wilkins muttered as she adjusted the silver nitrate plate of her camera.

The indecisive grey-yellow light that trickled through the conservatory glass was all wrong. She glanced at her sister Lily, Duchess of Lennox, who sat posed amid the palm fronds with her baby son on her knee, the snowy white folds of her lace dress and his creamy blankets bright against the dark green. But the murky light made the contrast blurry and hazy.

'It's not at all what I envisaged.'

Lily laughed and bounced the baby, making him laugh, too. How lovely Lily looked since her marriage, Violet thought with a happy but also envious pang, glowing with contentment that softened the elegant edges of her always dutiful, always kind nature. She and Rose, Violet's twin, who was already married despite their age of only eighteen years old, both had that smiling air all the time now.

It made Violet happy because she loved her sisters so fiercely—the daughters of 'Old King Coal' Wilkins had always stuck close together, in the face of their mother's ambition and their father's benign albeit wealthy neglect, of societies that rejected and embraced them in turn, and whenever desires turned and turned again all around them. Her sisters were always there, always loved her.

Even though Lily was a duchess now, and Rose was Lady James Grantley, sister-in-law to a duke, while Violet was still just Miss Violet Wilkins, which had never and would never change.

If only that wretched light *would* change…

'Oh, Vi, even you can't control the weather,' Lily said. 'We're lucky to have any sunlight at all.'

'This wretched English weather,' Violet

murmured. She'd been in England for many months now, staying behind with Lily after their mother saw two of her daughters married and then sailed back to Newport. England *was* wretched in some ways—the food, the damp chill of the air, the quiet whispers in stuffy ballrooms about 'unfortunate' American manners. But there were her sisters and nice strong tea, fascinating and picturesque history everywhere she turned, art and music, and lovely images she could turn into photographs. Here, no one cared if she wandered outside all day with her sketchbook, finding scenes to choreograph and photograph later. Her darling brother-in-law Aidan even let her set up a darkroom in an old potting shed so she didn't have to rely on a London studio to develop her plates.

No, England was home now, for better or worse. She couldn't envisage going back to stifling New York or Newport now. For all its hierarchy and gossip, there was a strange freedom to England that Violet had never known before.

If she could just find a way to hold on to it. Everyone expected her to marry now, with her sisters both wed and her fortune just waiting in a bank vault, but Violet couldn't even begin to imagine wanting to marry. Running a vast house like Lily, helping a husband's academic career like Rose with her Jamie and his classics studies. Violet's time, her energy, would be pulled away from her darkroom, bit by bit, until she had nothing left for her art. She had to work hard and steadily to master the complicated process of light and chemicals necessary to produce the images she saw in her mind. The sense of shadow that created the image of three-dimensionality, of life itself caught forever.

She was a long way from where she wanted to be, from bringing the images she imagined to reality. A long way from her great dream of being included in the Photographic Society of London's annual exhibit. She hadn't yet found the perfect subject to capture their attention. It would take much practice. But she was determined. She dared not even think yet of the vaunted Solar Club, which admitted only twenty-five members and barely any women at all, but some day...

'I heard that the French use phosphorescent flashes to create light effects,' she said. 'Perhaps if I…'

Lily laughed. 'Oh, no, Vi! That would frighten poor Babykins to bits and possibly set fire to the castle.'

Violet smiled at her nephew and went to adjust the edge of the long white wool blanket as she waited for the light to change. He gave her a precious, gummy grin and grabbed her finger. How she adored him! He had become her favourite photographic subject, his merry and patient little nature so perfect for her camera, such a joy to be around.

'I would never want to scare my little pumpkin,' she said. 'And I doubt I could! He's such an imperturbable little soul.'

'That he is, my wee angel,' Lily said with a Madonna-like smile. She bounced him in her arms, making him chortle. 'My happy little soul.'

'Just like his sweet mama,' Violet told him, checking the light against Lily's hair, darker than Violet's bright red and much deeper than the wispy platinum curls sprouting on the baby's egg-like head. 'You're the best boy in all the world, aren't you, my darlingest nephew?'

He laughed and kicked, reaching his plump arms up to his auntie.

'How he adores you,' Lily said happily. 'You must find someone nice and give him some cousins soon, Vi!'

Startled, Violet reared back as if suddenly burned. Of course, she was often asked about marital plans, in every letter from her mother, from Lily's mother-in-law, the formidable Dowager Duchess, and even, very gently, from Rose, who thought every marriage must be as seemingly blissful as her own. And it often came up in conversation with all the London mamas who were certain their sons would make the best use of her Wilkins money. But never from Lily.

Violet tried to laugh. 'You will have to look to Rose for nieces and nephews, Lily.'

'But Rose lives so far away! They never leave London. And she and Jamie are so wrapped up in their books, not to mention that Rose's beauty is becoming more admired every day. She's in demand among society now. We never see them. Babykins does need someone to be his friend.'

'What if I married someone and lived far away?' Violet said lightly. She went back to her camera, trying to ignore the fidgety discomfort such conversations always gave her. 'I might go off to India or Africa or something.'

Lily gasped. 'Did you accept Colonel Hastings, then?'

Violet laughed. She had many suitors, none of them quite right, none of them capturing her imagination, and Colonel Hastings was one of them. He was a widower in the colonial service who made no secret of the fact that he needed a wife before he went back to the Punjab or wherever it was. He was rather dull, but he was better than Lord Anderbrook, who only talked about cricket, and that dour Mr Frye, who lamented his crumbling Jacobean manor house. At least Colonel Hastings did have interesting tales of his travels, and India would make for some intriguing photographic studies. But he was quite thirty years older than her. If she had to marry, she wanted someone exciting, or at least very interesting.

'No, I'm not engaged to the Colonel, or anyone else,' she said. 'I'm much too busy right now.'

Lily sighed. 'Yes. I suppose we should get your Court presentation finished before we think about marriage. Has your gown arrived from Worth yet?'

Violet shook her head. 'Not yet.' The presentation was another thing that interested Lily far more than Violet, but at least, unlike marriage, it would be over quickly. Once she got past the lessons in proper curtsying and all the dress fittings, it would be only one day packed into the stuffy palace with all the other young ladies trussed up in trains and feathers and pearls. Dull, but perhaps it would open more doors, let her meet more people, go more places. Artistic, interesting people and places.

Lily shook her head. 'It must arrive soon! Or you won't have your proper train to practise your walk.'

Violet laughed. 'I do know how to walk, Lily!'

'Backwards, with a three-foot train?'

Lily did have a point. Violet had no desire to topple over in front of the Prince and Princess of Wales once she made her curtsy. She might be called 'The Wild Wilkins', but she didn't want to embarrass Lily.

'I'll tie a tablecloth around my waist and we'll practise walking the gallery after tea,' she promised. 'If I can just get the perfect angle on this photograph first...'

The baby was beginning to fuss, and Lily popped a teething ring into his mouth, but they knew it was only a matter of time before Nurse would have to be called. For a long moment, as Violet adjusted the tripod, there was only the sound of his soft baby sighs and the drip of water on the plants, the heady, earthy, rosy scent all around them.

Then Lily spoke again, just as Violet dared hope the dreaded marriage talk was put aside for the moment.

'But I did hear that Aidan's old friend, the Duke of Charteris, is returning home soon,' Lily said casually. Too casually. 'His estate at Bourne Abbey is not far away at all. And they say he's interested in a grand political career. He'll be wanting a most intelligent wife.'

'The Duke of Charteris?' Violet gasped. 'I'm surprised Aidan would be friends with someone like that.'

Lily's eyes narrowed. 'You've met him?'

Violet shook her head. 'Not at all. I just hear—things.' She remembered whispers about the Duke of Charteris, the wealthy and powerful owner of one of the oldest estates in the area, which had been in his family since the Reformation. She had been very intrigued by engraved images of the old abbey and by the glimpse of towers and chimneys she sometimes got in rides over Aidan's estate. They would make lovely photographs. But the Duke himself, though young for his title, as Aidan was, seemed rather fearsome. Ambitious, intelligent, serious. Handsome but humourless.

Though, to be strictly fair, most of the tales she'd heard had been whispered by a young lady at a garden party, a Miss Lowestoft, who seemed as if she might have a small axe to grind with the Duke. Perhaps she'd set her cap at him? That was where Violet first heard the 'Duke of Bore' title, but he *did* sound serious and tiresome. Not the kind of man she would want to be friends with, or marry, even if she could then live near Lily.

'I haven't met him yet, either,' Lily said. 'He was abroad at the time of our wedding. But Aidan seems to like him. He's travelled a great deal, though not quite in the same adventuresome way as Aidan. They say he is very intelligent and steady.' She paused. 'And handsome.' Before he'd returned to England following his older brother's death—when he had met and married Lily—Aidan had been a renowned explorer, wandering alone through deserts and jungles. 'I doubt he can be *very* dull. And maybe someone with a steady nature would do you some good.'

Violet sighed. She'd heard that all her life, every time she tore her skirt climbing over a fence or fell from a galloping horse or danced until dawn, all while laughing too loudly or giving her opinion too freely. Someone steady would give her life balance, they said. A strong husband was clearly needed. 'You sound rather like Mother.'

Lily laughed. 'What a terrible insult, Vi!

I've a mind not to shelter you under my roof any longer. But just this once, she might be right. A good, steady, calm husband could be a help to you, a fine partner in life. If you love him.'

'Well, I have never been in love. Not like you and Aidan, or Rose and Jamie.' Violet felt a sudden, sharp, unwelcome twist at those words, at the thought that she had never known such contentment as her sisters. She covered it by moving her tripod again. 'And I'm sure I never will be. I just want to get into the Photographic Society, or even perhaps the Solar Club.'

And to do that, she needed to perfect her technique, find just the right exciting subject to grab their attention. A woman's artistic work had to be twice as good, twice as interesting, twice as *artistic*, twice as hard to ignore, in order to get half as far.

The light at last shifted, the clouds scurrying away to leave the sun clear and shining and silvery, falling perfectly on Lily's sleek hair and white skirts. Violet happily left the marriage talk behind to focus on the image before her. She gestured for Lily to hold up the baby just so.

She did love taking portraits above all, capturing the essence of people on her plates, their expression, their style. She wanted to catch all the beauty around her, freeze it for all time, remember the feeling of the light and life itself. It was almost like magic.

'All right, now, Lily, hold very still. And one—two—three.' She released the brass lens, just as the baby howled.

As she finished and Lily stood to stretch her legs and swing the baby in a playful arc to make him laugh again, Aidan appeared. He was such a good match to her sister, so tall and golden and full of energy. He bounded up to his family to kiss them. Lily had certainly found her own 'steadying influence', her other half. Violet very much doubted there was such a man out there for her.

'I'm sorry to interrupt, Vi,' he said, contrite when he saw she was still behind her camera. Unlike most men, Aidan took her work as seriously as he did his own and revelled in studying her finished images.

'Not at all! We're just coming to an end.

I'll have to run off to the darkroom now,' she answered.

'Do you have just a moment?' he said. 'I have a bit of news and I think you should both hear it.'

Lily clutched the baby closer. 'Bad news, darling?'

'Not at all. Quite the opposite.' He held up a letter, close-written, copperplate lines on thick, creamy paper, edged in dark red with a gold crest. 'A letter from the private secretary at Buckingham Palace. We're requested to be among the party accompanying Prince Alfred to St Petersburg for his marriage to Grand Duchess Maria in January.'

'St Petersburg!' Lily gasped. She handed the baby to Aidan and took the letter, scanning its message. 'Oh, I have longed to see it. The golden domes and frozen rivers, the ballrooms! And a royal wedding? But whatever shall I wear? There's barely time to order new clothes!'

Aidan laughed. 'I take it you consent, then, Lily?'

'Of course! One must take advantage of

some of the perks of being a duchess, you know.'

'How exciting for you, Lily darling,' Violet said, feeling joy and envy strangely mingled.

'And you, Vi,' Aidan said.

'Me?'

'Oh, yes. The invitation includes you, since you are to be presented soon, and Lily will need a suitable companion.'

'Vi, just imagine!' Lily cried. 'Us together in St Petersburg. Skating on the Neva, dancing at balls with princes...meeting the Tsar. The Wilkins sisters! What will Mother say? Oh, I must send for the dressmakers and milliners at once. You can wear your presentation gown at the wedding, I think, but I must have something new.'

She rushed out of the conservatory, leaving Aidan with the now fussing baby and making him and Violet laugh. Violet still felt dizzy with the grand news. She'd read all about the wedding plans, of course, the highest-ranking royal bride in generations, the lavish plans in Russia, the buzz over it all. She'd never imagined she would see it for herself.

'Am I really to go with you?' she whispered.

Aidan grinned. 'Of course. It will be a very busy time, I'm afraid, lots of protocol to remember. They're even stricter about such things at the Winter Palace than here. I will need your help and so will Lily. It should be lots of fun, too, though.' His smile widened. 'I know you'll like the fun parts.'

Violet laughed. Oh, yes, she *did* enjoy fun. As Lily said, there would be balls and skating, no doubt sleigh rides and banquets and fascinating people and lovely clothes. But she feared there would be so much boring etiquette, enough to make her Court presentation pale. She dreaded embarrassing her sister. Still, at least it would not be boring. It would be something to remember always. 'When do we leave?'

'Very soon, so get your wardrobes together! We'll go to Berlin for a few days with the Prince and Princess of Wales to meet his sister Crown Princess Vicky, and then on to Russia. It will be deep winter there, I'm afraid.'

Violet thought of the sables and the silver

fox stole in her wardrobe, sent by her father last Christmas. They were probably nothing compared to what Grand Duchess Maria would have, but warm and cosy nonetheless. 'I'm sure we will be just fine. More than fine! It will be a great lark indeed.'

'I knew you and Lily would think so. Life is never dull with the Wilkins sisters. There *is* just one thing…' Aidan said this as Lily came back to join them.

'What?' his wife whispered. They both glanced at the baby and her eyes widened. 'We'll have to leave him!'

'Not for long,' Aidan hurried to assure her. 'Only for a very few weeks. I have arranged to come home directly after the wedding, when the couple leaves for their honeymoon. If you like, he can stay with my mother while we're gone. I know she's a tartar…'

'But she does love him,' Lily said sadly. She nodded and smoothed the baby's wispy hair. 'I know we must do our duty, and Russia in winter is no place for him.'

Aidan kissed her and gave her a reassuring smile. 'Not for long.'

As Aidan left to take the baby to his nurse,

Violet took her plates and hurried outside to her darkroom. She had learned her art via instructions in photographic pamphlets, on the old-fashioned, very complicated collodion wet plate process. She had somehow persuaded her father to buy her a bulky, heavy camera and she suspected he was probably quite sorry for that now; she knew he'd only bought it in the hope that it would distract her from mischief. But once the newfangled dry plate technique became available, she had jumped on it and found someone at an art gallery to show her how it all worked.

There was much less messing about with chemicals, much less ruination of images. The camera itself was far less cumbersome, more portable, and the exposures were easier to control. It was all so much easier. But Violet still enjoyed the quiet moments developing the images in her small darkroom, watching magic happen right in front of her. Magic that she created herself.

As she watched Lily's pale, oval face come to life, it suddenly struck her that a series of royal portraits would surely be just the thing to catch the attention of the Photographic

Society! The Grand Duchess and Prince Alfred, the Prince and Princess of Wales, maybe even the Tsar and the bride's many Grand Duke brothers, in all their wedding finery. It would be perfect. And they did say the Prince had inherited an interest in photography from his late father, the Prince Consort. If she could meet with him...

She would have to find a way to persuade them. She just had to!

Chapter Two

'William! Dearest brother. You're home at last. How very brown you have become under the Egyptian sun. It does suit you.'

'Hello, Honoria. That does tend to happen under the hot sun. But I went there to work, not to go sightseeing.' William, Duke of Charteris, kissed his sister's cheek and gazed behind her at the rows of servants, waiting to greet his return to Bourne Abbey.

He tilted back his head to study the house, so placid and steady under the grey English sky, unchanging, perfect, sheltering, just as it always had been. The Palladian mansion his grandfather had created hid the ancient walls of the old abbey behind its facade, pale stone juxtaposed against crumbling brown brick and cloister walkways, a double set of steps soaring up to symmetrical windows draped in green brocade, chimneys spilling welcoming silvery smoke.

He'd thought of it all so often on his travels. It had seemed like a dream, unreal even though it had been his world since birth, had always been his birthright, his responsibility. His whole reason for being. The house, the vast gardens, the farms, the hundreds of people under its shelter. All his great task in life.

For a while, under that sun, with sights older even than Bourne, he had felt—different. Lighter. Out of himself. He'd laughed and danced, climbed the pyramids under the sunset light to watch the moon rise, to drink champagne at their pinnacle, no longer the 'Duke of Bore' that he knew some called him at home. There had been work, of course, hard work, laying the groundwork for the political career his late parents had always wanted for him, but there had been fun, too. He wasn't quite sure he'd ever grasped the meaning of *fun* before.

Now that was all over, Bourne was before him again, always waiting for him, always needing him. He could almost hear the ornate iron gates at the foot of the winding, white gravel drive clanging shut.

But there was love, too. A deep, great swelling of it for his home, which had been there all his life, never changing. He belonged to it far more than it could ever belong to him.

Honoria took his arm and walked with him up the marble steps towards the open front doors and the waiting, wide-eyed staff, a great black-and-white double line of them.

'Glad to be home, Will darling?' she said.

'Very. You've kept it up very well, I see.'

Honoria laughed. She'd been widowed now for a few years and visited Bourne whenever she could. It was her home, too, and he always knew he could count on her. 'I did my best. You'll find one or two tiny little redecorating schemes inside, nothing too extreme. Just because Bourne has been here for centuries, that doesn't mean we must always put up with mildew!'

He glanced down at her, startled. Honoria was ultra-fashionable, one of the leaders of style in London. Her dark hair, so like his own, was twisted on top of her head in elaborate braids and curls fastened with pearl combs, and her lilac silk-and-cream-lace gown was straight out of *Les Modes*. He could only wonder what she and her town decorators might have wrought in Bourne's corridors and darkened staterooms. Even his mother, the sainted late Duchess, still venerated in the neighbourhood, hadn't dared touch one brocade curtain or soot-stained painting.

'I said don't worry,' she said with a laugh. 'Nothing too modern, I promise.'

'Your Grace,' Higgins, the ancient butler, said, stepping forward with a low bow. 'Welcome home.'

'Thank you, Higgins. I'm very glad to be here. I've missed you all.' They greeted the line of servants, from the housekeeper to the tweenies and the old man who wound the hundreds of clocks, which took a great deal of time, but at last William was alone with his sister in the drawing room with a tray of sherry.

'You see,' Honoria said, gesturing around the large, cube-like room with its old, soaring plastered ceiling, its two marble fireplaces crowned with the gilded ducal arms and held aloft by carved gods and goddesses, the clusters of sofas and chairs and small alabaster tables scattered about the faded carpets. 'I haven't changed much. Just some new upholstery, new glazing at the windows to keep out those infernal draughts. I brought those paintings down from the attic and had them reframed. I thought they were much more cheerful than Papa's old dead pheasant pictures, so dreadfully depressing.'

'Indeed.' He had to admit he did like the changes, the paler colours in the new satin cushions, the smiling portraits and green landscapes on the striped green silk walls. He glimpsed a gleaming new grand piano set near the newly glazed windows, along with a gold harp. 'Those are new, too, I think. Where is Mama's old pianoforte?'

'Oh, these are Pauline's. You remember her, I'm sure. Cousin Rannock's girl. I've been looking after her while he's out in India. She's ready to be presented at Court.' Honoria poured out two drinks in the cut-crystal sherry glasses and handed him the larger one. 'So sad, her mother dying so young, and me with no daughters of my own...'

William smiled at her and sat down on one of the newly covered sofas by the fireplace. He had to admit that they were quite comfortable, where once he had sunk down on the old springs. He was happy for his sister; he knew her lack of children had been a sorrow. 'I'm sure you're having a thoroughly awful time, organising clothes and parties and such.'

Honoria laughed. 'I do so enjoy *organising.* Speaking of which…'

He froze with his glass half-raised. He knew that tone of hers. 'Oh, no, Honoria.'

'Oh, yes, Will. Pauline is going to be presented at the next Drawing Room, and it would be so lovely for her if you came with us. Your connections to the royal family would be very useful to her, and it would do you good to show your face at Court again— if you really do want a political career. And there will be eligible ladies there, you know. I did leave most of the redecorating here for the next Duchess.'

William swallowed a large gulp of the sherry, wishing it was something stronger. He imagined the crowds of a Drawing Room, the stuffy air, the giggling young ladies and their beady-eyed mothers, the long, dull hours of waiting about at a formal presentation. He still hadn't quite recovered from Honoria's, years ago. 'I don't really see how such an afternoon would do me good. Or Pauline.'

'Of course it would, silly! I saw dear Bertie at dinner at Lady Riverby's a few weeks ago and he was so full of compliments about your work in Egypt. He'll want to hear all about it, after you show your face and remind him that you're home. And half the Court will be gone soon, off to the snowy wilds of St Petersburg for Affie's wedding.'

'Oh, yes. The Grand Duchess. I had forgotten about that.'

'So the sooner you see Bertie the better. And besides…'

He didn't quite trust the gleam in her eyes. 'Besides?'

'Well, what I said about a suitable duchess. You don't want the best debs of the Season to escape, do you? The prettiest and smartest will be snapped up right away.'

He stared down into the dregs in his glass,

swirling the amber liquid. 'I am in no great hurry to marry, Honoria.'

'You should be! Darling, you are over thirty now. I know you've been terribly busy, but tick-tock. Bourne needs a mistress, an heir, and you need the help that the right wife could give you. She could look after the estate when you're busy at Westminster, be a good hostess for you. It's so very important.'

'You can be my hostess.'

Honoria gave a little snort. 'I have my own home, in case you've forgotten! My own duties. I am very happy to help out for now, but I haven't infinite time. Besides, don't you want a companion? A partner?'

He thought of their parents, seldom speaking, seldom smiling at each other. Bourne had been their lives, not each other. 'Of course, I know all that. But it must be the right person.' Once, long ago, when he was young and foolish, he'd thought he had found her. The Honourable Daisy Dennison. So pretty, so flighty, so full of laughter and gaiety.

But he had been wrong. Terribly wrong. And he had realised that duty was everything, his whole life. Even one moment of frivolity in Cairo couldn't change that. He was the Duke of Charteris and he could never forget that.

Not that Honoria was wrong. His first duty was indeed to secure the future of Bourne, to see to his family's security and honour. A wife was necessary for that and one day soon he would have to find a lady of good sense and breeding, of good family, who knew how the ducal world worked and who would not expect too much from him. A lady who would be his partner in the business of the estate, be a good mother to his heirs. He couldn't imagine finding such a rational being in the crowds of giggling, romance-minded debs at the Drawing Room.

He went to pour another drink. 'I will start looking next year, perhaps, when things have settled down after the royal wedding.'

'You cannot keep putting it off, Will. It was very sad, what happened with Daisy all those years ago. Bourne has been without a duchess too long. You are more concerned with duty than anyone I know. I've been giving it a great deal of thought...'

William laughed. 'I am sure you have. Do you have lists?'

'You know I do. Lists are the best tool of any organised mind.' Honoria pulled out a sheaf of papers from her sewing box, spilling pieces of half-finished embroidery on to the faded carpet. 'I also have many friends in London and I've been looking over their sisters and cousins. No one is *quite* perfect, I fear, but there are some good possibilities. The Marquess of Wolverton's daughter is making her debut, for instance, and Miss Mayne. She only has the teeniest bit of a squint...'

'And you once said Lady Marienne has the worst dress sense in all of London.'

Honoria rustled her papers. 'Well, such things can easily be taken in hand, you know, with a few visits to my dressmaker. And her father will soon be head of the Foreign Office, they say. So very useful.' She narrowed her eyes as she looked up at William. 'Even Aidan is married now, you know. And has a child and heir.'

'Aidan,' he said with a laugh, taking another sip of his drink. 'It is quite hard to believe.'

'You know it's no jest. It was quite a lovely wedding. I forgot you've been gone so very long. Even though the new Duchess is American, she is very beautiful and well mannered, and so rich. His castle roof has been saved. They do seem terribly fond of each other, so sweet.' She fanned herself with her lists.

'Honoria. Bourne is not in need of American dollars.'

'No, but maybe *you* would like a bit of American spirit in your life. It's become all the rage, you know, American girls. There's Jennie Jerome, who they say will marry Randolph Churchill, and I have heard Lord Mandeville is courting some wild girl from a Louisiana plantation. And you don't seem interested in anyone on my lists.'

William couldn't think of anything worse than wild American 'spirits' around Bourne. 'An American would scarcely know where to begin when it comes to a place like Bourne or Charteris House. The way things have been done here for centuries, the ins and outs of political life...'

'Oh, well, have it your own way. But do say you'll come with Pauline and me to London. She could so use your support, and I will enjoy your company.'

'I'll think about it, Honoria. And now I think I'll go upstairs and change, have a quick ride to inspect the home farm before dinner.'

Honoria knew when to leave him alone with his thoughts. She nodded and picked up her embroidery. 'Of course, darling. We can go over the estate books after dinner. I think you'll be quite pleased.'

William knew he would be, he thought as he made his way upstairs to the Duke's chamber just beyond the old Elizabethan Gallery. Honoria was a sensible, smart manager and really, if he was going to let someone find him a wife, she would be fine for the job. Her social circle was wide, and she knew well the demands of running Bourne. He knew it had to be his task alone, though, to find someone quiet and dutiful, who knew what was expected of such a title and responsibility.

In his chamber, his valet had already been unpacking, and riding clothes were laid out for him. As he shrugged out of his travel suit, he glanced in the dressing table mirror. He looked the same as ever, the same as the portrait of his father that hung in the long line of dukes in the gallery: dark, almost black hair, high cheekbones, green eyes. He didn't look too bad, he thought with a laugh. Surely there was some sensible lady somewhere in England who wouldn't mind taking him on.

His gaze caught on a midnight blue gleam amid the brushes arranged across the table, a jewelled scarab he had found in a Cairo marketplace. He picked it up, turning it on his palm, and for an instant he was back there, in the shimmering heat, the warm, spice-scented air. A moment of heady freedom. That was behind him now. The reality was England and Bourne, searching for brides, duty.

He dropped the scarab and walked away to take those duties up once more.

William rode Zeus, his favourite gelding, hard over the well-beaten paths through the ancient woods of the Bourne estate. He remembered long hours tramping the same ways with his father and the gamekeepers, learning every inch of the estate, all of its history and meaning.

'This will all be your responsibility one day, William,' his father would tell him gruffly, pointing out the game hides, the fields, the tenant cottages, the towering chimneys of the house itself in the distance. 'The family name, the future of it all, is in your hands once I am gone. You are my only son. I must know that you can be utterly relied upon to see it safe.'

Even as a child, William had been able to see the solemnity in his father's eyes, the worried lines around his mouth. His father's own brother, the late Uncle Henry, had been utterly unreliable. He had even eloped with the lady meant for his own nephew, the roué. William heard his parents' whispers even from his mother's sickroom when he was young, the tense anger and worry over all the money his uncle gambled away, the loose women, the rumours that floated out of Monte Carlo and Venice. William couldn't understand it all then, but he heard well the worry of it all. The despair. His uncle threatened the first object of all their lives—the prosperity and future of the dukedom and of Bourne.

William had vowed then that he would never be like his uncle, never cause his family and all those who depended on them a moment's worry. He was alone in the world; he alone could maintain it all. And he had never faltered in that promise, not through Eton and Oxford, his frail mother's death, his uncle's scandalous demise in Marseilles and finally his father's death, which left it all in William's hands.

He had repaired the house, which had been rather neglected after his mother's death, saw to Honoria's schooling and marriage, maintained the farms and tenants and servants, and took a few steps towards political influence, though by then he was still only barely out of school himself. There hadn't been a moment for a free breath and never one for laughter or fun.

A duke could not afford fun.

He turned Zeus out of the thicket of trees and on to a high clearing, drawing the horse in so they could sit for a moment and watch the house, so peaceful and eternal in the distance. As much as he had enjoyed his travels, he had missed home. Those familiar walls, a shelter since birth to so many people, were his to maintain for now and in the future. He could not fail.

He laughed. No wonder Honoria decried his lack of 'fun'. There was simply no space for it here. No way to give even an inch or give in to a baser nature as poor Uncle Henry had.

But she was right about something else, too. He did need a wife. Bourne needed a duchess, especially if he was to rise in politics and bring honour to his family. He had put it off long enough.

Oh, there had been a woman or two in the past, all knowing their place in his life and his in theirs. Finding relief in each other's company for a few hours. And they were still friends. 'How ladies do love you, Will, though who knows why,' Honoria had once teased. 'You could have a pretty wife with one snap of your fingers!'

But who wanted a spaniel, summoned with a snap, for a wife?

Someone dutiful, yes, who knew the depth

of the task she took on, who was equal to it. But someone with ideas of her own, too. Someone who could improve Bourne. Who could make him smile sometimes.

Was there a ballroom or tea party in London where such a lady could be found? He remembered Honoria urging him to attend the royal Drawing Room. He closed his eyes, imagining a long line of girls waiting to try on the strawberry leaf coronet, and he laughed. That seemed as good a matchmaking plan as any.

He wheeled Zeus around and galloped away from the view of the house, along a rougher path that skirted the fields. He had certainly missed this; there was nothing like a fast gallop on a misty English afternoon, no one in sight, just the endless rolling fields, the smell of fresh air, burning leaves somewhere in the distance, the crisp wind catching at his uncovered hair. The horse moved beneath him as if they were one, wild and free, if only for that moment.

He drew up at the top of a hill just at the edge of Bourne land. Beyond a low grey stone wall was Aidan's estate. He should go call on his old friend, see how he was settling into English life again after all his years of exploring, wandering, seeing so many wonders. Once, William had quite envied Aidan that freedom, dreamed of what it must be like. But Aidan had been a second son, not meant to shoulder the burden of a dukedom until his brother died. William hoped his friend didn't feel trapped now.

Yet he had a wife now, a pretty American, Honoria said, even a child. Perhaps Aidan wasn't so unhappy after all.

As William studied the house in the distance, his attention was caught by a bright flash of movement in the grey-green meadows. He shielded his eyes from the glare of the light and saw it was a lady making her way slowly towards the castle. She wore a blue-and-white-striped gown, the ruffled hem trailing behind her. Her red hair blew in the breeze like a banner, uncovered by any hat, and she dragged a strange contraption with her, a tripod and a medium-sized box with a handle. He remembered men with just such a thing at the pyramids, taking photographs, but he had never seen a lady with one.

Aidan's wife? She did seem eccentric enough to be an American. Yet strangely, William hoped she was not. Something about her, that waving, brilliant hair, like something in a Millais painting, that strong, free independence of her stride and her fearless posture, caught at something inside of him. He longed to ride down to her, to see her face clearly, to hear the laughter from her wide red lips that the wind seemed to snatch away.

Who *was* she? What was she doing, so close yet so far away? He watched, enraptured, as she waved one arm as if to test the wind then threw back her head to look up into the sky. The lace-edged sleeve fell back, revealing a slender arm and a gold bracelet. As she looked up into the meagre light, William could see her more clearly, her face illuminated like a cameo in the grey day. Her chin was lightly pointed, her cheekbones high and elegant, her full lips curved in a whisper of a smile. He could even glimpse a spray of freckles over her straight nose. Her pose indicated intelligence, defiance, concentration.

She shook her head, took up her equipment and hurried away. William wanted to call after her, follow her, but he stayed frozen where he was. No lady on a country ramble wanted a gentleman to chase her down, surely even one as bold as that redhead obviously was. He was never in the business of frightening ladies, not even one who intrigued him so. And he was so rarely *intrigued*.

Besides, she might indeed be Aidan's new wife. Something sank in him at such a thought. Not that he himself could marry an American. He had already told himself that.

He spun Zeus around and galloped back towards Bourne. It was nearly dinnertime and perhaps Honoria would know something about the red-headed lady. He feared he wouldn't be able to get her out of his mind for quite a while.

Violet had to stop on her path back to the house, caught by the afternoon light shimmering like rose gold on the fields. It seemed to ripple like some rare beaded fabric. There was no time to set up her camera, so she took a sketchbook from her satchel and sat down to try to catch it in quick pencil strokes to remember later.

As she drew in the impression of light, caught up in images of rare beauty, she suddenly realised she wasn't quite alone in the silent afternoon. A figure on horseback appeared on the pathway below her perch, outlined in sunlight that turned him golden, like a pagan idol. Violet shielded her eyes to study him.

And what she saw made her gasp. That glimmering light made him seem truly godlike, with tousled dark hair over a noble brow, riding so smoothly and carelessly, as if one with the horse, tall and lean and powerful. She wondered if he was truly real at all.

For an instant, her fingers froze on the pencil, as if time had stalled. Then she drew even faster, trying to capture his image before he rode away. She'd seldom seen anything quite so beautiful.

As she sketched an impression of his features, chiselled as if sculpted just so beneath the brim of his hat, he suddenly raised his hand and waved at her. Violet was tempted to duck, but then she told herself sternly that there was no way he could see her blush from there, no way he could see that she drew his face so she could always remember it. Instead she waved back and he laughed before he galloped onwards. That laughter made him even more handsome, made him glow from within.

Who on earth *was* he?

Chapter Three

'Oh, Vi, do sit still! It will all be quite crooked if you don't, and everything must be perfect,' Lily beseeched, watching from across the bedchamber as the hairdresser pulled and prodded at Violet's aching head.

'Oh, Lily, dear, I've been sitting here forever,' Violet muttered. She fiddled with the items scattered across her dressing table, the silver-capped pots of creams and powders, the ribbons and engraved brushes and perfume flagons. Silver-framed photographs of her sisters gazed back at her, happier, freer moments at the seaside and in the garden, where no one tortured them with knife-like hairpins.

Where she could glimpse the most astonishing men sometimes.

'I told you, perfection takes time and nothing less than perfection will do for today,' Lily said. She was already dressed, perfect as she always was in silvery-lilac satin embroidered with pearls and sequins in lily patterns over her skirt and the three-yard, fur-trimmed train. Her brown hair was swept high and fastened with the three feathers, held with the famous Lennox diamond-and-pearl tiara. Violet would wear the diadem her mother had given Lily for her wedding.

Violet winced as another pin pierced her scalp.

'My art cannot be rushed, *mademoiselle*,' the little French coiffeur muttered, his waxed moustache quivering, as he ruthlessly twisted up another red curl. 'I have seldom faced such a challenge...'

'The flowers have arrived!' Rose cried, rushing in followed by maids bearing fragrant cardboard boxes. Violet's twin would stay behind at Grantley House to put the finishing touches on that evening's ball, but she, too, was impeccably dressed, in a grey sateen skirt and starched shirtwaist, a red Indian shawl draped over her shoulders. The perfect scholar's wife.

'Oh, thank heavens for that,' Lily gasped. 'One can't go to the palace without the right bouquet.' She lifted out the large, trailing arrangements, white roses interspersed with violets for Violet and a sheaf of lilies for her. 'Did the flowers for the drawing room at Grantley arrive, too?'

'Oh, yes, I was just there and the florist's assistants are hard at work.' Rose clapped her hands as Lily held the bouquet up to the gown displayed on the dress form as seamstresses put the finishing touches on the hem. 'It is quite perfect.'

Violet tried to twist around to look, too, but the hairdresser sternly held her in place. It *was* a beautiful dress, she had to admit that. From Worth in Paris, creamy white, swathed from one puffed shoulder to hem with tulle dotted with satin violets that twinkled with amethysts and pearls and clear beads that shone like tiny diamonds. More velvet violets lay across the low neckline like a wreath.

Once she was at last dressed, her satins and tulles smoothed and the requisite three feathers fastened in her hair with the tiara and a row of pearls around her neck, Violet stood very still in front of the looking glass. She could hardly believe it was *her* standing there, this slim lady so perfect in her jewels. She hardly dared move an inch, scared she would ruin it all, especially since they had been up since dawn creating it all. She was sure she would disappoint her sisters, as usual, with some wild jape.

'Oh, Vi, how beautiful you look.' Lily sighed, dabbing at her eyes with a lacy handkerchief. Violet was sure no one could look as beautiful as Lily herself, the perfect Duchess. The perfect lady Violet could never be. 'If only Mother could see you!'

Violet gave a choked laugh. 'She would only think I had been switched by fairies or something.'

Lily and Rose laughed, too, and they kissed Violet's cheeks, careful not to mess up her fine feathers. 'Well, as long as they wait a few hours to trade you back again. I know the palace will be tedious, but it will all soon be over and then you can do just as you like.'

Violet frowned. If what she *liked* was to marry an Englishman, or go to Newport to let her mother brag about her daughter being presented at Court, maybe Lily was right. But that was assuredly not what Violet wanted.

Though maybe her sister was right after all. The more famous people Violet met, the more likely she was to find good subjects for her photographs. Maybe it would not be wasted time at all.

As she smoothed her satin-and-tulle skirt, Rose handed her the long kid gloves. Only Lily and Violet would go to the palace, but Rose had to be prepared to host the ball afterwards. If Jamie could just be lured from his library to play host.

'Oh, Vi.' Rose sighed. 'You are so very beautiful, truly. Like a princess. No—a queen!'

'Queen of a desert island, maybe,' Violet said. But she was secretly pleased. Though they were twins, she'd always been sure that Rose was the beauty, dainty and quiet and bookish, and Lily of course was a goddess who had captured the heart of a handsome duke. But today, after all those preparations, she had to admit she wasn't so bad herself. It would never do to subject herself to this every day, as surely someone like Princess Alexandra must. But for once it was rather fun.

Rose and a maid each took a hand and carefully rolled on the skintight kid gloves, fastening the tiny pearls to her elbows. Lily handed her the pearl drop earrings from her own jewel case and Rose handed her a fan, which was Brussels lace with a mother-of-pearl handle.

'There...' Rose sighed dreamily '...now you are absolutely perfect.'

'Until I put my foot through my train while walking backwards from Their Highnesses,' Violet teased.

Rose and Lily gasped. 'Oh, no!'

Lily giggled. 'I nearly did so myself when the Dowager Duchess presented me after I married Aidan. I was so very nervous, I was sure I would faint!'

'You would never have dared in front of the Dowager Duchess!'

Lily shook her head vehemently. Lily might be Duchess of Lennox now, and her mother-in-law a countess after her remarriage, but Agnes was always *the* Duchess. Perfect and formidable, behind all her style and airy charm. Lily was lucky her mother-in-law had gone off to run a new estate far away in Scotland, leaving Lily in charge of all the Lennox houses. But the Countess and the Earl were meant to be at Rose's ball that night.

As Lily helped Violet step into her pearl-encrusted, white high-heeled shoes, Rose cried, 'I almost forgot! A letter from Papa and Mother came this morning. I forgot with the excitement of the florists.' She took a pale blue missive sealed with their mother's distinctive green wax from the pocket of her skirt.

'A letter? How odd. We just got a telegram yesterday,' Lily said, fussing with the feathers in her own hair and straightening her diamond necklace.

'I suppose Mother has more advice to give,' Rose said. 'It must be quite killing her not to be here!'

Curious, Violet reached for a penknife and cut open the letter. She read it with growing horror.

'Oh, no!' she gasped when she reached the second page. The sting in the scorpion's tail her mother often hid until the end.

'What is it?' Lily whispered. She and Rose knew well how their Southern belle mother Stella operated—sweet as peach pie, until the bitter tincture appeared.

'Mother says Papa is coming over on the *Oceanic* after we get back from Russia,' Violet said. 'And he's bringing Harold Rogers with him.'

'Mr Rogers?' Rose said, puzzled. Her hands froze in fussing with the puffs of tulle on Violet's shoulder. 'But why would Papa's business partner be coming here? He never leaves the Park Avenue offices.'

'To—to marry me, Mother says!' Violet wailed, her stomach so tight she was sure she would be sick all over her expensive new finery. 'Now that I'm of age and presented at Court, Mother says it's time I made myself useful by bringing the business closer together. But, but why *now*? Now, when I can finally see a way to be happy!'

'Oh, Vi, my darling, I am sure that can't be what she means,' Rose said, taking the letter to read herself. Her eyes were wide, her slim hand with its gold band and ruby engagement ring shaking.

'Mr Rogers is thirty years older than you,' Lily protested. 'We've known him since we were toddlers! They can't mean for you to marry him!'

Violet thought of Harold Rogers, the times he had come to the Newport house, the way he smelled of camphor, his yellowed teeth. Ugh. Papa said he was a wizard at foreseeing good investments, but Violet cared nothing for that.

'Well, it does seem to be what Mother is saying,' Rose whispered sadly.

Lily's lips tightened. She was usually the sweetest, kindest of the Wilkins girls, but when her protective instincts were up, she could be a dragon more than even Stella Wilkins could imagine. 'Well, Mr Rogers can come here whenever he likes, but he is not here now. You are in *England*, Vi, and Aidan is a duke, which is no small thing. And after today you will be officially known to the royal Court. We will find you an earl or marquess to marry. Preferably one with a powerful seat in the Lords. Then we will just see what the likes of Harold Rogers can do.'

'What a snob you've become, Lil,' Rose said admiringly.

Violet could feel panic sweep over her like a cold wind, her parents and Mr Rogers and her sisters pressing all around her until she was sure she would disappear under them all. 'But, Lily, I don't…'

Lily gently pressed a finger to Violet's lips, careful not to disturb a curl or a hint of the subtle pink lip rouge. 'Don't worry, darling. Just think about today. This is so very important. Mother and Papa aren't even here. They can do nothing. I am a duchess now, and Rose's husband is related to a duke. I can surely use this to help my family. They can't hurt us.'

They couldn't hurt Lily or Rose, but Violet wasn't yet married. They *could* hurt her. Without her allowance, and denied her inheritance, she had nothing, no career. Her options were limited.

But Lily was right. She had to get through today. It was vital that she do well at Court. It was her great hope now.

She took up the fan and the bouquet and stood very still as the maids smoothed her tulle-edged train. She would grit her teeth and get through it all with a bright smile. She was a Wilkins girl after all, and they never gave up.

Tomorrow—she would work out how to deal with Harold Rogers.

The line of carriages backed all the way up the Mall and beyond, a creaking, creeping train of gleaming black and blue and burgundy barouches and landaus, some with coronets emblazoned on the doors and liveried footmen perched behind. None was as grand as Aidan's crest, none of the horses as pretty as his matched bays, but it wouldn't buy them even an extra inch through the standstill scrum. The palace was still so far away, a shimmering mirage of pale stone and gleaming windows and empty balconies that seemed to laugh at so many overdressed supplicants.

Violet sighed and sat back against the tufted leather seats of the carriage. At least Aidan, or rather Lily, had ordered the best. They could be bored in relative comfort, ermine rugs over their laps and warmed bricks under their satin shoes, as well as a picnic basket waiting beneath the seat. But she had to be very careful to sit up straight and not brush her feathers against the carriage roof.

She sighed again and drew her fur-edged cloak closer around her. 'Whoever devised such a torturous process?' she grumbled. 'Why couldn't we all just wander by in our walking suits and say, *How d'ye do, Your Highnesses*?'

Lily laughed, squinting a bit as she filled in the word puzzle on her travel desk. Her tiara gleamed in the light. 'History, I suppose. Tradition. If you had been presented to Queen Charlotte in the last century, you would have had to practically kneel on the floor when you curtsied, then stand up again. It's not so very bad now.'

'Well, it makes absolutely no sense.' Violet wiggled her aching toes in the satin shoes, which seemed to be growing smaller by the moment, and wished she could loosen the thousand pins in her aching head.

'Nothing about the English aristocracy makes much sense, darling. But I've learned to live with it all and so will you.'

'Unless I am married off to Mr Rogers and shipped back to moulder in Newport.'

Lily gave a firm shake of her head, her feathers waving. 'That will not happen. Not while Rose and I have breath in our bodies.'

Violet glanced out of the window, glimpsing some of the other girls in their own carriages, so pretty and placid and golden in their pastels and feathers and pearls, so very English. So content with their lot. Why could she not be that way? She never had been. 'But why Mr Rogers and why now? They never even hinted at such a thing before. Do you think Papa's business is in some trouble?'

Lily frowned in thought, tapping at her crossword with her little gold pencil. 'Papa's business affairs have often gone up and down, but he always recovers. I'm sure Mr Rogers just harboured some secret passion for you, Vi, and now that you're of age...'

Violet laughed to think of old Mr Rogers, with his dry, silent ways, harbouring a 'passion' for anyone, let alone a girl his daughter's age whose skirts were always splashed with photographic chemicals and whose hair was always tangled. No, she was sure there was more to it than that. But Lily was right—today was not the day to worry about such matters. She had enough to twist herself into knots over with the palace looming before them.

'Do you have any more sandwiches in that basket?' she asked Lily.

'You ate the last one before we even turned into the park,' Lily said. She pulled a flask from the basket her cook had packed so carefully early that morning. 'There's tea and maybe some seed cake. But have a care—there's bound to be only one or two chamber pots and hundreds of nervous girls.'

'Ugh. A whole palace and no sufficient indoor plumbing?' She sipped very carefully at the cold tea and touched her temples with dots of Lily's rose water.

At last they glimpsed the gates of Buckingham Palace, tipped with gold, emblazoned with the royal arms, and the broughams, landaus and hansom cabs followed four lines to roll slowly past the guards in their red tunics and bearskins into the cobbled courtyard. Violet's stomach lurched and she rather regretted that bite of seed cake, but her boned bodice held her upright.

They finally reached the front doors and Violet alighted from the carriage to follow Lily and the long line of other white-clad debs into the palace itself. She stared at the furniture, marble-topped tables holding large Chinese porcelain vases of white and pink roses, portraits of William IV and Queen Adelaide peering down at them. There were rows of satin chairs embroidered with *VR* and crowns in gold, reminding her of where she was—a royal home. They snaked their way up a horseshoe-shaped flight of stairs, slowly wending towards the throne room.

When they at last reached the head of the queue, maids waited to smooth skirts and straighten feathers, to fold the long trains over ladies' arms while a stern-faced major-domo checked their cards. For a panicked instant, Violet was sure she'd forgotten that vital square of pasteboard, but Lily had them tucked into her beaded reticule. They were ushered along with the other ladies, like a kind of pastel, bejewelled line of peacocks, through a side door and a small, scarlet-carpeted antechamber. They burst out on to a soaring double staircase with gilded banisters and red carpet, watched by portraits of long-dead kings and queens, lit from a domed skylight that made the ladies' diamonds sparkle.

But no matter how grand, it was just as packed full, just as stuffy. The warm air smelled of woollen uniforms, furs too long packed away, the heady lilies in tall silver vases, the ladies' myriad perfumes, the sweat of fear and lemon polish.

Violet tried to take a deep breath, to ignore the claustrophobia of the space and examine all her fellow debs. They were, after all, her fellow inmates of this luxurious prison. There were diplomats and cabinet ministers in dark suits and sashes of orders, some older men in full Court dress of black satin breeches and silk stockings, cocked hats under their arms, even swords gleaming at their hips. There were also Scots officers in their glorious kilts of reds, greens, blues and tans, vying for attention with the ladies in their satins, jewels and feathers.

The Coldstream Guards band, in their red dress uniforms, played a lively, popular dance tune as cloaks were taken and tiny glasses of sherry handed out. Violet wondered if it was to be the only refreshment offered all day. Her feet already ached in their new heeled shoes, but she was entranced by it all. Everywhere she glanced she saw new inspiration for photographs, new ideas, new art and furniture and people.

At last they were formed into lines again, two by two with their sponsors, and led slowly up the staircase. Violet's hands, damp and shaking in her gloves, clutched at her fan and flowers. At the top landing, they handed their cards from the Lord Chamberlain's Office to the equerry at the doorway to what she thought must be the throne room itself. But, no. There were five more drawing rooms for waiting.

'It's all quite absurd, isn't it!' the lady in front of Violet said with a weary giggle.

Her spritelike beauty matched her musical laugh; she was tiny, fresh-faced and pugnosed, with a froth of pale gold curls beneath her bandeau-style tiara and feathers, her pure white satin gown embroidered with silver.

She pulled a flask out of her bouquet of white roses and offered Violet a swig.

Violet was quite sure it did not hold tea and she did very much want some, but she feared being sick all over the fine palace rugs. She declined even though Lily wasn't paying attention, talking to some of her own friends.

'I'm Thelma Parker-Parks, by the way. The Honourable, but that sounds so silly,' the sprite said. 'Didn't I see you at Lady James's tea party last week?'

So this was the notorious Miss Parker-Parks. That made sense. 'Oh, yes,' Violet said. 'Lady James is my sister. I'm Violet Wilkins.'

Thelma's already large hazel eyes widened. 'The American! Wild Wilkins. Of course. How very wonderful. I am quite dying to hear all about America. I bet you don't have nonsense like this there. So archaic. No curt-sying to President Washington?'

'Well, Washington has been dead for decades, so no. But they do have their own little traditions, especially in New York.' Like Mrs Astor and her Four Hundred, which Violet's mother ached to join.

'But not as silly as this, I'm sure.' A plump

older lady in gold brocade and lace called to Thelma, who waved at her impatiently. 'In a moment, Mama, I am talking to someone!'

Violet, no matter how bold she was in her manners, couldn't quite imagine talking to her mother like that and she was rather impressed. Thelma turned back to Violet with a roll of her eyes. 'You will come to Parker House soon, won't you, and meet some of my friends? They're rather a younger, arty set, lots more fun, none of this stuffy nonsense. They would love to know a wild American.'

A wild American? 'Well, I...'

Thelma caught Violet's gloved hand in hers, nearly crushing her fan. Despite her dainty, sparrow-like appearance, she was rather strong and her hazel eyes were beseeching. 'Oh, do say yes, please! I could certainly use a new friend. Mama is always after me to marry some unsuitable boy or other now and it's so dull. And I know we shall be good friends, Miss Wilkins. I can always tell.' Her lips suddenly turned down and her eyes hardened. 'I will be a duchess one day and it could be very soon now, you'll see.'

'Thelma!' her mother snapped and, with

one more giggle and waggle of her fingers, she skipped away to her place in line.

'Was that Thelma Parker-Parks?' Lily said, a strange strain in her voice. 'Do you know her?'

'Not really. She says she was at Rose's tea party and invited me to meet some of her friends.'

Lily carefully smoothed a creased bit of satin at Violet's sleeve, not quite meeting her eyes. She had a worried expression on her face. 'I would be careful around her, darling.'

'But why? She seemed a bit—changeable, but interesting. London can be so dull.'

Lily's lips tightened. 'They say she is rather fond of the card rooms. Most impracticable, considering her family hasn't much money. And there was the matter of a broken engagement. To a duke. She was sorry she let him go afterwards, of course, but it was done.'

'Really? A gambler and a jilt?' Violet gasped. 'She said she was practically engaged again. To another duke, maybe?'

Lily glanced up in surprise. 'A duke? How many can there be in London, and who would take her on now? Which one was it?'

'She didn't say.'

'Interesting,' Lily muttered, straightening her tiara. 'Well, we shall see when the announcement is in the papers, won't we? In the meantime, I don't think her parties are any place for you, Vi.' As Violet opened her mouth to argue, Lily shook her head firmly. 'We cannot afford any scandals in your first real Season. Especially if you want to attend the royal wedding.'

Violet nodded. A scandal would certainly be the perfect excuse for Harold Rogers and her parents to whisk her away. She had to be very careful. No matter how much she wanted to go to a fun, artistic party.

There was a great fanfare of trumpets, and all the rustles and laughter stopped. A major-domo in the red-and-gold royal uniform opened a set of gilded doors, and a silent procession of nervous debs and their sponsors inched slowly forward, trying to avoid each other's trains. Footmen waited with golden rods to drape those trains over the girls' left arms, bouquets clutched in the right. One by one, their cards were handed again and names were called out.

'Miss Agatha Peterson and the Marchioness of Eastley. Lady Mary Cartley and the Countess of Peterloff...'

They all vanished into the main throne room, two by two.

Then it was Violet's turn. Lily handed over their cards and two footmen in their red coats and powdered hair bearing gold rods of office smoothed their skirts behind them and made sure Violet's train was properly arranged. Something like a thin sheet of ice seemed to come down over her, after all those hours of practice in Lily's sitting room, and it seemed to her as though she watched herself from high above. As though she sat among the painted cherubs of the plaster ceiling and watched it all as in a theatre. The royal family were gathered on a dais at the far end of the vast room with its slippery parquet floor and velvet curtains muffling any daylight.

She carefully removed one glove and glided slowly to the dais, praying she would not trip, would not rip her gown, lose her feathers, laugh or scream or otherwise disgrace herself.

She bit her lip and studied the people waiting for her, as she would for a photograph. Prince Bertie and Princess Alexandra, who presided over such official events since the Queen stayed in seclusion still, were the only ones sitting down, on red-and-gold high-backed chairs. The Prince was indeed rather large, his coat and satin waistcoat straining against the ribbon and star of the Garter, his bearded face red, but he smiled kindly. The Princess was even more beautiful than in her photographs, slim as a reed, dark-haired, faintly smiling as her husband did. She was dressed in a gorgeous gown of dark purple satin trimmed with black beaded lace and covered with diamonds, a spiked tiara on her hair. The ladies-in-waiting and equerries clustered behind them, looking rather bored.

Off to one side was Prince Alfred, the new bridegroom, wearing his naval uniform and a full, almost bushy beard. She wondered if he would still have it at his wedding. Next to him was a lady Violet recognised as one of the younger Princesses, the lovely Louise, who whispered to her brother and made him laugh. To either side of the dais was a crowd of courtiers, watching, watching, always watching.

One man caught Violet's attention for an instant, making her falter. Was he real? How could anyone be so very handsome, so very haughty-looking? With such very green eyes? She could see the piercing light of them even from where she was. And he looked rather familiar…

Of course! He was the man on the horse, the gorgeous stranger. But now he looked so very stern. She looked away sharply, hoping he did not notice her.

'Her Grace the Duchess of Lennox, presenting her sister Miss Violet Wilkins,' the major-domo announced.

Bertie's small blue eyes brightened and Princess Alexandra smiled vaguely.

Violet curtsied low to Bertie, holding up her head with one of her most practised smiles, praying she would not wobble. Bertie's smile widened enthusiastically, and he reached out to raise Lily up and kiss each of her cheeks, a great honour usually reserved for royalty itself, along with Lily, it seemed. 'My darling Duchess Lily, the *American*,' he said, with his rolling *r*'s. 'We have seen too little of you this Season!'

'I have been rather busy, sir,' Lily said with a laugh. Restoring a crumbling ducal castle and creating a new baby duke-to-be had indeed kept her busy, Violet thought.

'But we shall all be in St Petersburg together soon, yes? And we have your lovely sister with us now.' Bertie reached out to clap the shoulder of Prince Alfred, whose golden naval epaulettes shivered. He was much slimmer than his older brother, though perhaps getting a bit plump since leaving his ship, with handsome eyes above his beard and tanned skin from all his travels. 'Though why he must go all the way to those snowy steppes to find a bride...'

'The Duke and I are most grateful to be invited,' Lily said with a sweet smile. 'And of course so is my sister Miss Wilkins. She longs to see Russia.'

Violet offered her own quivering smile and imitated Lily, holding out her bare hand for the Prince and Princess to take and curtsying again, as low as she dared. If only she didn't tumble over! She trembled and noticed Princess Alexandra giving her an understanding smile.

'Your Royal Highness,' she murmured, managing to lift herself up again in one piece.

'Lovely, lovely,' the Prince said, his beady eyes taking her in from feathers to shoes. But she knew she was safe enough; they did say he only liked married ladies. 'You are so like your fair sisters. We do like Americans here at Court.'

And then he turned away and Lily and Violet made their obeisance to the other royals. At last they came to the bit Violet feared the most, walking backwards out of the room.

She put on her glove, held out her arm and let the page drape her train back over it, neatly folded. Carefully, carefully, most especially to avoid that green-eyed man's regard, hardly daring to breathe, she slowly backed out of the vast room and found herself in one of the anterooms where another glass of sherry waited on silver trays.

'Very well done, Vi!' Lily said.

Violet let her breath out with a great whoosh—as much as her tightly boned bodice would let her. She had done it! She hadn't fallen or laughed loudly or made a gaffe. Even better, she'd seen several people she would love to photograph. Lords and ladies... princes and princesses.

The man with the green eyes.

Relieved, she let go of her long train and reached hungrily for a biscuit. As she followed Lily across the room, she heard a terrible loud noise, the rip-rip of satin cloth. But she was quite frozen in place.

So close to success, so close!

She clenched her gloved hands into fists and slowly turned.

A man stood behind her and not just any man, but the one from the throne room. The one on the horse. And he was far too close for comfort, yet he did not smirk and tease like all those annoying creatures who thought it such a good joke to make fun of her at parties. He looked terribly abashed, as if he was as shocked as she was. And, up close, he was even more handsome than her glimpse in the throne room had revealed. His hair was so dark as to be almost black, his face lean and sun-browned, his eyes vivid.

Yet he seemed so much stiffer than when she had first seen him.

But the embarrassment quickly vanished, as if behind a grey, flat cloud, and he straightened to his full, very-high-indeed height and gazed down at her almost as if the rip was her own fault.

Violet prickled at the thought, at the way he looked at her with those emerald eyes. How dare he regard her thus, like she was a stupid, clumsy creature! She was no ballet dancer, but she knew how to behave properly. He should be falling all over himself in apology. Instead he just kept watching, as still as a Greek statue and just as coldly handsome. *Blast him!* For he really was too gorgeous for her presence of mind.

He was tall and slim, but with narrow hips and wide shoulders that rippled slightly with powerful muscles under his correct, beautifully cut black superfine coat and a sparkling array of orders. The blush sash of the Garter lay like an azure river over one shoulder, so Violet knew he was someone very important indeed.

She peeked up at him carefully and saw

a face hard-carved in elegant, lean angles, like an ancient cameo of a god or emperor, cheekbones that could cut glass and a square jaw with a dimple on one side—of course he had an adorable dimple, the blighter. His skin was lightly sun-touched and it set off those bright green eyes and impossibly long, sooty lashes, with arched dark brows. His glossy almost black hair was brushed back from his forehead in a slight widow's peak.

Violet was quite enthralled. How she would love to photograph him! The shadows and angles of him would look so perfect. On the other hand, *he* was so perfect, so impeccable in every way, so very still, he made her feel quite blowsy even in the finest gown she had ever owned. She was just glad she was wearing gloves to hide the tremor of her hands.

She smoothed her hair beneath the feathers she feared must now lean quite precariously and scowled up at him. 'Pardon me, sir!'

He unfroze at last and gave a little bow. 'I do beg your pardon, ma'am. It is quite crowded in here. I had forgotten what these Drawing Rooms were like, or I would never have agreed to attend, even for my sister and cousin.'

Violet unbent a little. 'It is rather like a zoo, though not nearly as amusing. I was forced to come by my sister. One does not ignore a royal invitation, she says, even if one is American! What's your excuse, then? Your family, too, I guess?'

A smile seemed to quirk at his lips, which were of course also full and lovely, but he quickly suppressed it. 'My cousin is being presented and my sister bullied me into giving my support. Sisters, above royalty, must be obeyed, I see.'

Violet bit back a snort. 'They certainly are in my family! Though I'm the middle one, no one bothers to obey me, since I have a beautiful older sister and a winsome younger one. Even if she really is only younger by fifteen minutes.' She realised she was rather babbling, but she couldn't help it. He really was gorgeous. She studied him from under her lashes, wondering if she was boring him.

He certainly didn't look as if he had trouble getting people to listen to him. Indeed, every inch of him, every smallest movement, every flash of his eyes, spoke of wealth and power, and of an ease that meant it all must be inborn. Yet he wore it all lightly, seemed not even to notice it. It must have been draped over him like an ermine blanket since he was born.

Yet there was something deep in his eyes, a darkness like a shadow, almost hidden. She wondered what it could be and couldn't help but be intrigued.

As if his thought was indeed a command, a footman in that scarlet royal livery appeared beside him with a tray of champagne glasses where everyone else had weak sherry. He took two and handed one to Violet.

'Do accept my most sincere apology,' he said. 'I promise I am not usually so oafish.'

Violet could well believe that. She doubted he had an oafish bone in his tall body. She took a sip of the champagne. It was rather good, sharp and bubbly on her tongue. 'I do accept, thank you. As you said, such a crowd.'

'Do tell me where you purchased your frock and let me send a replacement.'

Violet laughed to think what Monsieur

Worth would say to hear his creation called a 'frock'.

'That is kind of you, but I couldn't accept.' Pearl embroidery and velvet roses with long trains would quite be in the way for taking her photographs. And Lily would be scandalised if a Worth gown appeared from a strange man.

'You're American, yes?' he said suddenly, his eyes narrowed, and Violet felt her cheeks turn warm. She didn't really mind all the giggling speculation over Americans and their dollars, but somehow she did not like it from *this* man. She hardly knew why it mattered; he didn't really seem like the sort who appreciated much.

She took another sip of the champagne. 'How can you tell? My accent? The six-shooter I pack at all times? I have been told my accent is rather charming, by those who try to be kind. My governess tried to knock it out of me.'

'I've just been travelling, so I am quite attuned to many accents at the moment. I met people from all over.'

So that would explain the sun-gold cast

over his cheeks. The sun never seemed to show itself much at all in this grey place. Perhaps the Greek statue was more than he appeared? 'Were you in India?'

'Egypt.'

Egypt. It rang a bell somewhere in her mind. Hadn't she recently heard gossip about someone who'd just returned from there?

'Chartie, darling! There you are!' Thelma Parker-Parks, Violet's new acquaintance, suddenly appeared to weave her arm through the Greek statue's and smile up at him winsomely. 'Honoria was looking for you. Oh, I see you have met my new little friend!' She gave Violet a strained smile. 'Oh, my dear Miss Wilkins, whatever happened to your sweet gown? How awful!'

'Miss Parker-Parks, how interesting to see you again,' he said tonelessly. 'I fear I was the boor who stepped on her train, yet we have not even been introduced. Perhaps you would do the honours?'

Thelma looked as if she would rather eat lemons, but she finally nodded and smiled. 'Of course. Chartie, may I present Miss Violet Wilkins? Miss Wilkins, the Duke of Charteris. He has been friends with my family for donkey's years.'

He turned to Violet in astonishment. 'You are Aidan's sister-in-law?'

Violet nodded and tried to smile. What a strange situation this all was. She wished she knew what was really happening. And he was what some in society called the 'Duke of Bore'! What a joke for the gods to make him so gorgeous. What a waste.

'And your estate marches with his. I have heard of you,' she said. That was why he had been riding there that day, of course. She should have made the connection sooner.

'I was most sorry to be out of the country for his wedding. It did seem sudden. Is the Duchess here? She must have presented you, I am sure, Miss Wilkins.' He scanned the crowd over Violet's head, as if quite unaware of the effect of his words. It seemed 'sudden' that Aidan had married. Did he mean anything negative in this observation about Lily, the loveliest, sweetest woman in the world?

But then again, he didn't know Lily. He knew nothing of any of her family.

'Yes, she was indeed my sponsor. She insisted on it. She is just over there.' Violet waved at Lily, who stood across the room talking to Princess Alexandra, shouting into the Princess's deaf ear as Alexandra went on serenely smiling beneath her sparkling tiara. How tedious it must be to be royal!

Or to be a duchess, especially if one was married to someone like Charteris. But Miss Parker-Parks didn't seem to think so. She clung to Charteris like a snail.

'I should like to meet your sister, Miss Wilkins,' he said.

'Chartie, Honoria did say she needed you most urgently,' Thelma said.

'Are you coming to my sister Lady James Grantley's ball this evening, Your Grace?' Violet asked. 'You can meet her there and see Aidan. I am sure he will be glad to make your acquaintance again. He does talk often of your boyhood.' She imagined Charteris must have been rather different in that boyhood, for he did seem a strange friend for the adventurous, humorous Aidan.

'Yes, of course. I shall see you all there. Once again, do accept my apologies, Miss Wilkins.' He bowed and walked away with

Miss Parker-Parks chatting up at him, joining two ladies across the room. One had to be his sister—she was dark and pretty like him—and the younger, a blonde in white silk, their deb cousin.

Violet felt as if she had been swept up, whirled around and plunked down again. She pressed her gloved hand to her aching forehead.

'Was that the Duke of Charteris you were talking to just now, Vi?' she heard Lily say. She turned to see her sister giving her a curious smile, taking a fresh glass of champagne from the obliging footman.

'Yes. The so-called Duke of Bore.'

'I'm sure he can't be that bad!'

'He stepped on my train!' Violet pointed out the rip in the satin and tulle, but then she felt she had to confess, 'Though he did offer to send a replacement.'

'A replacement from Worth! How extraordinary. But then he *can* afford it. I think I should like to meet him.'

Violet didn't tell her what he had said, about being surprised at Aidan's sudden choice of wife. 'He'll be at Rose's ball. What were you talking about with Princess Alexandra, then?'

Lily sighed and took another sip of champagne. 'Poor Princess Alexandra. She only hears two words out of five, but she does try. She's so sweet and pretty. I fear her lot is not always an easy one.'

Violet thought of the rumours of Prince Bertie's behaviour, all the women and the baccarat and the theatre. Yet another reason to avoid the perils of marriage. 'Aidan would never...?'

'Oh, no,' Lily said firmly. 'Aidan is made of very different cloth indeed. Which is why I want you to get to know his neighbour. He would never be friends with a cad.'

Violet remembered the Duke's cold, beautiful green eyes. 'I don't think Charteris is much like Aidan.'

'No?' Lily said curiously. 'Well, Vi, appearances can be deceiving at first. You should remember that.' She put down her empty glass. 'Come, we should be going now that we've done our duty. And you should revel in your success! The Prince thought you quite the prettiest deb of all and even the Princess was very complimentary...'

William watched Violet Wilkins move away across the crowded room, her bright hair like a beacon, and suddenly remembered well where he had seen her—crossing the field near Bourne, dragging a camera behind her, her hair loose, free and lovely as if she was part of the sun and earth itself. Sketching, laughing, so free. Even here, in her feathers and satins, she was different. A fairy creature.

'Well, she is most...er...extraordinary,' Thelma said, her usually champagne-like voice flinty. He remembered well how quickly she could change. She linked her gloved fingers around his elbow.

Extraordinary—that did not even begin to describe Violet Wilkins. She was like a queen of ancient Britain, not a part of the modern crowd around her at all. She was not tall—in fact, she was quite slim and small. But she held herself as if she was tall, her feathered head high, the torn train over her arm, her cheeks rosy pink. The crowds instantly parted for her, Boudicca crossing the Thames. She was rather magnificent.

And, if he was not mistaken, she had no great liking for him. Even when she had heard he was a duke the icy shards in her blue-grey eyes hadn't quite thawed. She didn't seem impressed at all.

Maybe it was because she was an American and her brother-in-law was a duke, too. But Aidan was a most unusual duke and always had been. William often wished he could be more like his friend, free, open to exploring his own soul. But Aidan had been a second son who never expected the title and William had had too much to worry about to explore his own 'soul'. Too many people relied on him.

But Violet Wilkins looked as if she could rule a kingdom without blinking an eyelash. She was herself and perfectly so. But who was she, really? William found he longed to know and it was a feeling he had never experienced before.

'She is certainly quite beautiful,' he said.

Thelma huffed, her fingers digging into his arm. 'Beautiful? With that red hair? What an extraordinary idea. But it seems we are to be overwhelmed with Americans now. England will never be the same! The Jerome woman, for instance, and her sisters. So vulgar!'

Aidan would never marry a 'vulgar' woman, he knew he couldn't. But Miss Wilkins did not seem vulgar. Just…carefree. Free. 'Indeed.'

Thelma giggled. 'Well, we know you never would, Chartie. You know your duty. You'll be at Lady James Grantley's ball tonight? She's another Wilkins heiress, you know. Lord James's fortunes have certainly improved since they married, I must say. He may be a dean at Oxford soon! Whatever that means.'

'I look forward to the ball. I enjoy Lord James's learned conversation.' He watched Violet Wilkins as she stopped to talk to her sister and his own cousin Pauline, making the shy girl laugh. Yes, he did look forward to the ball, for once. He never really looked forward to any society party—they seemed like such a waste of time when there was so much work to do at Bourne. But tonight might be interesting indeed.

Chapter Four

Rose's house was a wedding cake of a structure, whirls of white plaster icing outlining balconies and window frames and chimneys, in a row of other such houses. It was the perfect place for a pair of scholars such as Rose and Jamie, her bespectacled, distracted, kind husband, to be quiet and placid and content behind velvet window draperies. Now those curtains were thrown back, glowing amber lights flowing from every door and window on to the pavement below.

Music drifted out in silvery ribbons: Chopin, Mozart, pattering country dances. Lines of carriages crammed into the narrow lane to disgorge crowds of men in greatcoats and silken top hats, ladies in fur-edged cloaks, their high-piled curls filled with fluttering aigrettes and winking, jewelled tiaras. Their laughter twined with the music. Rose's house was one of Violet's favourite places, pretty, comfortable, filled with books and flowers and modern paintings and the quiet affection between Rose and Jamie in every corner, redolent with Rose's own sweetness, her own angelic spirit.

Yet it seemed different tonight. Crowded, noisy, everyone watching, smiling at her, whispering about her, speculating about her future now that she was 'out'. She really was out now; of course they would wonder who she would marry. And marriage was the last thing she wanted now. Until she could establish her career.

She stepped down from the carriage behind Lily and Aidan. This gown was also by Worth, but not as grand as her presentation gown. It was cloud-white taffeta, trimmed with yellow satin ribbons, a swirl of velvet violets over the skirt and forming the straps of the bodice. More violets were twined into her hair, twisted into careful ringlets by the maid with her iron rods, and she held a bouquet of violets in her gloved hands. Purple silk shoes carefully stepped over the blue carpet laid out on the stone steps to the front door. She followed Lily's rose-pink-and-cream-striped skirts into the small entrance hall, where they left their fur wraps.

'Darlings!' Rose cried, dashing down the winding staircase, a vision in spring-green muslin and white lace, a tiara of seed pearls in her loose curls. She looked like a vision of spring, a Lady of Shalott amid the stylised flower draperies and faded carpets of her house. 'There you are at last. I heard you were quite the Diamond of the Drawing Room today—even the Prince and Princess raved about you.'

'Oh, hardly,' Violet said, laughing as she kissed Rose's cheek. 'But I did manage not to fall.' She thought her sister looked so lovely, prettier than ever; she would have to bring her camera and take her portrait tomorrow.

'An achievement indeed. Well, now that is all behind us. Come and have some wine, Jamie ordered it from Germany, and something to eat. I've laid out such a grand buffet.' Rose took Lily and Violet's arms and led them through the chattering crowds to the dining room. 'Jamie is just finishing up some work in the library, but he'll come out soon to make the toast, and there will be dancing. All night, if we like!'

She led them into her drawing room, transformed to a ballroom for the night. It was a long, narrow room, with a large carved wooden mantelpiece at one end and tall doors opening to a small garden at the other. Rose's fine artistic taste had made it a bower of violets, piled in Chinese vases and silver baskets, sweeping along the walls, curved into bowers in each corner, sweetly scenting the evening air. The furniture was removed and gold and white draperies and chairs lined up along the edges of a parquet dance floor. A small orchestra played behind a bank of ferns and refreshment tables were laid along two walls, piled with bowls of white soup, lobster patties and mushroom tarts and lemon cakes. Footmen passed by with trays of champagne glasses.

'Oh, Rose, it's so gorgeous.' Violet sighed. Her twin always made everything she touched lovely.

'Only the best for my sisters! Oh, here, try a salmon croquette. I know they're your favourite. Look, there's Lord and Lady Am-bleby! How interesting her gown is. Have you ever seen such a shade of green? And Mrs Hunter-Smith, and Lord Westley. How handsome he is.' Rose lowered her voice and added, 'They say the Prince and Princess of Wales may come later.'

Violet almost choked on her salmon. 'Surely not to my lowly deb dance.'

'He probably wants to discuss plans with Aidan about the St Petersburg journey. But it hardly matters *why* they're here, their ap-proval will be your making forever. Suitors will be lined up, yours for the choosing, Vi! Oh, no, no, those strawberry cakes must go here...'

As Rose went to straighten the cake mishap and Lily talked to Lady Ambleby, Violet was left alone for a moment next to the windows.

She studied the guests carefully over the gilded edge of her wine goblet, which was rough-hewn and medieval in style, just like all the uniquely artistic objects Rose and Jamie collected around themselves. They always declared they were just simple scholars, but their house, their clothes, everything around them was full of artistic beauty, only theirs and impossible to replicate. Violet hated to admit it, but she did rather envy them. They had created their own world, their own sort of marriage. If only she could find something, someone, like that!

As a footman handed her a fresh glass, she watched the colourful crowd, dancing, munching on lobster patties, laughing, chatting, a glamorous, carefree evening. A violet-scented chilly breeze stirred at the half-open window, puffing out the embroidered silk curtains, revealing and concealing a few people strolling on the terrace under the light of painted paper lanterns. It really was an enchanted night, filled with flowers and wine and laughter, the kind of night her sisters were so good at creating.

Violet ached to be a part of it all, *really* a part. But so often in the centre of a merry crowd, she felt she was watching from above, not really there, not really belonging. She only belonged when she looked at things through a camera. And she had no camera now.

She glanced at a group on the other side of

the room and wondered how she would arrange them for a portrait, the ladies' skirts swagged and draped with flower wreaths and tulle, the men so dark, their faces lit with laughter. They made the perfect society tableau, like the scenes that sold in stationers' windows. And there was that girl from the palace, Thelma Parker-Parks, like a silver-and-white doll in a rose-pink gauze gown, her fairy floss curls bound by a wreath of diamonds and rubies made to look like carnations. All an illusion. Though she giggled with her tall, blond, sunburned companion—was he that tennis player everyone was reading about?—she kept watching the door.

Violet turned away to see Lily dancing a Viennese waltz with Aidan, the two of them spinning in slow, lazy circles, watching only each other. It wasn't the 'done' thing for spouses only to dance with each other, but the two of them never cared.

The drawing room doors opened, and everything seemed to swirl to a stop, mid-dance-step, mid-word. Violet turned herself to see Rose hurrying to greet Prince Bertie and Princess Alexandra. For an instant, even

Violet was frozen in astonishment. The royal couple had really come to *her* ball? And with quite a crowd to accompany them! She could scarcely believe it.

She set down her nearly empty glass on a footman's tray and drifted in a haze towards the door where Rose, Lily and Aidan were with the royal newcomers. Jamie was still nowhere to be seen, no doubt losing track of time in his books.

Princess Alexandra was just as lovely as she'd been at the palace and seemed even taller, even more slender, in a beaded gown of guinea-gold satin and tissue, the low-cut bodice draped in pearls, diamonds and topazes, her famous high pearl collar at her throat. Her dark hair was piled high beneath a diamond fringe tiara, long chandelier earrings catching in her curls, and she nodded and smiled prettily at Violet's curtsy.

Unlike his wife, Prince Bertie was no fairytale idea of royalty, but he was presentable and amiable enough, his portly figure encased in a perfectly cut evening suit and sumptuous gold brocade waistcoat. His sparse, pale hair and copious reddish beard gleamed on his egg-shaped head, his strangely baby-like red lips pursed as he surveyed the company, his icy blue eyes narrowed. A cigar dangled from the corner of his mouth.

'Lovely, lovely indeed,' he said in his slight German accent, patting Violet's hand as he drew her up from her curtsy. 'Always do love a party at Rose's, y'know. She's one of the best hostesses in London! And one of the prettiest. Grantley was wise to snap her up. Now, who will snap *you* up, Miss Violet? Who do you have your pretty eye on?'

'No one at all, Your Highness. I confess I'm more interested in photography at the moment.'

'Photography, eh?' His pale brows arched. 'You don't say. Affie here is most interested in that, as well. Got it from our father. Didn't you, Affie?' Bertie waved forward his younger brother, Prince Alfred, the Duke of Edinburgh and soon-to-be bridegroom. Like his brother, Prince Alfred was stocky and solid, brown-bearded, his cheeks sunburned from all his years aboard ships. His pale eyes sparkled with bluff humour, putting Violet at ease.

'Didn't I what, Bertie?' he said merrily. He seemed to have been imbibing a bit before the ball, but he also seemed friendly and eager to join in the conversation. The happy almost married.

'Have an interest in photography, Affie. Just as this young lady is. Miss Violet Wilkins, this is His Royal Highness Prince Alfred, my most unfortunate younger brother.'

'Indeed I am, Miss Wilkins, though I do consider myself most fortunate now!' Prince Alfred offered his gloved hand to Violet. 'And photography is quite astonishing, don't you think? A most wondrous blending of art and science, the present and the future.'

'That is exactly what I feel, Your Highness,' Violet said eagerly, feeling a strange warmth towards this weather-beaten, bluff Royal Navy man.

'Oh, Affie,' said one of the silk-draped women, a lady Violet recognised as one of his sisters. Princess Helena? She took her brother's arm with a careless smile. 'You can bore this poor girl all about it on the long journey to Russia! Now, I want a dance, and you are my chosen partner.'

'It is indeed a long journey.' One of the ladies-in-waiting sighed. 'I'm not sure why we *all* must go. The Queen is staying comfortably at home. All that way just to freeze in the ice and snow!'

'Because, Lady Morris, Grand Duchess Maria is the Tsar's only daughter and respect must be paid! You're marrying above yourself, eh, Affie?' Bertie said, heartily clapping his brother's shoulder. 'And Alex here wants to see her sister, the Tsarevna, don't you, my dear?'

'Oh, indeed,' the Princess said, waving her painted silk fan lazily as she studied the party. 'It's been an age since I've seen my darling Minnie.'

'Russian hospitality is most lavish, I hear. Second to none, I dare say. The best food and wine, the biggest ballrooms, the prettiest ladies in the grandest gowns and jewels,' Bertie said, taking his cigar out of his mouth and popping it back in. 'And you'll have Charteris for company, eh? Gracing us with your presence for once, Duke?'

The Prince drew forward a gentleman from the back of the crowd and Violet was startled to see it was the man who had torn her train at the Drawing Room. The too-handsome, too-cool-eyed Duke of Charteris. And he was just as handsome and cold this evening, his dark hair combed back from the sharp angles of his face in glossy waves, his eyes seeming to see everything around him despite his not moving. 'Your Highness?' he said, in that echoing, low, rich voice.

'Charteris, the Princess has said she never sees you dancing at parties and it distresses her. Why don't you dance with the lady of the hour here? She's most pretty, quite the prettiest of the Drawing Room, what?' Bertie said. 'I see a tray of mushroom vol-au-vents over there, so delicious, my favourites, Lady James, as I am sure you knew.'

'And the music is a mazurka, Duke! It's always a favourite of mine,' Princess Alexandra said, clapping her gloved hands.

Violet realised she had no choice. She had to dance with the lead-footed Duke by royal command. And a mazurka, too! So complicated and quick. Why couldn't it have been a sedate waltz?

He didn't look much happier than she was

at the order, his eyes darkening. 'Of course. Would you do me the honour, Miss Wilkins?'

'Yes, thank you, Your Grace.' Violet curtsied and took Charteris's hand under Bertie's beaming blue gaze, letting him lead her to the floor. His hand did feel strong and warm under hers, steady, and he smelled wonderfully of sandalwood soap, like a winter English forest. Why did he have to be so very tall?

They took their places in the forming figures of the dance, waiting for the music to begin in earnest. Violet felt herself fidgeting most ridiculously under his steady watch and she glanced down the rows of dancers to distract herself. Thelma Parker-Parks was at the far end of the line with an officer in a dashing red coat, but she did not seem happy. Indeed, she stared at the Duke with burning eyes as her handsome partner tried to converse with her. And Jamie had appeared at last from his library, talking with Rose by the open window, but neither of them looked very happy.

Oh, dear, Violet thought ruefully. Was her ball cursed?

'You don't have to see out the *whole* dance set with me, Your Grace,' she offered to her quiet partner. 'We could easily tiptoe towards those terrace doors and you could slip outside.'

His lips quirked in an amused expression, a dimple set deep in his cheek flashing in and out. Against her will, Violet found herself rather fascinated by that smile that wasn't quite a smile. 'And what would you do then, Miss Wilkins?'

'Go upstairs to look at my photo albums until supper, perhaps. My sisters wouldn't miss me until then.' She laughed as he spun her around, his strong arms holding her above the tug of gravity, keeping her safe and free. It was an amazing sensation and she suspected she could never have such a thing with any dance partner but him.

'You really are interested in photography, then?' he asked curiously.

'Oh, yes, it is quite fascinating!' The music blasted out again, loud and quick and merry, and she took his outstretched hand. 'I could happily work in my darkroom all day! What are *your* interests, then, Your Grace? For I know we should converse during the dance.'

He looked a bit surprised, as if no one had asked him that before. But surely he must have interests? 'I'm too busy with my estate and work to think about hobbies.'

He spun her around, lighter and more graceful than she would have expected after the train-stepping incident. 'I like to think of my photographs as more than a mere *hobby*. I'd like to be just as—as recognised as Julia Margaret Cameron, or Clementina Hawarden, and join the Photographic Society to show my work, when it's good enough.'

He looked down at her, his arched dark brow making him look curious. 'You don't think it's yet good enough?'

Violet shrugged and turned a double twirl in the dance, his hands gently leading, letting her fly while he held her steady. She almost laughed at the delightful feeling. 'My range of subjects is limited and I could use a real teacher, I think.' She thought of the trip to St Petersburg, her hope in finding new inspiration there. *He* would make a gorgeous model, too, with those elegantly carved angles to his face, those deep, glowing eyes. If she could ever persuade him, which she probably couldn't, as he was so *busy* with important work. Glancing up into those eyes, that unbearably handsome face, she feared he never would and perhaps she did not have the skill to capture him properly.

The music came to an end and she curtsied to him, strangely reluctant to let go of his hand, to spin free again.

'Violet! Oh, I do beg your pardon, Your Grace, but I fear I must steal my sister away for a moment,' Rose said with a laugh. 'There is someone she simply must meet.'

Violet dropped another quick curtsy to the Duke, still feeling a bit shaken by the way his touch made her feel. 'Thank you. For the dance.'

'You are quite welcome, Miss Wilkins,' he said. As Rose led her away, she couldn't help but glance back, only to find him watching her. As if he were trying to read her, *see* her, deep inside. It was most disconcerting.

'What other important personages have

you lured here tonight, Rose?' she whispered, resolutely looking forward again. 'The Queen herself? The Pasha of Turkey? I was just dancing with a duke, you see.'

Rose laughed. 'Better! It is Mrs Prinsep of Little Holland House, where I have been a guest often lately. And she has brought her sister, Mrs Cameron.'

'Julia Cameron?' Violet gasped.

'Yes, that is her over there, see?' She gestured to a lady Violet probably would not have noticed. She looked so different from any image she might have had of a famous photographer. Violet had thought she would be stately, elegant, but Mrs Cameron was small, weather-beaten and dressed in a careless old brown wool gown, an old-fashioned lace cap on her greying hair. Violet thought her quite marvellous.

'She's asked if we will be at the Photographic Society exhibit,' Rose said. 'Jamie has procured us tickets.'

'No!' Violet gasped. 'Has he really? I've been longing to see it.'

Rose laughed. 'Truly. He is useful sometimes. I do hope you'll enjoy it.'

Violet sighed happily. 'I'm sure I can hardly fail to.'

'Wonderful! Now, do come meet Mrs Cameron.'

Violet fairly floated out on to the terrace, still giddy from meeting Mrs Cameron and hearing her speak of her own photographic techniques, and then there was the prospect of seeing the exhibit still to come. There she might meet other people who could teach and encourage—or discourage—her in her work. It was quiet outside after the clamour of the dance, Rose's small garden lit with Chinese lanterns strung through the trees, small moonlit bowers arranged with cushioned, wrought-iron chairs and sofas. The evening breeze, cold and crisp, was scented with vases of greenery and violets.

She wrapped her arms around herself and twirled down the shallow stone steps on to the grass. If she could meet *real* photographers, and then take some splendid, unique images in Russia, surely her hopes had a chance of coming true? Surely she would have an opportunity to do what she wanted?

She hummed along with the echo of the dance music and swirled on to one of the seats near a tiny summer house. She could see the silhouettes of the partygoers through the windows, dancing and laughing, the ladies' gowns like teacakes, and it all looked like a dream. Her sisters' lives were lovely; London was lovely and she had enjoyed every minute of her time here. Yet still she longed for something more, something just out of sight, out of reach.

She sat back on the striped cushions and smoothed out her satin-and-tulle skirt, thinking of museums and paintings and photos, thinking of what she wanted to achieve with her own art. Prince Alfred was quite right; it was a moment of the present that could be carried, perfectly whole, into the future. And she wanted to be a part of that.

Suddenly, there was a rustle and a burst of giggles from the summer house, which Violet had thought was empty. She drew in a deep breath and slid down low in her seat, not yet ready to make conversation again. Surely whoever it was would soon go back inside.

'Charteris is in fine looks tonight,' one

lady giggled. Violet smelled a whiff of cigar smoke, like that which had hung around Prince Bertie. Were the ladies hiding in the summer house to smoke? She rather wished they had invited her, even if they *were* talking about the Boring Duke. The Duke of Bore.

The man whose looks, whose hidden thoughts behind Those Eyes, were not really entirely boring.

'Indeed,' said another, and her silvery voice told Violet it was Thelma. She sounded terribly smug about something. 'He always is.'

'You will look very nice together, I'm sure,' the first lady said.

'And I shall teach him charming manners! A man with political ambitions should draw everyone close to him, shouldn't he?'

The first lady giggled again. So maybe Violet wouldn't wish to join them after all, if all they were going to do was giggle incessantly and talk about the Duke. 'Just as you do. No one can resist you, Thelma.'

'My mother always did say I was born to be a duchess.' The ladies laughed merrily.

Were they planning to catch themselves

a duke in a trap? Or maybe Charteris was actually courting one of them. Violet felt a strange, cold pang at the thought. She would ask her sisters; they always knew the gossip.

But the party had grown so crowded when she slipped back inside and she couldn't see Lily or Rose anywhere. The laughter and music was louder, the smell of flowery perfumes thick in the air. She didn't see the Duke anywhere, either, and she hoped he was well away from Thelma Parker-Parks.

Mr Hamilton, one of Violet's casual suitors, a handsome but silly young man, grabbed her hand as she hurried past. Tucked under his other arm was one of Rose's large silver tea trays, and she noticed several giggling people clustered nearby on the stairs, calling out to Hamilton to hurry.

'Come along, Miss Wilkins!' he said merrily. 'We're going to go sledding.'

'Sledding!' she cried with a laugh. 'What, are you making a blizzard now?'

'Harry over there said he used to do it all the time in his nursery! Sliding down the stairs on a tray. He says it's dashing great fun.'

Violet suspected Harry and Hamilton and

their friends were rather cup-shot on the champagne and on Rose's planters' punch, but she had to admit it did sound rather fun. She glanced around but still couldn't see her sisters. But she did see Charteris, standing in the drawing room door, watching them in silence. Did he disapprove, then, the Duke of Bore?

She lifted her chin, reacting as she always seemed to when someone disapproved—she wanted to do the forbidden thing even more. Show them she did not care, even when she did. 'Certainly, Mr Hamilton! It does sound like good fun.'

They climbed to the top of the narrow, polished staircase and lined up three to a tea tray on the last landing. Hamilton pressed cheekily close to Violet's back as she tucked in her skirts, making her giggle—she must have too much champagne bubbling in her veins, too. Rose had appeared on the landing, as if she had been in one of the chambers there, and cried out that she would join them.

Rose sat in front of Violet, taking the steering into her capable little gloved hands. Rose had always been slim as a reed, much thinner than Violet, but now she felt quite delicate, the bones of her shoulders fragile through her satin gown, arms like a delicate bird's. A few curls of dark red hair escaped from her sapphire bandeau and she smelled of a rich jasmine scent. It made Violet feel rather worried suddenly.

Rose was Violet's twin, her closest other self ever since they were born, yet she'd felt too often lately that Rose was holding something back even from her. But tonight they were as close as ever, laughing together, leaning against each other.

Harry gave their tray a great push and they were off, flying over the stairs, barely stopping in their accelerating flight. Violet and Rose shrieked with laughter; it really was like sledding down the snowy hills behind their Newport house when they were children and would go there for quiet winter treats as well as busy summers. It was wonderful! Like flying!

They landed hard on the marble floor of the entrance hall and spun around and around until Violet's head felt giddy. She tumbled down and lay flat on her back, laughing and laughing until her whole body ached and she couldn't stop.

Suddenly, a hand appeared above her, tanned golden, with a few fine dark hairs at the wrist, impeccably manicured with a gold signet ring on the smallest finger, steady and strong. 'Miss Wilkins? Are you quite all right?'

Violet stared up and up into the bright green eyes of the Duke of Charteris. His brow arched as he watched her, expressionless. It made her feel suddenly sober. He had probably never had fun like that, not even when he was a child.

'Miss Wilkins?' he said again. 'May I be of assistance?'

Violet slowly reached up and took his hand, almost as if a spell compelled her to, and even beneath her glove she could feel the heated *life* of him, the raw strength. His fingers closed around hers and he raised her to her feet, as if she was as light as swansdown. Only once he was sure she stood steady on her heeled shoes did he step back, to a safe distance. She felt suddenly chilled and wrapped her arms around her waist.

He gave her a half-smile and she could suddenly see why Thelma Parker-Parks might desire him. Even if she did not. Not even a little bit, not at all.

The lady doth protest... some little voice whispered in her ear, and she tried to laugh such disquieting things away. She couldn't like the Duke; he would never like her back.

'Thank you, Your Grace,' she said. 'It's such fun, you should try it!'

Charteris shook his head, that hint of smile vanishing. 'Such nursery pastimes have never held much attraction to me, I fear, Miss Wilkins. But to each their own, yes?'

Violet bristled a bit, even if he was rather correct. It was a bit nursery. But still, there was no harm in a bit of fun! Thelma was welcome to him.

Before she could say anything else, Thelma herself came to take the Duke's arm, smiling and dimpling up at him. She really was very pretty, so golden and delicate, as Violet had never been. Perhaps the Duke would not mind so much if she *did* catch him.

'Charteris,' she cooed. 'They are starting the

last waltz before supper, and you did promise to be my partner.'

'Of course, Miss Parker-Parks.' He took her arm and let her lead him back into the drawing room, smiling in silence at her chatter and giggles.

Violet turned back to the stairs, where others were lined up to take their turn. Jamie was talking to Rose, his handsome, thin, scholarly face serious, but she shook her head, her chin set, and hurried away from him to Violet.

'Everything all right, Vi darling?' Rose asked, smoothing her hair carefully under that jewelled band. Her laughter from the ride down the stairs had faded and now she looked rather worried, though she tried to hide it behind a smile. Where Violet was all prickly angles and energy and fire, so much she often singed herself with it, Rose was like her name—sweet, fragrant, elegant, a peacemaker. Was something amiss with her now?

'Everything is very all right, Rose, my love. You give the best soirées in London.'

'So they say,' Rose murmured doubtfully, and Violet kissed her cheek quickly, eager to make her sister smile again. And so she did, though it seemed wavery. Jamie had vanished again. 'Shall we check on supper?'

Violet nodded. She glanced back to see the Duke taking his place in the dance with Thelma, so tall, so straight, so very correct. She didn't know why she should care if he disapproved of her, but that cold disquiet in her core still shivered there. And she could still feel that touch of his hand on hers...

Chapter Five

'I don't suppose I could persuade you to go shopping instead? To tea at Gunter's?' Lily teased as their carriage rolled along towards Pall Mall, slowly because the traffic was thick there. The buildings were beyond elegant and the ladies who strolled past were lovely in their furs and silks.

'Not a chance of that, Lily! I've been counting down the hours to this ever since my dance at Rose's,' Violet declared. A photographic exhibition, where she could take her time to study other work. Maybe even speak to other photographers, as she had with Mrs Cameron at the ball! It made all those garden parties and Venetian breakfasts and musicales she'd endured all year seem quite worth it.

She'd been trying to stay home as much as

she could, practising with her camera, studying albums, and she'd seen few people. Certainly not the Duke of Charteris, though she had watched for him when they went for rides in the park. Probably he was too busy with all his 'important work' for such frivolities. Maybe he was engaged to Thelma now. She shouldn't care and she didn't. Really. She did not.

Or maybe just the tiniest bit, when she couldn't sleep at night and she would think she saw his emerald eyes in the shadows. It was most annoying.

Lily laughed. 'I'm sure it will be most interesting. And your work is sure to be in the next exhibition!'

Violet wasn't so sure about that. She still had problems with her technique, ruining more plates than she would like. It was so hard to make her visions appear before her in reality. But events like this would help her learn, and she had to stop thinking about the disapproving Duke and concentrate on that.

At last they drew up outside the pale stone mansion that once housed the Society of Female Artists. It was one of the first times such an exhibition of a new medium was being held for the public and the line out of the doors was rather long already. Violet recognised several Earls and their Countesses, wealthy art collectors and the quiet editor of *Photographic News* already taking notes. She practically jumped down from the carriage to hurry and join the queue.

Once inside the grand, cold marble foyer, the corridors stretched to either side, long and crowded, filled with enticing objects three deep on the blue silk walls. Lily was quickly distracted by a group of her friends, but Violet happily wandered on by herself, entranced by what she saw.

The earliest photos were displayed near the front, by Oscar Rejlander, a great pioneer of the photograph as an artistic image rather than a mere mirror. The first was rather small and faded, depicting a chubby cherub who reminded Violet of her nephew looking up with a palette and brush in his hands. *Art Must Assist Photography*, read the placard, *1856*. But right next to it was an image that showed Rejlander must have rather changed his mind. *The Infant Photography Giving the*

Painter an Additional Brush—a tool for art, not secondary to painting. Violet had read that Rejlander had combined four negatives together to make the image. She found the technique fascinating and wished she could work out how to do such a thing.

In the next room was a row of portraits, some of them even by ladies. Clementina Hawarden, a viscountess who had died in 1865 at forty-two, had a row of glowing images of her daughters, from toddlers to young ladies. Not stiffly posed as young noblewomen in silks and feathers, but natural girls going about their days, sitting sewing by the fireplace, brushing hair in a mirror, leaning against each other laughing. Like real life itself, like Violet and her sisters. Just what she wanted to create.

Mrs Cameron's photos were very different. They were blurry, full of motion and feelings, telling a whole story.

At the end of the row were two portraits of a girl. *Julia Jackson*, the card said. She was beautiful, her face sharply carved and full of sadness, evoking emotion in the viewer.

'Do you like it?' a woman asked.

Violet, so absorbed in the images, was startled by the sound. She turned to find a lady smiling at her. She was tall and slim and elegantly dressed in a purple walking dress and flowered bonnet.

'They're lovely,' Violet answered honestly. 'I love the blurriness at the edges, the sense of motion. The life.'

The woman smiled. 'Some critics say it lacks womanly delicacy.'

'They are quite wrong. Sometimes I think *only* a woman can see another person so deeply. Men are always in too much of a hurry to really look.' Except for Charteris and those glowing eyes that seemed to see too much. Seemed to look too deeply. She tried to push aside thoughts of him and turned back to the photographs. 'Though I do like Mr Dodgson's work.' She gestured to the opposite wall, which held a row of Mr Charles Dodgson's work. There was a dark-curled little girl clutching her doll, looking melancholy beyond her years, and a group of people in a rowing boat, laughing in the diffused sunlight. The technical process of it all was amazing.

The woman's smile widened. 'Yes, indeed. Life. We must drink it in deeply wherever we can find it. That portrait is my niece, by the way. She's such a beauty. Mrs Cameron, who has just left for Ceylon, is my sister. You may have met her? I'm Mrs Prinsep.'

'Mrs Prinsep!' Of course Violet had heard of her. One of the Pattle sisters, as close as Violet was to her own sisters. Her home at Little Holland House was famous as a centre of artistic life, its gardens and corridors packed with painters and writers, full of creative thought. Full of an informal, even scandalous spirit. Rose had said she had been there herself a few times, welcomed for her beauty and sweetness, and Violet longed to see it for herself some day. 'It's an honour to meet you. I'm Miss Violet Wilkins.'

'Ah, yes, Rose's sister. I've heard you are interested in photography yourself.'

'I merely dabble. I was hoping to learn a great deal from today's exhibition.'

'Then you must join us at my house soon! Perhaps after you all return from Russia? I shall send you a card. I warn you, we are very casual there. You'll meet all sorts of people.

But Rose does seem to enjoy it. Until later, my dear!' Mrs Prinsep waved and sailed away, making Violet laugh.

Violet also left the main gallery, turning into a small chamber, and laughed again at what she found. It was a collection of nude images, ladies posed as classical goddesses in nothing but laurel wreath headdresses. She glanced over her shoulder and found she was alone for the moment and could take a peek.

'Why, Miss Wilkins, how very shocking,' a wry, teasing voice said. Violet whirled around, her face growing too warm, and she found the Duke of Charteris watching her from the shadowed doorway. He leaned there lazily, his arms crossed over his chest, his eyes gleaming, a panther stalking her through a thicket of scandalous photographs.

'I—I...' she stammered. 'I was looking at Mrs Cameron's portraits out there and stumbled in here by accident. Much as you yourself did, I'm sure.' She laughed, forcing away that trace of embarrassment. 'But perhaps there should be some photographs of *men* in the altogether, yes? I could correct that in my own work.'

His smile widened with a flash of humour so warm she wanted to draw closer and closer to it, bask in its beauty. It was all too rare. But maybe if he smiled too much, ladies fainted at his feet and it was a nuisance to walk past them. She was glad she had made him laugh rather than shocked him. 'Of course. You're in here merely by accident. And I would be interested to see your work.'

'I'm surprised you're here at all. I wouldn't have imagined photography was an interest of yours.'

'Oh, I do have *some* interests, Miss Wilkins. You would be quite shocked.' He held out his arm lazily. 'Shall we? I would quite like to see Lady Hawarden's work.'

Violet took his arm and led him around the exhibits, talking about what she admired in a few favourites, the techniques she imagined had gone into each one. She feared she was prattling too much, but he nodded and frowned and smiled, asking a few intelligent questions, as if he was interested in what she had to say. It was quite dizzying and she found herself laughing at some of his wry jokes. She was—could it be *comfortable* with the dour Duke? The thought made her feel quite discombobulated and she excused herself to visit the withdrawing room at the end of the gallery.

Violet sat down at one of the little tables behind the japanned screens, glad of the moment alone to rest her feet. What a ninny the Duke must have thought her, chattering on so much about photographs! Surely he was used to ladies who were very different from her, sophisticated and well informed on many stylish topics. Maybe society women were what he really admired, fashionable and smiling and light.

Not that she *wanted* him to admire her. Of course not, she told herself sternly. He was not at all the sort of gentleman she was interested in, if she was at all interested in romance yet. Seeing the exhibition showed her she needed to work so much harder at her art.

But then, he, too, seemed interested in photography, which was most surprising. Maybe he was right—maybe there was far more to him than she had first thought. He was actually rather easy to talk to, a good listener, informed on so many topics. His smile was lovely indeed, his eyes concentrating only on her, only on what she said. Such attention felt intoxicating.

Yet she could never fit into his real life, his life as a duke. This was a moment out of time. She knew that very well.

The door opened and she heard a burst of giggles, though luckily she was hidden behind her screen of silence. She sank down lower on the bench and heard someone exclaim about what a 'bore' photography was, what a shame it was becoming fashionable so one must pretend to like it.

'Then why ever did you want to attend, Thelma?' a lady said, with a rustle of muslin skirts and a clatter of bottles as she rummaged on a dressing table.

Another woman laughed and Violet realised it was that silly Thelma Parker-Parks, who was chasing Charteris so shamelessly. Just Violet's luck to be trapped, caught listening to the girl for a second time.

'Because it *is* becoming all the rage, you know, looking at photographs,' Thelma said. 'And you never know who you will see at fashionable artistic things!'

'And it has quite paid off, has it not, Thelma dear?' her friend teased.

Thelma laughed, a brittle, snappish sound. 'Indeed. Wasn't the Duke most charming? He said he'll be at the little dinner-dance for Prince Alfred later.'

'And did he ask you for the first dance?'

Thelma laughed again. 'Oh, Bea dear, he need not *dance* with me. We have talked of this. I will send him a note to meet me in the garden at Marlborough House. A terrible emergency. A twisted ankle, I think. He would never leave a lady in distress.'

Violet's thoughts whirled. This seemed like a real plan on Thelma's part, not just the vague hopes she'd heard at Rose's party. Poor Charteris.

'And then what?' her friend Bea gasped.

'What do you think, silly? You shall then come outside to take the air and bring a group with you—maybe even the Princes! You will catch us kissing. I shall be a duchess in no time. But your timing must be just right.'

Violet pressed her hand to her mouth to hold back a gasp. It *was* a plan, a dashed unfair one!

'Thelma! You wouldn't.'

'I would,' Thelma said coldly, no longer at all the airy-fairy princess. 'A lady must look after herself these days. He admires me, I'm sure, and he needs a wife. I would be a darling duchess. I'm just…helping him along a bit. Poor men, such dears, stumbling about in the world, but sometimes they must be shown what they need. What they really want.'

Violet was quite sure that, of all men, Charteris was quite capable of knowing his own mind. And the minds of others, too, drat him. Stuffy he might seem, but no one deserved such a trick played on them! To be saddled with an unwanted spouse for life. What a terrible plan on Thelma's part.

Though maybe he really *did* want Thelma Parker-Parks, as she seemed so convinced. Violet had seen no signs of such a thing, but romance was not really her area of expertise. What should she do?

'No one can resist you, Thelma,' Bea said.

'With your help, of course, darling Bea.'

There was a rustle of skirts, a last giggle, and the door clicked shut behind them as they left the withdrawing room. Violet buried her face in her hands, her head aching as she tried to decide what to do next. Her sense of American justice wouldn't let Thelma's plan just come to pass, but how could she stop it? How did she help a man she wasn't even sure she liked? But there was something about Charteris, something intelligent and all-seeing and fascinating, and he deserved so much better.

She knew she had to do *something*. She smoothed her hair beneath her little, tip-tilted, feathered hat and powdered her cheeks with some of the rose powder on the nearest dressing table, hoping to look less flushed and confused and more composed, until she could work out what to do. How she hated all this plotting and scheming! No wonder she preferred photographs that could be composed and arranged.

Somewhat tidier, she hurried back to the galleries, looking for her sister. Maybe Lily and Rose could help her, surely they would know what to do? They were practically English themselves these days and were successfully navigating their way through society.

The corridors were less crowded now, quieter, and she didn't see the Duke anywhere.

'Oh, Vi, there you are!' Lily called. 'Have you quite looked your fill? I'm parched for some tea.'

For an instant, Violet did consider telling Lily what she had heard. Wasn't Aidan friends with Charteris? But something held her back at the last minute, something about the air of privacy Charteris always wore.

'Yes, of course, tea sounds lovely,' she gasped.

Lily frowned as she studied Violet's face. 'Are you quite all right, darling?'

Violet made herself smile. 'Just a bit tired.'

Lily tsked. 'And no wonder! What a terrible sister I have been, dragging you all over town. We shall just have a good rest before Prince Alfred's party. Tea on a tray and a good book!'

Violet nodded. Thelma had said she would enact her silly plan at the party. That would give Violet a bit of time to decide how to act, work out what to do. How to help the Duke, if she could.

Chapter Six

William studied himself in the looking glass, automatically straightening his cravat, tugging at his cream brocade waistcoat, tucking away the ruby-studded pocket watch that had been his father's and grandfather's. It was always the same when he went to a party, he looked just the same. Fashionable but never flashy, proper, well-tailored, just as a duke should be. Just as he had been taught all his life.

Just as *he* should be, at his core. As he always was. And yet, walking through the exhibition with Violet Wilkins, watching the way her eyes gleamed and her hands fluttered with excitement as she talked, as she led him through a different world, made him feel—unsettled. As if something, a new fire, was igniting deep inside of him, something that was well hidden the rest of the time. He'd never felt quite like that before, as if life itself had revealed a new light, just for that one bright moment. The shadows gone, the steady thrum of duty interrupted, only there for one flaring instant.

Then she was gone and that light gone with her. All was just as it had been before he saw her looking at those scandalous photos. He'd never thought himself an imaginative man; he had no time for such things. Bourne was all he knew, his world and work. Yet perhaps he had become a fanciful man now, after the brilliant sun of Egypt. Maybe he imagined things in her eyes, bright, exciting, unknown things.

Violet was not quite beautiful. But she *was* pretty, with her vivid hair, her sparkling eyes, the splash of freckles on her nose, her air of energy and health and vivacity. She burned with vitality, as if time could not contain her, could not limit her. She didn't seem to care what people thought of her, as a duke could never afford to do, not if he had ambitions in the world.

She was so different from anyone he had

ever known. Unfathomable, even as he tried to read her. She did seem to have such a passion for her photography, far beyond the polite artistic accomplishments of other ladies. She seemed to feel, in fact, as he did about Bourne. That it was something she *must* do, must work on, must be a part of, no matter what.

Listening to her, talking to her, was like standing in the Cairo sun too long, or drinking too much brandy. It could so easily consume him, destroy his careful control. He couldn't afford that.

Yet he did wonder if she would be at the party, if she would talk to him, dance with him. Smile at him again.

'Don't be a fool, man,' he told himself sternly. A woman like Violet Wilkins, an American with raw energy burning through her veins like champagne, could never be a good duchess. Could never happily live with such duties, with a man like him. She was too *much*.

Honoria was right. He needed a quiet, sensible wife, and soon. But no sensible woman he had ever met had eyes like Violet Wilkins's.

* * *

Violet held up one necklace to her throat, then another and another, unsure which went best with her pale blue silk gown trimmed with darker blue velvet ribbons and crystal-dotted lace roses. She just couldn't make up her mind, and that was nothing like her.

She enjoyed clothes—they were just like another form of art, especially when she considered how they would look in photographs. Yet she herself could usually choose her attire quickly and go on to more interesting activities. Tonight, though, she felt like a ditherer.

She glanced at the French enamelled clock on the mantel, with its cavorting cupids and blooming roses. Almost time to leave, those gilt hands said. Everyone told her Princess Alexandra was always late to everything, even a ball she was hosting, but her guests could not be. They had to be at Marlborough House on time or they wouldn't be let in. She looked back down at the jewels scattered on her dressing table. Which ones, which ones?

She feared she knew the reason for her uncharacteristic indecision: William, the Duke.

Would he be at the party, as Thelma seemed sure he would be? Would she have to tell him about what she had overheard, and would she be in time to help him? How could she even begin to warn a man that he was about to be trapped into marriage?

But she was afraid it wasn't just *how* to tell him that was making her so nervous. It was facing the man himself.

The Duke of Bore. How silly she had been to think that of him! Or at least *just* that. He was serious, that was true. His rare smiles were like jewels dropping into her hands, brighter than the necklaces before her now. They made her feel so silly, made her want to do and say the most ridiculous things just to see that smile again.

And when his hand touched hers—it tingled, just like photography chemicals, only softer, warmer. What could that mean?

She thought of her sisters and their husbands, how happy they seemed. She was not completely averse to marriage. But it would have to be to just the right man, one who understood her, who allowed her to be herself, who she could understand and help, too.

She knew also what she did *not* want and it wasn't a solemn man with the many duties of a dukedom on his shoulders.

And it definitely wasn't her father's old business partner, either, no matter what her parents said.

Violet sighed. Harold Rogers was a problem she would have to solve another time. She couldn't think about that now. At least her parents and Mr Rogers were an ocean away right now. Her most vital problem was warning Charteris about Thelma Parker-Parks and her silly plan.

And not daydreaming about his touch, his smile, his blasted adorable dimple all the time. She had ambitions of her own. After seeing the beautiful works at the exhibition, she was determined her own photographs would be among them one day soon.

If she could just stop imagining a photograph of the Duke himself, posed like one of those naughty images in the back room…

'Oh, just stop it!' she cried, banging her silver-backed hairbrush on the dressing table.

'Stop what? Are you ill, Miss Violet?'

the maid asked, bringing in Violet's newly stretched kid gloves.

'No, no, I'm just being silly,' she said, quickly collecting herself. 'I just can't seem to decide on a necklace.'

'Really?' The maid sounded puzzled. It usually took Lily much longer to get ready for a party than Violet. 'Why not the pearls, then, miss? You can never go wrong with pearls.'

Violet studied the tangle of necklaces, the three strands of creamy pearls with a sapphire-and-diamond clasp that had been a present from her father. It reminded her of the Duke, strangely. Elegant, timeless, quiet, but with a sheen that drew a person closer, made them want to see more.

'Yes,' she said. 'You're quite right. The pearls it is.'

Chapter Seven

As Violet handed her fur-edged blue velvet wrap to a footman, she stared around her at the entrance hall of Marlborough House, the Prince and Princess of Wales's London residence. She knew she shouldn't stare like a milkmaid, but she couldn't help it. It was just so very grand. So—so royal. It had none of the shabbiness at its edges like Buckingham Palace, but was immaculate and elegant in every way, all bright colours and sparkle.

The footman led them up a staircase and into a drawing room, where the butler waited to announce the guests. In line ahead of them, Violet saw an elderly royal aunt, a marquess and two earls. No Duke, though, and no Thelma. She fidgeted with her lace fan, worried about the night ahead.

At last they reached the doorway, and the

butler called out, 'Their Graces the Duke and Duchess of Lennox and Miss Violet Wilkins.'

The Prince of Wales headed his own receiving line, portly and genial in a stiff evening suit bearing the blue ribbon of the Garter order and plenty of gleaming medals. His wife, the Tardy Princess, was nowhere to be seen yet. 'Aidan, my dear chap! I hope you're up for a hand of whist after dinner, eh? No baccarat with Mama just around the corner at Buck House, I'm afraid. And you've brought your beautiful wife and sister-in-law to grace my little drawing room. I'm overjoyed. My own wife shall be down—well, soon, I'm sure? You know my sister, Princess Helena, I think.'

The Princess, with a plain face and slightly outdated brown silk gown, as if she cared more for horses and dogs than fashion, gave them a pretty smile, and there were bows and curtsies all around. Violet was glad of all that practice for her presentation.

'And you've met my brother Prince Alfred, the bridegroom,' Bertie said, gesturing for his bearded, sparkly-eyed brother in his naval uniform to step forward. 'We can hardly drag him away from his old ships, but true love did the trick, eh? Been angling to marry his Grand Duchess for years.'

'It took that long to persuade her, I fear,' Prince Alfred said with a hearty laugh. Violet nodded slightly. She had heard the gossip. The Tsar wasn't sure a mere English prince would be good enough for his only daughter and Queen Victoria thought Russia a fearsome, barbaric place. But then the two lovebirds blotted their copybook in some way and so a marriage was reluctantly arranged. But, no matter how reluctant, it was all full steam ahead for the grand nuptials. 'I am a lucky man indeed now. You'll be at the wedding, I think, Lennox? And you, Miss Wilkins?'

'We are honoured to be invited, Your Highness,' Aidan said. 'My wife has never been to Russia.'

'You will enjoy it, Duchess, like nowhere else. Very grand they are, not like Mama's little court.' The Prince smiled at Violet. 'And I seem to remember that you are the one who shares my interest in photography, Miss Wilkins?'

'Oh, yes, Your Highness,' Violet replied

eagerly. 'We just visited the new exhibition today. It was wonderful.'

'I am hoping to visit there myself tomorrow. I look forward to hearing your thoughts about it, Miss Wilkins.'

Violet knew it was not the moment to ask him about wedding portraits, but maybe soon. At least she had made a start; he had remembered who she was, and she had done nothing to embarrass herself or Lily.

Yet.

'I would enjoy that very much, sir,' she said with one more curtsy.

More people waited behind them, so they moved into the drawing room to take glasses of champagne from more footmen in the scarlet royal livery and to look around. But she didn't see the Duke anywhere.

'Aidan, darling! How grand to see you. I didn't know you were here,' a woman trilled, and Violet felt her stomach flutter with nerves all over again. She turned to see Aidan's fearsome mother, the Dowager Duchess of Lennox, now remarried and a countess, but everyone just called her Duchess Agnes. And she was *very* much the Duchess tonight, in a dark red gown beaded with green and black, feathers nodding in her pale hair, her eyes sparkling and sharp. 'And your little sister-in-law, how lovely. You do look nice tonight, Violet, so sweet in blue.'

'Thank you, Duchess,' Violet gritted out.

'Mother,' Aidan said warily, kissing his mother's powdered cheek. 'I thought you were in Cannes for the Earl's gout.'

'Oh, we were, but it was too, too dull. There's no one there at all right now, so empty. All anyone can think about is this Russian wedding! I understand you are going?'

'Yes, Lily and I, and Violet,' Aidan said.

The Duchess gave Violet a suspicious glance. 'Really? All of you? Oh, I do wish I could attend, to keep an eye on you! But the Earl is still too unwell, the poor darling. I am quite on my own tonight.'

'I'm so sorry to hear he still feels ill, Mother Duchess,' Lily said. 'It's too bad you cannot be at the wedding.' But Violet was sure she wasn't *that* sorry; Duchess Agnes's eagle eye would be sure to put a damper on any St Petersburg fun.

'Ah, well, you must tell me all about it when you return,' the Duchess said, her gaze sweeping the room. She waved at a group of ladies in the corner, including Princess Helena. Two of them hurried towards her. 'Have you met my friend Mrs Palmer and her daughter Beatrice? Bea just made her debut, as you did, Violet, dear.'

Beatrice Palmer giggled and Violet was startled to realise that this was Thelma's friend, the proposed note-passer. 'How do you do,' Violet said carefully.

'The Duke of Charteris and Lady Honoria Browning,' the butler announced, and Violet felt her hands tingle under her gloves, as if he had touched them again. She patted at her pearl necklace, the upsweep of her hair, and glanced at the doorway.

The Duke was bowing over Princess Alexandra's hand as she smiled at him, a small smile on his own face, that wretchedly adorable dimple flashing in his cheek, his eyes so brightly green she couldn't bear to look away from him. But then those eyes caught hers and his smile widened, and she felt quite ridiculously warm and flustered. She turned away, but she could still sense him looking at her. It was all so silly—and yet so giddily delightful...

At the gleaming dinner table, Violet was happily surprised to find herself seated next to Charteris, so close she could smell his sandalwood soap, sense him close to her. But she had been led into dinner by the gentleman on her right, a rather deaf elderly marquess, and was obliged to try to converse with him during the soup course.

As they shouted to each other about the weather and sipped at the lobster bisque, Violet was all too aware of the Duke beside her. She longed to warn him about what she'd heard, but at the same time she rather dreaded it. How did a person say to someone *Whatever you do, don't let yourself marry Miss Parker-Parks!* It sounded quite ridiculous, even in her head.

Yet she couldn't let that happen, even to the Duke of Bore. Besides, as she'd already admitted to herself, she now rather suspected he wasn't quite as boring as all that. He deserved better than to be stuck with such a wife forever.

At last the soup was cleared and the fish course, salmon in dill sauce, was brought in. Footmen poured out a new wine, a crisp Rhône white, with a double-large glass for Prince Bertie, and Princess Alexandra turned to her other side to converse with the man on her left.

As Violet turned to the Duke, she caught a glimpse of Miss Parker-Parks on the other side of the table and further to the left. She stared at them with burning eyes beneath her sweep of blonde curls.

'Did you enjoy the rest of the exhibition, Miss Wilkins?' the Duke asked.

'Oh, yes, very much. In fact, I'll have to go back for a second, closer look,' she said. 'I have so much to learn about technique and subjects for my own work.' She studied his face in the amber light, particularly noting those wonderful angles and sharp edges to his jaw and nose, his jewel-like eyes. Yes, he would make a marvellous image himself, perhaps as a classical Greek hero.

'I, too, enjoyed it. Bourne Abbey, my family's home, is filled with beautiful art my grandfathers collected, and I'm ashamed to say I've never appreciated it as I should. But I am learning to. There is a Raphael, several Van Dycks, even a Rembrandt. And some French landscapes my mother liked, beautiful, gorgeous colours.' He sounded somehow lighter tonight, happier. She even glimpsed that enticing dimple as he flashed her a quick smile. It made her more determined to try to save him from marriage. 'Perhaps I should add some photographs to the collection, something modern and different. A portrait of my sister, for instance.' He gestured down the table towards Lady Honoria, who would indeed make a fine portrait image, with her angular face and dark hair, so like her brother.

'She would make a very photogenic subject, I think. And you should have your portrait done, as well.'

He laughed, a dark, deep sound that seemed a bit rusty at the edges, as if he didn't laugh enough. She longed to hear it again and again. 'Me? Oh, no, Miss Wilkins. I would not want to frighten any visitors who are shown around Bourne by our housekeeper. It's bad enough I must have a painting done for the gallery—at least the artist can soften my scowls a bit.'

'Did you find anything for your collection while you were in Egypt?'

'A few things. A group of scarabs and some fine rugs. It was all most astonishing there. The light and the sparkle on the river. The pyramids against the sunset. You would certainly find many subjects for your camera there, Miss Wilkins.'

'I'm sure I would. I do dream of such travel,' Violet said with a wistful sigh. But he did not seem like the usual sort of tourist. 'Why were you there, Your Grace? Perhaps you have an interest in work for the Foreign Office?'

He shook his head, the light glinting on his glossy hair. 'I am only interested in helping my home county, helping Bourne and its people, however I can. The House of Lords, perhaps, or the Home Office. It's my duty. That couldn't be achieved in diplomacy, no matter how interesting that might be. Education for my tenants' children, proper work for them, things of that sort.'

Violet nodded. So he, like her, had ambitions and plans, hopes. Different ones, of course, but she heard the passion in his voice, the determination to see those visions come true. It surprised and moved her. Most of the noblemen she had met in England did not seem to care so much for their people, only for what they got out of their estates.

The footmen cleared the fish course and brought in sorbet. She realised with a shock that time grew short and she would soon have to talk to the deaf marquess again. She had to speak to the Duke *now*.

She quickly touched his wrist with her fingertips, the shock of bare skin on bare skin making her almost gasp. She pulled away and peeked up at him, only to find him frowning at her curiously. 'Your Grace, I must tell you something,' she whispered. 'If Beatrice Palmer gives you a note, do not do what it says.'

His brow quirked. 'Miss Palmer? I barely know the girl.'

'It won't be a note *from* her. Just ignore it.

Please.' Violet saw the Princess turn her tiara-topped head and knew she had to follow. She nodded at Charteris, hoping it looked meaningful, and turned, hoping that he would at least ignore any note for the time being.

That he would save himself.

After dinner, in the pale blue-and-cream ballroom, Violet watched the dancers twirl around the floor, in a kaleidoscope of vividly bright gowns and flashing jewels, black coats and sparkling medals, under the light of the massive crystal chandeliers. Lily, as usual, danced scandalously with her husband, while Miss Parker-Parks twirled with an officer in a red coat. She couldn't see Charteris, but at least he was not with Thelma.

Despite the rest of the courses at dinner, and there were many, for Prince Bertie's legendary appetite was not overstated, she hadn't been able to tell him more in a discreet fashion. They'd been reduced to talking about Egypt and the weather.

She wandered around the edge of the dance floor, marvelling at the paintings on the silk-papered walls, Renaissance Madonnas, fields of French flowers, Gainsborough portraits, Queen Victoria glowering from over the fireplace and cabinets filled with porcelain and enamel and jewelled snuffboxes. Princess Alexandra sat beneath her own portrait, a full-length vision of white tulle and brown curls, talking with two of her ladies. Prince Bertie and his brother and equerries guffawed and gulped great quantities of brandy punch, studying the young ladies seated on the gilt-and-satin chairs with their mothers, waiting for the next dance to begin.

The music ended for the waltz and sets were formed for a country dance, the brilliant gowns and black coats shifting and changing like a sunset. Violet wished she could capture such motion with her camera.

'Miss Wilkins. May I have this dance?' she heard someone say behind her.

She whirled around to find the Duke watching her, a smile touching his lips, his hand held out. To her.

'I—yes, thank you, Your Grace,' she said. 'Though I must warn you, I am not very graceful, as I am sure you remember. Your toes may not be happy afterwards.'

'Now that I cannot believe.' He offered his arm and Violet slipped her hand around his elbow, feeling the power and heat of him through her glove. She knew he could not spend all his time at a desk, not with his lean strength that was against her.

She took her place opposite him in the line and glimpsed Miss Parker-Parks in the crowd. She glowered at them, but there was no time to worry about it. The orchestra launched into the lively tune and she and the Duke were the lead couple. He took her hands and twirled her in a circle, making her laugh. Her blue silk skirts billowed like a cloud, buoying her up, and the room spun.

He let her go and they passed between the next couple until they came together again. Holding hands, they hurried down the line and passed again, so fast she was dizzy and held on to him tightly. As she'd remarked before, he was a surprisingly good dancer, fast and graceful, and he held her so lightly she barely had to think about what she was doing. Normally dancing was chore, a tedious time of counting and thinking and hoping she wouldn't step wrong; now it was a delight. He caught her around the waist and spun her again, and she let her head fall back to watch the royal chandeliers turn into stars.

The dance ended and they were the last couple in line, near a set of open glass French doors. To her surprise, he didn't let her go, but held her hand and drew her through those doors on to a night-dark terrace, lined with potted palms and people whispering in the shadows.

'What is...?' she said.

He reached inside his coat and brought out a small, folded bit of paper. 'Miss Palmer gave this to me before the dance.'

Violet swallowed hard and nodded. At least she had been able to warn him at dinner. He did seem rather a chivalrous sort of man, this lord of a great estate with great responsibilities; he might have thought Thelma really needed his aid. 'From Miss Parker-Parks?'

'Asking me to meet her in that teahouse over there, that she is in trouble and has a favour to ask.'

'You aren't going, are you?'

'Certainly not. I must marry one day, but it must be to the right lady. Not a flighty sort who would try to trap a man she barely knows, like this Miss Parker-Parks.'

And not to a woman like Violet. Independent, temperamental, *American*. She knew what he meant. She nodded again.

'How did you know?' he asked.

'I overheard them in the ladies' withdrawing room at the exhibition,' she said. 'I was behind a screen and they thought they were alone.'

'It was my lucky moment, then. You are my guardian angel, Miss Wilkins.'

Violet laughed. No one had ever called her *angelic* before. 'A good deed in a wicked world, Your Grace. That's what my old nursemaid would say when she tried to make me behave. But I just couldn't let that happen to you, to anyone. I know what it's like to be herded towards a marriage one doesn't want.'

'Do you indeed?' he asked, his tone curious.

She leaned on the stone balustrade of the terrace, staring out at the dark trees and flowerbeds as she shivered in the evening breeze. He immediately took off his light wool evening coat and draped it over her shoulders, surrounding her with his warmth and his sandalwood scent. She drew it closer, but it made her want to shiver again, being so very near him.

'Y-yes,' she said. 'My father wants me to marry one of his business partners, you see. A certain Mr Rogers. He is much older than me and he would never let me carry on with my photography, let alone advance with it. He would insist I go back to America.'

'I see.' He was quiet for a long moment. There was just the sound of the wind around them, the incoherent echo of laughter from the ballroom. Somehow that silence didn't feel uncomfortable; it wasn't a space she had to fill, but just a place to *be* for the moment. A place where she was not alone. 'It sounds as if we both require time to set our lives to rights.'

'Yes.' Violet sighed. 'Yet I fear time is something neither American dollars nor an English dukedom can buy us.'

'Perhaps. Or perhaps not.'

He sounded as if something was ticking over in his mind and she studied him curiously in the half-light. His face seemed even sharper there, more sculpted, his eyes more glowing. 'What do you mean?'

'I have a rather outlandish idea.'

'You, Your Grace?' she said with a laugh. 'I don't believe it.'

'It's not usual for me, I admit. But I feel I need to thank you for saving me tonight, and this might be a good thing for us both.'

Violet studied him carefully. 'I am intrigued.'

'I think we should get engaged.'

'No!' Violet cried. Whatever she had imagined he might plan, this was beyond any wild idea. Her—a duchess? Lily was a very good duchess. Lily was also a gentle soul and a perfect lady who worked hard at it. Violet would be terrible.

And to be with *him*…

Well. She had to admit that part might not be as dull as she once would have imagined. He had depths she hadn't noticed before, as well as that handsome face. But she couldn't marry him.

She started to give him back his coat, to run back into the ballroom, but he stopped her with a hand on her arm. His touch was light, but it held her still, frozen in that moment, marvelling at the way it felt.

'Hear me out, Miss Wilkins. I don't mean *really* engaged. Of course I don't mean that,' he said.

Violet bit her lip. 'You don't have to sound *quite* so appalled. Then what do you mean?'

'I mean we announce we are betrothed, but that we want to wait to arrange a ceremony until after the royal wedding in St Petersburg. My sister and your parents wouldn't pester us any longer and we would gain some time to arrange our lives more to our liking. You with your art, me with politics.'

Violet was startled. 'I have to say, that's rather clever of you.'

He flashed her that enticing, dimpled smile. 'I have been told I am not all that stupid, for a duke.'

'No, you're not. Stupid is the last thing I would call you.' A fake engagement, to hold off real life for a while. It wasn't such a bad idea, was it? A very good one, really. 'How would we get out of it at the end?'

'Nothing easier. Once you have seen off this Mr Rogers and become well known for your photographs, you will cry off. Say we don't suit each other. You miss America, or any excuse you like. It would be a topic of gossip, which I admit I do not relish, but not for long. Then you can go abroad, if you like. Go to Egypt to photograph the antiquities.'

'It just might work, I think. Until after Prince Alfred's wedding, you say?'

'As long as you like, really, Miss Wilkins. I am in no hurry.' He leaned on the cold stone next to her, his arms crossed. 'Perhaps you are thinking Prince Alfred might be of some assistance in your work? He did inherit his father's love of photography.'

'I had considered such a thing, yes. If I could publish an album of photos of the new royal couple, of St Petersburg, I could certainly gain some notice. And I will come into my own settlement of money in a few years.' *If* she could avoid marrying Harold Rogers. Her parents loved her and her sisters, but they were strict, too. Her mother especially had always been very determined to arrange her daughters' lives to her own liking. Lily's grand title was a protection, but it wouldn't always shelter Violet.

She would so hate to lie to Lily. But surely it would not be for long and her sister would understand in the end. She, too, had escaped their parents. And Violet had no ideas for gaining time for herself. Her parents would surely not make her marry Mr Rogers if they thought they could have *two* duchess daughters.

'I could call on Aidan tomorrow,' he said, gently coaxing. She imagined few ladies could resist such a soft tone in that deep voice, such a look in those eyes.

'Very well, Your Grace. You have a deal.' She held her hand out for him to shake.

He bowed over it instead, his lips brushing warmly, softly, over her kid-sheathed fingers. There was that dratted tingle again! 'I think you should call me William.'

She nodded slowly, dazedly. She couldn't quite believe she was doing this, but here they were. Fake betrothed. 'Yes, indeed. William. And I am Violet. Let's hope this really works...'

Chapter Eight

'Did you know that Aidan is in the library with the Duke of Charteris?' Lily said, her embroidery needle flashing in and out of her canvas.

Violet pretended to study the photographs she was pasting in her new album. 'I saw him come in earlier.' She had been waiting for him all morning. She'd barely slept the night before—the dance, his touch, their strange bargain were all swirling around in her head.

'I wonder at their being so secret. Some political scheme, maybe? Do you think I should send tea in?'

Violet smoothed down the image of Lily in her white gown with the cooing baby on her lap. It was really very good, one of the best she had done. It captured Lily's sweetness and humour, the tenderness of mother and baby as he reached out his tiny hand to her. She could get better at her photography, if she just had the time. She knew it. And this plan, wild as it was, could give that to her.

It was time for the curtain to rise and the play to begin.

She smiled brightly at her sister. 'Maybe we should find some champagne?'

Lily looked doubtful. 'Oh? At two in the afternoon?'

'Well, you see, Lily darling, last night at Marlborough House the Duke proposed to me. And I accepted. So, if Aidan agrees today in Papa's place, I do think a bit of champagne might be nice.'

'Engaged? To Charteris?' Lily's sewing fell to the floor and her jaw dropped. Violet was sure she'd never seen her ladylike sister quite so discombobulated. 'But you barely know him!'

'I know him as well as Rose knew Jamie, or you Aidan. He is young and handsome and interesting, and he *is* a duke.' All very true. He was also secretly a very sly devil. Not the Duke of Bore at all. 'He is surely a hundred times better than Harold Rogers. And we'd be neighbours, you and I! You did say he is friends with Aidan. Aidan would never be friends with anyone terrible.'

'Of course not. Charteris is very far from *terrible*. And I would adore having you near me always, Vi! But he is—' Lily broke off, reaching down to retrieve her embroidery.

'He is—what?'

A door shut somewhere in the house and there was the echo of voices. Aidan and William would be with them soon. Lily gave her a strange little smile, half happy and half worried, and shook her head.

'I have heard he is a good man. His tenants love him,' Lily said. 'And if you think he will make you happy, that is all that matters to me. I've only ever wanted you and Rose to be happy, more than anything in all the world.'

Violet felt the prickle of tears behind her eyes and blinked them away. 'I *will* be happy, Lily, you'll see.' Maybe not the way Lily imagined her happy, but she would make it happen. 'I will make you proud of me.'

'Oh, Vi.' Lily dropped her sewing again

and hurried across the room to kiss Violet's cheek. 'I am always, always proud of you.'

Aidan and William came into the drawing room, which Violet was glad about as they stopped her before she could cry. William smiled at her, a small, secret smile she couldn't help but answer. 'I see Lily has heard the good news, too,' Aidan said with a laugh. 'My best wishes, my dear sister.'

'Thank you, Aidan.' Violet smiled as he kissed her cheek. He really *was* a good brother to her. A good husband to Lily, a good father, a good duke. He made her sister so very happy. She couldn't help but love him for all that, but there was also a pang of wistfulness, of envy, as she watched him put his arm around Lily, the two of them beaming. Would she ever find happiness like theirs?

Then she remembered she really was supposed to be happy just like them in that moment and she turned to William. He arched his brow at her as if in question and she nodded. As if they could read each other's thoughts now. They had made this strange bargain and she would keep it. It was the only way to win the right to choose their own lives now.

And for a fake fiancé, he was a very fine one indeed. As handsome as the night and just as alluring. And she did love to tease him! Maybe this time together could even be rather—fun?

He took her hands in his and she was surprised to feel that she was shaking. He bent his head slowly towards hers, as if to kiss her cheek, but she suddenly felt flustered and drew back a bit so that his lips brushed hers.

She tilted her face closer up to his, her eyes fluttering closed, and felt his lips touch hers again, lingering too long for mere politeness. She shivered with the rush of emotion that poured through her and reached out for him. But it was all over much too soon.

When he drew away, Violet felt her knees tremble and she sat down hard on the nearest satin-cushioned chair. She felt so dizzy, the whole room spinning around her, as if the world had gone off its axis with that kiss. Who would have known he could do *that*? Make her feel that way?

He seemed unsure, as well, confusion on

his face for the first time she had ever seen. He turned away and leaned over to examine the photo of Lily and the baby along with the array of other photos Lily had displayed in silver frames. 'You took all of these?' he asked, and Violet nodded. 'They are exquisite. I never realised photographs could capture so much of life.'

Violet wondered for a moment if he was making fun of her in some way, but his expression was serious and intent as he studied the images. Perhaps he really could see what she'd tried to do with them, really could appreciate them. She felt a tiny, warm touch of pleasure at his admiration. 'Thank you! See this one? It's of the fields near your own home, at sunset. The light turns everything so golden, like a fairyland.'

'It's my very favourite time of day there,' he said. 'You've caught it for all time. Amazing.'

'Well, I shall ring for that champagne,' Lily said happily, and Violet glanced at her sister. Lily's smile was broader now, real and glowing, as if she imagined she saw something reassuring there in Violet and the Duke's kiss. Something—romantic.

Violet felt her cheeks turn hot at the thought. It *had* felt romantic, hadn't it? As if that moment was strangely real. She couldn't let herself believe that, not for an instant.

William sat down beside her and took her hand lightly in his. When she tried to pull away, his touch tightened, grew warmer, and he gave her a teasing little smile. And she had imagined *she* would be the one playing mischief!

'You'll be able to plan a grand wedding, darling,' Aidan said to his wife. 'Not like ours at the tiny chapel. Maybe Westminster Abbey?'

'Oh, no...' Violet began to say. She knew that once her sister started making plans she was unstoppable, and the last thing Violet wanted was to talk about satin and orange blossoms! And the Abbey, as if...

As if she would be a real duchess.

'We want to wait until after the Russian visit to think about all that,' she said.

'True, there is sure to be a great deal of inspiration to be found in a royal wedding,' Lily said happily. 'You will want some kind of artistic gown and the most interesting flower arrangements, no fusty old lilies. But I hear the Prince and the Grand Duchess are having *two* ceremonies! The Orthodox one and an Anglican one led by Dean Stanley. Queen Victoria insists on it.'

'I think one should do it for me,' William said.

'And then you will be our neighbours! How grand it will all be,' Lily said. The butler came in with the champagne and Lily handed it around as Aidan poured. 'To true love, yes?'

'To finding one's real self,' Violet answered.

She took a sip of the delicious, bubbling golden liquid and wished she could gulp it down. She needed a steadying hand now. This was all harder than she had thought it would be. Especially with William there beside her, so close, yet still so far away. So warm and real, yet such a dream.

As Lily chattered about the forthcoming journey to St Petersburg and Aidan refilled the champagne glasses, the butler appeared at the drawing room door again. Behind him, in the entrance hall, they could hear some kind of commotion, a clatter, a cry.

'I beg your pardon, Your Grace,' he said. 'But it seems there are some unexpected guests.'

'Guests?' Lily said with a laugh. 'Well, who could it be? The Queen? Princess Alexandra? Anything is possible today.'

'It's us, my darlin'!' a sweet voice, dripping with Southern magnolias, cried. Violet shot to her feet, going cold all over, as their mother appeared in the doorway. It was the indomitable Stella Wilkins, so small and lithe in her fur-edged cloak with a feathered hat on her golden curls. Her smile was wide and sparkling. Right there, like a dream. Or a nightmare.

Violet was sure she was imagining things. Had she actually drunk too much champagne? But Lily looked just as shocked as Violet felt and Stella rushed in amid a cloud of lilac scent to kiss Lily's cheeks. She turned to Violet, her smile just flickering the merest bit. 'How happy I am to see my beautiful daughters again. And I brought you a surprise, Violet!'

'I—are *you* not the surprise, Mother?' Violet gasped.

Stella laughed, like silvery bells. 'Oh, I *did* want to surprise you, of course. It's all such fun. We sailed on the *France* last week, that new ship, you know, so luxurious and fast.'

'We, Mother?' Lily said.

Stella turned and waved at the doorway. Their father stood there, Coleman Wilkins, 'Old King Coal', as large and hearty and bluff as ever in his brown overcoat, sweeping off his hat to reveal his halo of wispy hair. 'Hello, my prettiest girls!' he boomed.

And behind him was—Harold Rogers. As thin as their father was portly, he was pale beneath too-dark hair, his eyes watchful. He was as beaky as a buzzard, she thought. He smiled at Violet, too brightly for her taste, too—too knowing.

Violet reached again for William, blindly, instinctively, and he caught her hand in his. She suddenly felt steadier with him beside her.

'And Mr Rogers, here to claim his bride,'

Stella said, steel under the flowers of her voice. 'But I see we are already celebrating something! Champagne in the afternoon, Lily darlin'? I thought you English always had tea?'

'It's true champagne is not our usual, but Violet had such good news,' Lily said. 'She has become engaged to Aidan's friend and neighbour. This is William, the Duke of Charteris. William, these are—our parents.'

'How do you do,' William said with a bow to Stella. He still held Violet's hand, as if he sensed she needed him in that moment. 'I am terribly sorry I haven't yet written to you, Mr Wilkins, as I should have. This has been rather sudden and I was so anxious to secure your daughter's hand that I turned to Aidan for permission first. I realise you do not yet know me, but I hope now you are here I may reassure you.'

He seemed to be the only steady, calm person left in the room. Even Violet's mother, always so supremely confident, so in control, so organising of everyone's lives, looked flummoxed. Her pink lips parted. Her cheeks flushed rose-red, her gaze darting between William and Violet.

'You're engaged to a—a duke, Violet?' she whispered. 'There's to be another duchess in the family? No one has done a double like this that I know.'

So Lily had been right. Being a double duchess-mother seemed to spark Stella's interest immediately. But Violet's father did not seem so very convinced. He scowled at them darkly and she almost wanted to run and hide under a desk, as she had when she was a child.

'Violet, I am quite sure we wrote to you that Harold here had asked for your hand,' Coleman said sternly. 'It was all most satisfactorily arranged.'

Violet glanced at Harold Rogers, who watched her with narrowed eyes, very still and silent. 'I'm sorry, Papa. But my feelings for William had already…'

'Your *feelings*?' Coleman snapped. He had always been a distant but indulgent father most of the time, leaving the strictness to his wife and lavishing his girls with gifts whenever he was home, which was rarely. But when he did make an order, he expected it to be followed immediately. He looked shocked and furious now that one of his daughters would flout that. 'Feelings don't come into business, Violet. Business that has kept you and your sisters in diamonds and furs all these years.'

'Coleman,' Harold said quietly. 'I am sure this is not the moment. We're obviously interrupting a time of celebration.'

'I'd certainly like a bit of that champagne, Lily darlin',' Stella said.

Coleman nodded brusquely and turned to scowl at William. 'May I have a word with you, then, Your Grace? In private?'

'Certainly, sir,' William said. For some reason, Violet couldn't quite let go of his hand. He gave her a small smile and whispered, 'So that is…er…your almost-fiancé?'

Violet nodded. 'Isn't he quite ancient?'

'And dreadful. Don't worry. We have a bargain, right?'

A bargain. That was all.

'You can always trust me to keep my word,

Violet. Your father might be the richest man in New York...'

'Fourth-richest.'

'Well, first or fourth, he doesn't frighten me. Trust me.'

Violet looked up into his green eyes, green as springtime, clear as a mountain stream, and somehow she realised she *could* trust him. He had a quiet inner strength that was like huddling close to a fire in winter.

'Shall we use my library for this conversation, then?' Aidan said.

She nodded and let him go. He and her father, along with Aidan and Harold Rogers, vanished to the library, and Violet's mother plopped down next to her daughter with a glass of champagne.

'Another duke!' She sighed. 'Just imagine. How ever did you do it, Violet?'

Violet almost laughed. At least her mother seemed to be coming over to her side. Considering Violet had inherited her own sense of determination from her wilful mother, that was no small thing.

But she still didn't like that gleam in Harold's eyes as he watched her. Not at all.

* * *

'Only a trial, private engagement,' Coleman said angrily, his voice blurry behind the closed door as Violet strained to hear more. 'I know you have a high-and-mighty title, but I have plans for my daughter and surely her mother and I know her best…'

Charteris's reply was indistinguishable.

Violet slowly backed away from the library door and tiptoed towards the drawing room. She heard her mother and Lily chattering there, but she couldn't face them and their happy wedding plans yet, couldn't sit and smile and nod about veils and bouquets. So much had happened so quickly and her head was whirling.

She ducked into a small breakfast room, which was silent and shadowed at that hour, the heavy yellow satin curtains drawn over the windows. She sank down into one of the chairs, her legs shaking. So, she was engaged now. She had bought a bit of time. How would she make the most of it? How would she make her dreams come true?

And how would she survive being close to the Duke—William—for so long? When he was close, he was all she could think about, curse him.

But she wasn't alone in the quiet very long. She heard a low, rough cough and a rustle at the door. She twisted her head around to see Harold Rogers there, watching her. How long had he been lurking? She shot to her feet, twisting her hands in the folds of her striped morning skirt as she made herself smile. Made herself appear oblivious. She wouldn't let him see how unsettled she really felt.

There was no real reason for him to 'unsettle' her, she thought, surely. On the occasions when he had come to their houses in America, he had seemed quiet, watchful, polite enough. He was her father's associate. She had never thought he would show an interest in her. Why would he? He didn't need her money; he was rich on his own. If he wanted a family, a pretty wife, surely he could find one, someone much prettier and more desperate than Violet. Money could do that.

Yet here he was, come all the way to England to see her, and her father seemed upset at the overturning of his marital plans for her. Much more upset than she might have expected. Why was that?

'Mr Rogers,' she said, as he stared at her.

'I'm sure you could call me Harold, my dear, after all this time,' he said softly. 'I thought we knew each other quite well.'

'Did we?' Violet said, puzzled. She couldn't remember any private conversations with the man at all.

'Of course. My plans with your father were so carefully laid, I was sure you would welcome them. Welcome me.' He moved closer, so slowly, so still, it was almost like watching a ghost glide inexorably towards her. 'Yet now I hear I must wish you happy.'

Violet backed away until she bumped into the table edge. He stood so close in that small room that he blocked her path to the door. 'I'm sorry, but I had no idea of my father's plans, or that you meant to propose to me,' she said. 'I truly never saw you in that light.'

'Never? Oh, my dear, you do protest too much. I'm sure you remember our dance at Newport.'

Violet didn't, actually, but she always tried

to forget about Newport life when she wasn't forced to be there. The constant changing of clothes, the tennis games and carriage drives and teas and balls, when she longed to run on the beach. She thought hard and remembered a party before they had left for Europe, before Lily married. It all seemed so long ago. Violet hadn't been officially 'out', but she was still brought down to greet guests at parties and she had waltzed with Mr Rogers that evening. It had been stiff, slow, strange. The way he'd looked at her...

She shook her head. No wonder she wanted to forget it.

'I was very careful over how I showed my feelings,' he said, moving even closer. 'You were quite young then. But I was assured you felt the same, my dear Violet.'

Violet was deeply irritated at being called 'dear' by him. She stood up very straight, her shoulders stiff. 'I had no idea of any such thing. And I am in love with someone else.'

He smiled, as one would to a stubborn child or pony. 'Dazzled by a title, perhaps, as ladies tend to be, but that is no life for you. I know, deep down, how suited we are to one another. How very good we would be together.'

Violet had heard enough. 'I am engaged,' she said and tried to push past him.

To her shock, he grabbed her arm, hard, and pulled her off balance against him. She stumbled and his lips came down on hers. It was so quick she barely knew what was happening, and it was bruising and rough. She tried to shove him away, cold panic threatening to wash over her. *Run!* her mind screamed, but she was frozen. How could such a thing be happening?

Suddenly, he was away from her, stumbling himself. She backed away, rubbing the edge of her hand over her lips, and saw it was William who had pulled Rogers from her. He was very still, his jaw stiff, his eyes glowing in that way she had come to long for— and also fear. William was not a man to be trifled with.

Rogers righted himself and smiled smugly. 'I was just wishing my old friend happy, Your Grace. A friendly kiss of congratulations. You are very fortunate.'

'So I am,' William said, so quiet, so lethal.

Once she'd believed him to be boring, but he was just restrained, reserved, and when that was unleashed she knew the world would shiver. 'And I do look after those I care about. I give you fair warning to show respect to my fiancée in the future—at all times.'

'Oh, no need for that. Ducal commands don't work on Americans, do they? It was merely a kiss—from *her* to me. You may find she will not be your fiancée for very long, especially if you don't take care.' He gave one more cold smile and marched out of the room, the door clicking behind him.

Violet sat down again and wished she could stop shaking, wished she could feel warm again. William went to the sideboard where a carafe of water sat, poured out a glass and pressed it gently into her hand.

'It's not brandy, but it will help for now,' he said. 'Take a sip, then breathe deeply. He's gone now and I will make sure he doesn't come back.'

Violet was touched by his quiet consideration, and his calmness steadied her. 'Thank you,' she murmured. She did as he said, breathing steadily, as deeply as her tightly laced bodice allowed, and she found it did help. She was starting to feel angry again rather than scared. 'I *didn't* kiss him!'

'I know,' he said, and the simple confidence in those words gave her even more strength.

'I never thought of him in that way. I have no idea why he would think of *me* like that! He's richer than I am.'

William sat down beside her, so close but not touching, just staying with her. 'You think your money is the only reason someone would want you?'

'W-well…' Violet stammered. 'It's certainly a consideration. I have red hair and I'm not very ladylike.'

He laughed. 'Red hair is quite extraordinary and you have great spirit.'

'Do I?' Violet considered this. She supposed she did, though it was not the kind of *spirit* that usually attracted a man. She was independent and tended to act sometimes without considering, though she was working on reining that in. But she didn't want to be very different from how she was and William didn't seem to mind that. It was very strange. 'Be careful, William. I might start to think you rather like me.'

'I do like you. Sometimes.' He poured her more water and smiled. 'You did say you needed a way out of engaging yourself to this Mr Rogers. I see now that was very true.'

'And you said you wanted to thank me for warning you about Miss Parker-Parks.'

'Yes. No Mr Rogers for you, no Miss Parker-Parks for me. Your father has agreed to a trial engagement between us, informal arrangements only until after the royal wedding, but I think we are safe enough for now.'

Safe. Yes, she did feel safe now—with him. She would never have imagined it before, that he would be her steadiest friend. The one she could be honest with, as she could with no one else right now. 'Thank you.'

He nodded. 'Shall we go to the drawing room? If you feel ready. I think your father and Mr Rogers were going to leave for their hotel.'

Violet nodded. 'Yes. You really are very kind, William, no matter how you try to hide it. Rather a Galahad.'

A dull flush spread over his sharp cheekbones, fascinating her. 'What are fiancés for, then? Just don't tell anybody. You would quite ruin my fierce reputation.'

Chapter Nine

'I can't believe we've actually been invited on to the royal train!' Violet exclaimed, watching the city flash past their carriage window as they made their way to the station. It had been quite the whirlwind in the last few days. Despite the fact that it was an 'informal' engagement, word had leaked out and letters and cards had flooded into Lily's house, along with flowers and invitations. Their father and Mr Rogers had luckily left London for urgent business in Paris, but their mother had stayed behind to shop on Bond Street and chatter more about lace. She and Lily were quite enthralled with the Westminster Abbey idea now.

Even such tiresome talk couldn't dampen Violet's enthusiasm today, though. Despite the grand, gilded boredom of her Court presentation and the dinner at Marlborough House, she was still quite fascinated by the idea of royalty. An actual journey on the royal train to Russia seemed very glamorous. And there was the possible chance to talk more with Prince Alfred about photography. It was a marvellous opportunity.

The chance to spend more time with William, on a quiet train with nothing to do but talk and look at him, had nothing to do with it, of course. Nothing at all. *At all.*

She peeked over at him where he sat beside her on the tufted velvet seat. She couldn't read his thoughts—he was once again the remote Duke, his face shadowed by the brim of his hat.

Lily sat across from them; Aidan would follow to St Petersburg in a few days because of business at his estate. Lily had cried bitterly when she left the baby with his nurse, but now she looked excited just like Violet.

'Do we have *you* to thank for the invitation, William?' Violet said. His shoulder brushed against hers as the carriage lurched, making her shiver. 'Ducal influence, politics, all of that? I hear the Prince of Wales has his own card room on the train. Scandalous. It sounds racy for you.'

'Because I hate fun?' he said, laughter hiding in his voice.

'Exactly so,' Violet said. 'And it sounds as if the Prince's life is nothing *but* fun. Do you not disapprove?'

'Violet!' Lily cried. 'Of course William likes fun. Or he wouldn't like *you*.'

Violet looked up at him. 'Do you like me, then?'

'I told you—sometimes I do. And I admit that the Marlborough House set is not my usual circle. All those late nights don't make for a productive workday. But I know Prince Alfred likes photography, as you do, and I thought you might enjoy talking to him when there's not such a crowd.'

'I—yes, I would, thank you,' Violet said. She wondered why she was still surprised by his consideration, his thought for her and others. William had shown her he did not have ducal self-centredness. It was one of the things she was starting to like, rather too much, about him. 'I'm sorry I teased you.'

He smiled at her and she shivered again.

'Not at all. And I am quite sure your brother-in-law had something to do with this invitation. A little bird whispered that Princess Alexandra is thinking of Lily as a Lady of the Bedchamber. Possibly even the next Mistress of the Robes.'

'I have only just heard of it myself,' Lily said. 'I do like the Princess. She is sweet and kind, even if you have to shout at her to be heard. But I don't know about the late nights at Marlborough House, either.'

'A Lady of the Bedchamber doesn't have such onerous duties,' William said. 'Just ceremonial, really. Standing beside her at Drawing Rooms, holding her bouquet sometimes. I doubt she expects you to be there all the time.'

Lily smiled. 'Perhaps when you are married, Vi and I can serve at Court together. So helpful to have such a wife when the husband has political ideas, isn't that so? And we would have so much fun!' She laughed happily, making Violet feel terrible that she would have to disappoint her sister later. 'Oh, that word again! Fun. But you will have to get used to it with a wife like my sister.'

'I look forward to it immensely,' William said, and he sounded as if it was true. Maybe he belonged at Drury Lane.

Violet bit her lip and turned back to the window, glad of the distraction from looking at him and talking about fun and marriage. 'Oh, look, we're here!' she cried in relief.

Violet had thought travelling with her sister the Duchess between her country home and London had been luxurious. Private train compartments, plush carriages, footmen and outriders. Yet it was nothing compared to being escorted on to the royal train, waiting in its own siding in solitary, gilded splendour. It gleamed dark red and gold, matched by a plush interior of velvet cushions and rich carpets.

The royal party itself had not yet arrived, and equerries and ladies-in-waiting sipped tea in the drawing room, greeting Lily with smiles as Violet took it all in. It was more like an extension of a palace than a train, with tables and sofas dotted around a fitted, wall-to-wall red carpet, sconces and gold-framed paintings gleaming with muted light on the silk-papered walls, the windows draped in velvet curtains.

If this train was so grand, what would the actual *palaces* be like in Russia, where everything was said to be so lavish and luxurious? What beautiful photographs they would make!

They were quickly seated near one of the satin-swathed windows. Tea was brought, fur rugs offered. Footmen in royal livery hurried past bearing notes and telegrams and hampers and small lapdogs. Everyone nodded to William, their gazes full of curiosity as they looked at Violet's hand on his arm, her glove hiding any ring or lack thereof.

She snatched it back, tucking it into her sable muff.

'Do you always travel in such great splendour?' she asked him. Even her mother, whose 'cottage' in Newport was modelled on the Grand Trianon, would have been aching to take notes for remodelling.

'Me? Certainly not. I'm not a prince.' He snapped open a newspaper one of the footmen had brought him. 'Far too elaborate. It takes up too much time. A normal train and ferry could get us to Berlin much faster.'

'So you would travel alone if it wasn't for my enthusiasm for photography?' she said.

'Hmph.' He rustled the paper impatiently, but she saw the smile he was trying to cover up. 'It does me no harm to put my face in front of the Princes, either.'

'No, I suppose not. But it doesn't really benefit you, only me. So it's very nice of you.' She studied an image on the front page of the paper, sketches of Prince Alfred and Grand Duchess Maria above an etching of her grand St Petersburg palace home. Violet hoped she would be able to give the papers something much better in a photograph, capturing the royal pair and the sweetness of their romance for everyone to see.

And, thanks to William, she might just have that chance. She put her hand back on to his arm. For an instant, he tensed, but then he relaxed back into that warm, steady strength she always felt with him. He gave her a curious glance over the paper.

'We're meant to be engaged,' she whispered.

'So we are.' He suddenly leaned over and kissed her cheek, making her laugh. She lightly covered the kiss with her other hand, as if she would hold it there.

Lily sighed happily.

Suddenly, there was a commotion outside and Violet turned from William and her confusion and delight over his kiss to peer beyond the window. The Prince and Princess of Wales, followed by the bridegroom, were making their procession on to the train.

'Oh, isn't this delightful!' Princess Alexandra said, clapping her mauve kid-gloved hands in wonder. 'A royal wedding journey... Oh, Affie. So romantic.' She turned her beaming gaze on to Violet and William. 'For all of us...'

The wheels of the train were clacking softly in the night beyond the velvet-draped windows when Violet joined the royal party for a hand of whist after a lavish, multi-course dinner. She soon found herself winning. She laid down another card and said carefully, 'I saw your engagement photographs in that magazine, sir.'

Prince Alfred laughed. 'Oh, yes. So horribly stiff, aren't they? I fear my Marie hates the way she looks in photos. But she also hates to sit still. She would rather be riding or skating, unless she's reading. She is a great reader.'

Violet thought of the Grand Duchess's image in those photos. She had indeed looked rather grumpy. Perhaps if she was shown actually reading a book, or somehow in motion? Like in Mrs Cameron's images, where that slight blurriness implied movement, action, time passing. 'I haven't met her, of course, but it seems to me she has a face full of energy and personality.'

'That she does, Miss Wilkins! Not a great beauty, maybe, but I was so caught up in her magnificent spirit the first time we met. I've never known anyone else quite like her.'

Violet smiled. She knew what he meant; she had never met anyone quite like William, either. Not that she loved him as the Duke loved his Princess, but still there was that glimmer about him, that spark of fascination she couldn't deny, couldn't quite stop thinking about. 'Perhaps, then, she just hasn't found the right photographer to capture that spirit? Angles and lighting can make such a difference in an image.'

Prince Alfred chewed thoughtfully on the end of his cigar and laid down another card. 'That is most true, Miss Wilkins, most true. It's a technique I have wrestled with myself. The light is always what bedevils me in my attempts. Tell me, what camera do you favour?'

'One from Charles Bennett now. I've tried several.'

'Fascinating. I learned on an old wet-plate monstrosity myself. It once belonged to my father, an old-fashioned, heavy thing. It made me find ways to work round problems, though. I like a scenograph now. Very up to date. You don't even need half the chemicals and the images are clearer.'

'I haven't yet had the chance to try it.'

'Oh, you must! It's lighter, too, perfect for a lady, I should think. I imagine your favoured medium is the portrait? Ladies are so good at arranging such things, especially with children. I tried once with my nieces and nephews, but found I haven't the patience.'

Violet laughed, trying to imagine arranging a pack of wriggling little ones in a proper photo. 'All portraits do take patience, sir. But I like them. I like looking deeper into people. I enjoy a landscape, too.' She put down another card. 'Perhaps the Grand Duchess would like an image of herself with her St Petersburg home in the background? Something to remind her of where she comes from. I do know how it feels when one is newly arrived in a foreign country to make a new home.'

'Oh, yes. You and your sisters are Americans. It's easy to forget that. One would almost think you were English.'

Violet bit back a sardonic smile at such a 'compliment' and took another card. 'Why, thank you, sir. Do you think people will say that to your bride?'

'No, no. Marie will never be anything but a Russian at heart, I think.' He laughed. 'I think it will be interesting to see her with my mother.'

'Then a photo of her old home will be welcome, I should think. Perhaps reading her favourite book?'

'A fine idea, Miss Wilkins. It will distract her, make her smile.'

'What are her favourite books?'

'Poetry, I think, and some of the classics. Romances, like Mr Scott. I haven't a head for them myself, I fear. Are you a great reader yourself?'

Violet shook her head. 'I fear not, though I do enjoy poetry. Some Walter Scott. My sisters are the readers, especially my twin, Rose.' It was why Rose had married her Jamie, for his great scholarship. That, and his lovely golden-brown eyes.

'Few of my siblings are readers, except Vicky, and Alice. She's our great intellectual.' He laid down a card. 'My sister-in-law is so fond of your sister the Duchess of Lennox. She says she's quiet and kind, and sensitive, as I am sure you are. Perhaps you're right and Marie would prefer a lady photographer. Someone to see her true nature.'

Violet glanced past the Prince to William, where he sat at the next card table with Princess Alexandra and Lily. She gave him a secret, triumphant little smile, and he nodded happily. Their own little success, together!

'Perhaps so, sir. I would be very honoured. Oh, look at this hand!' she said, laying down her cards. 'I think I win this round. Only fair since you've already beaten me twice.'

Later, as William escorted her to her berth, the party left behind them, she told him all about her royal conversation.

'I do think he is very close to letting me take a wedding photo,' she said, suddenly feeling nervous. It was what she had longed for, yes, but was she ready for such a task? Did she know enough? 'But I fear…'

'Fear what?' he said gently. 'Isn't this what you wanted?'

'Oh, yes! But what if I have this chance and find my work is not good enough?'

'It's not like you to lack confidence, Violet. I think you need have no fear of that. Your work is as fine as any I saw in the exhibition. At least I think so, though I am no expert.'

'How do you know?'

'I saw your portrait of Lily and her baby. It was tender and expressive, her gentleness shining through. Even if I had never met her, I would feel I knew her from looking at it.

You also have an eye for detail. The lace on her dress, the plants, were so crisp and clear, all adding to the atmosphere.'

Violet stared up at him in wonder. He saw all that, just from glancing at her photograph. He saw—her? 'Do you think so?'

'Oh, yes. Anyone would like to be seen so clearly for who they are, even long after they age and are gone.'

'But I know my sister very well. I don't know the Grand Duchess at all.'

'Then you must get to know her—as well as you can, anyway. Russian royalty can be even more prickly about protocol than the English, but they do say Grand Duchess Maria enjoys a good laugh and is very intelligent and active.'

'Prince Alfred said she doesn't like to sit still except when she's reading. And I don't find him or his brother at all prickly! They seem quite sweet, really.'

William laughed. 'That's because you are a pretty young lady.'

She laughed, too, both startled and pleased. 'You think I'm pretty?'

'You know you are.'

She shook her head. She didn't know any such thing. Lily was beautiful, with her chestnut hair and sincere, clear gaze; Rose had a calmness, a true sweetness, that made her glow like a Renaissance Madonna. Violet always felt like a ragamuffin beside them, her skirts torn, her hands stained with chemicals. But if *he* thought she was pretty, this man who seemed incapable of being dishonest, then maybe, just maybe…

'I wouldn't even have this chance if not for your entrée into the royal family, getting us on to this train,' she said, her cheeks warm. She was glad it was dark in the narrow corridor.

'Our bargain, remember? I couldn't let you down.'

'This is surely far beyond your side of any bargain!'

He leaned his palm against the panelled wall beside her head, so warm and close. 'If the Princes are happy, they're more open to listening to me when I want a favour. If his fiancée likes her fine portrait for their wedding, Prince Alfred will be even happier.

And the Prince of Wales is very fond of his siblings—he likes to see them content.'

Violet found herself drawn closer to him, brushing against him as the train swayed beneath them. She laid her hand on his arm to steady herself and found she couldn't, didn't want to, move away. 'Then we will *all* be happy.'

'Exactly.'

'But what sort of favour would you ask?'

'I'm not sure yet. Help for my people, more land, maybe, for a proper school. Their support in my campaign.'

Of course—help for his people. That was what he wanted, above all else. Just as she wanted her freedom. That was their bargain. But somehow there in the intimate darkness, just the two of them, it felt so very different. Like so much more, as though she was glimpsing his true self, his hidden self. 'That is why you want to be involved in political life, then? To make the lives of your people better?'

He gave her a surprised glance. 'Of course. Why else? It would be far easier, and certainly more enjoyable, for me just to stay at

Bourne and ride over my fields. To be the country squire. I can dispense charity and aid for them there as needed. My late mother is still renowned there for her charitable work and she had a deep concern for the people, a deep sense of duty. She showed me how to do that, how to care. But it is no longer enough for those of us with privilege to just dispense charity. Everyone deserves a chance to use their own talents to improve their own lives as they see fit, and that cannot happen without deeper, more fundamental changes. The reform bills and Factory Act were a start. We must continue on that course. I need all the influence I can find to aid in that.'

'Of course. You are very right.' She thought of her own life, and the lives of so many other women, trapped by who they were, by things they could not control, expected to be quiet and do as they were told, no matter what their own desires or their own talents were. She was very lucky; she had never had to worry about money. How much worse to be poor and trapped. How good he was to want to change all of that.

How good he was.

She saw now why he needed exactly the right kind of wife to help him in such an important course of action. He needed a gracious hostess, someone who was able to forge her own contacts, someone calm and smiling and organised, who knew how this English world really worked. This was a woman she couldn't be, no matter how hard she tried.

But that woman would be a lucky lady indeed, Violet thought sadly. This fine English woman who would be his wife. He was a man of principle and compassion, she could see that now. Not to mention as handsome as the devil.

'I was also brought up to dispense charity,' she said. 'Balls for aid societies, dispensing baskets of blankets and jam, hosting Christmas parties for orphans. But I think your methods are far preferable to my mother's. She only does it to look like Lady Bountiful in front of her friends. Do you even have any friends to impress?'

He laughed and she loved the sound of it. It was warm and rolling, like a summer sea. How she wanted to hear it again and again!

To make him laugh. To make him look happy. 'Jam certainly has its place.'

'Especially damson. My favourite.'

'Oh, yes. Or raspberry. My mother always did hand out Christmas hampers to all the tenants and pensioners. My sister does it now, when she can escape her own duties. They would be quite angry if we didn't continue that.'

The train, gently swaying until then, gave a sharp jolt and Violet was thrown off balance in her heeled evening shoes. She fell heavily against William, clinging to his strong shoulders to keep from falling.

He held her tightly and she was surrounded by his heat, by his touch, by his scent of sandalwood soap, and she couldn't move away. She peeked up at him and found he watched her intently, his eyes narrowed, his breath held just as hers was. She was filled with such a rush of longing she almost cried out with it. Her hands curled tightly into the fine fabric of his coat.

His arms tightened around her and she wondered if he could possibly feel just as she did in that moment. That one perfect moment out of time and place, where they were just William and Violet.

She went up on tiptoe just as he dipped his head and their lips met. It was just as she remembered from that startling kiss in Lily's drawing room—tender and sweet, yet firm and touched with flames. His evening stubble was deliciously rough on her skin. His scent enveloped her, carrying her away, up and up, as if they floated into the stars.

She wrapped her arms around his neck and those flames grew between them, igniting into a bonfire. She opened her mouth at the touch of his tongue, letting him in, letting herself fly free with him. She felt all her walls crumbling around her and it excited her even as it frightened her.

The train jolted beneath them again and she heard a muffled laugh somewhere in the distance. It seemed to wake her from the hazy dream of his kiss, at least a bit, and she let go of him, standing back until she felt herself braced against the gilded-and-silk wall. He stared down at her, his eyes burning, his lips parted.

'I don't—I don't understand what's happening here,' she whispered.

He shook his head, raking his hand through his dark hair, rumpled now from her touch. For just an instant, his mask dropped and he looked discomposed, unsure, *real*. Then the mask came back up and he gave her a wry smile. 'Neither do I.'

She spun around and rushed towards her berth beyond the next door, frightened and confused and so unbearably excited all at once.

She slammed the door behind her and leaned her forehead against it, trying to draw a deep breath, trying *not* to remember that he was just on the other side of that thin sheet of wood. It was certainly true that he was *not* the Duke of Bore. But she hadn't bargained on throwing her heart into this plan, too.

Chapter Ten

Violet drew back the heavy burgundy-red velvet curtains at the window of their chamber in the Neues Palais, just outside Berlin, where they would spend a couple of days before travelling on to St Petersburg. It was quite pretty with its three wings of mellow red brick, surmounted with a Baroque roof decorated with a large dome and rows of sculptures, set in elaborate gardens.

She remembered the Crown Princess herself, racing towards them at the station, a tiny figure swathed in furs and velvet, uncaring about waiting red carpets and brass bands, disapproving men in elaborate Prussian uniforms and shining medals. She just threw herself into her brothers' arms, crying, 'You're here, at last! My darlings! Tell me all about Mama, about home.' Just like Violet surely would have, if she'd been separated from her sisters so long.

'I would hardly have thought she was a princess at all. She wasn't even a fraction as stuffy as all those old, moustached men,' she said to Lily.

Lily laughed as she sorted through her jewel case, testing various necklaces against her dinner gown. The palace was so small—for a palace, anyway—and so full that they shared a small suite, just like when they were children. 'The poor Princess. They say she does love her husband, but she's very unhappy in Berlin. They're so stiff and formal, not like England, and her in-laws have taken her children away.'

'The poor lady,' Violet murmured. 'I'm sure she'll be happy to leave for Russia with her brothers, then.'

'I'm sure she will.' Lily joined her at the window, gazing down at the gardens which were pretty even in the middle of winter with their teahouses and English mazes. Princess Victoria suddenly appeared on one of the pathways, running with her brothers between the hedges as they laughed. 'And so will we! We can be children again, just like them.'

'I do like that. I think you'll enjoy it all much more when Aidan joins us, though.'

Lily laughed and wrapped her arms around Violet to draw her into a hug. 'I'm enjoying time with my sibling, just like Princess Vicky out there. You'll be a duchess soon, too. It's not always an easy job, but it has its rewards.'

Violet shivered as she remembered William's kiss, his touch. *That* would surely be a reward—if this was real. 'Does it?'

'Oh, yes. We're in a position to be of help, real help, to people who need it. Every charity wants us to be on their committees. You can choose what's important to you and where you can do the most good. Every arts committee in England will want you, darling. You're so creative! You have such a wonderful eye. Artists will be beating down your doors at Bourne all the time. Perhaps you could set up a salon? A place where all the best painters and poets could gather. You'd be so good at it all...'

As Lily went back to her jewel sorting, Violet stared down at the darkening garden where the royals had been running and turned her sister's words over in her head. A salon where artists could gather, where she could help them and seek their advice for herself—it sounded very nice indeed, like a dream.

She thought of William's words, of the work he did to be of use to his people, to help them make better lives. She certainly knew how hard Lily worked. Her old disdain towards women who sought to marry titles no matter what, and her perception of William as boring, was melting away now. Maybe there could be a point to it all.

And when he kissed her the way he did, held her close, looked at her in that way of his that said he saw her, saw *Violet*, not the Wilkins heiress—she wanted only him in those moments. She wanted to share in that life.

But it was a silly idea, a silly hope that slowly faded when she was away from him. She had fought so hard, was still fighting, to win her independence. To find her own dreams in life. This was just a little ruse to keep Harold Rogers at bay. A bargain, as

William had said. One day William would be gone from her life, surely off to marry someone else, a proper English lady. This was all just a strange interlude.

She bit her lip, hating the pang she felt at the thought of never seeing him again. That was not part of the bargain!

'What shall we wear tonight?' Lily asked. Violet heard the rustle of tulle and silk as Lily and the maid started sorting through trunks. 'Aidan tells me this Prussian court is far more etiquette-bound than in England! Even though this is Princess Vicky's own house and they say she hates the stuffiness of her in-laws, I'm sure all proper protocol will be on show for the Princes. I'd hate to wear the wrong thing.'

'So, no petticoat that plays "God Save the Queen" when you sit down? They say that's what Jennie Jerome wore. People expect Americans to liven things up.'

'Violet! You're terrible.' Lily laughed.

'I know, I'm sorry. I do know how proper you try to make everything.'

'I just never want to embarrass Aidan,' Lily said quietly.

Violet turned away from the window to see Lily staring wistfully at a pink satin gown in her hands. Lily *was* a good duchess, as Violet knew she herself could never be. She feared she would always embarrass someone, no matter how hard she tried.

'You could never in a million years embarrass Aidan! Even if you did wear musical underpinnings, he would think it the grandest idea ever. Besides, you are by far the most proper duchess I have ever seen.'

Lily gave a wavery smile. 'Thank you, darling Vi. I know you will always be my most staunch supporter.'

'Of course I am. The Wilkins sisters always stick together.' She sat down beside Lily, running a fingertip over a lace ruffle on the gown's sleeve. 'Is something amiss? Tears aren't like you.'

Lily glanced at the maid, who was arranging the dressing table across the room. 'I think I might be blessed again.'

Violet's eyes widened. 'Another baby? Oh, Lily! How wonderful. Does Aidan know?'

'Not yet. It's so early and I want to be sure. But I feel like I did the last time, wanting to cry one minute and laughing like a fool the next. And I want to eat sweets all the time.'

'Are you hoping for a girl this time?'

Lily smiled. 'Maybe. I know the Duchess says we need a spare heir...'

'Ugh, your mother-in-law,' Violet groaned. 'You shouldn't listen to her.'

'I don't. I want another Wilkins girl, yes. But you mustn't say anything yet.'

'I won't. I can keep secrets.'

'I know you can. You are the best secret-keeper I've ever known. But not even a word to Rose yet. Just for a little longer.'

'Why not Rose?'

'I'm sure you've noticed she's, well, not entirely herself lately.'

Violet frowned, remembering how thin Rose had seemed at the ball, how brittle her laughter, how preoccupied. Violet suddenly felt like such a fool. She had been so wrapped up in her own problems she hadn't been of more help to Rose, her own twin. 'She does seem rather delicate. She's always been so sensitive, so sweet, but now...'

Lily nodded. 'She hasn't become pregnant and Jamie is always so buried in his studies.

If not yet having a baby is what's bothering her, I don't want to add to her worries.'

'I do see, yes, of course.'

'We'll tell her when we get back from St Petersburg.'

'Oh, Lily, speaking of Russia, are you quite sure you should be on this journey? In winter?'

'Of course! It's my job. Aidan needs me here. And you heard William, Princess Alexandra wants me as one of her ladies. I can't let them all down. You'll see. William needs you, too.'

Violet was quite sure William needed no one at all, especially not a hoyden like her. 'I'm not sure I could be of much use to him. Not like you are with Aidan.'

'Nonsense! He is very lucky to have you, my sensible, artistic sister. You'll never let all the folderol go to your head, and he'll always be able to count on you for clear-sighted honesty, which is what a duke needs. They're too often up on their ducal clouds, you know, so no one dares to be really honest with them.' She held up the pink gown. 'Now—this one, do you think? Thank heavens I can still fit into my dresses, after having so many made for this journey! You could wear the white taffeta with the pink velvet roses. They say Princess Alexandra and her sister the Tsarevna like to wear coordinated gowns...'

Lily had been right, Violet thought as she looked around the Neues Palais ballroom. The Prussian court was bound up so tight in their etiquette, she wasn't sure how they breathed. The Marble Gallery, with its checked black-and-white floor, its roaring fireplaces set within carved mantels, and rows of polished mirrors interspersed with gilt-framed paintings, was charming, but no one seemed to look around them at all to admire it.

The air was thick and overly warm, sticky with the scent of trailing arrangements of gardenias and orchids all along the dark blue flocked walls and heaped like waterfalls in the corners. Roaring fires snapped and flared in the vast stone grates, making the atmosphere smoky and hot yet strangely letting cold draughts sweep along ladies' bare shoulders, making them all blue and goose-pimpled under their jewels.

But Violet had to admit that Princess Vicky, despite her large, sad eyes, was very charming, with a sweet smile and welcoming air.

'Oh, yes, dear Will's new young lady!' she had exclaimed when Violet curtsied to her in the receiving line. 'How pretty you are, just as he said.'

Will? Some of Violet's astonishment that anyone, even a princess, would be so informal with William made her laugh. The thought that he considered her *pretty* made her feel filled with a strange, giddy pleasure.

'You must forgive me, Miss Wilkins, but he was one of our few approved playmates when we were children. I boiled eggs for him in my playhouse at Osborne. He's so dear, so hardworking. And he says you take photographs! Just like my dearest Papa. Marvellous. You must show me some of your work.'

Violet had stammered an agreement before she moved along the line. Perhaps this was what Lily meant by spouses being of use to each other, how they might act as partners in the world. It was a most extraordinary thought. Oh, she saw that Lily and Aidan were together in all things, but she'd never really experienced such a feeling before. Their parents were not 'partners' except that Stella ran Coleman's houses. She had nothing to do with his business dealings, nor he with her society world.

Violet had imagined that all marriages were like her parents'—separate, the woman shuffled off to the home and parties. And with Harold Rogers, that's exactly what it would be. But with William...

She peeked at him over the edge of her lace fan. He was talking with Crown Prince Fritz, who was as portly and bearded as his brothers-in-law, but with a nice smile, and nodding solemnly at something the Prince said. William caught her gaze and gave her a nod and a little, speaking smile. He started towards her across the crowded room, but was stopped by several people. She wondered how many of them called him 'Will'.

Violet turned to Lily next to her. Her sister chatted and laughed happily with two of Princess Alexandra's ladies-in-waiting, not giving a single sign that she felt at all out of sorts.

'How grand it all is,' Violet said, gesturing

to the rooms with her fan, the ladies blazing with diamonds, the men covered with their medals. Who would have ever thought that they, the daughters of 'Old King Coal' Wilkins, would be in such a place.

One of the ladies laughed. 'Oh, the Neues Palais is pretty, I grant you, Miss Wilkins, and these Germans do try hard, but it is all nothing at all next to Russia. Wait until you see the Winter Palace. It is all most breathtaking.'

'Especially when they want to show us how far above her new English family the Grand Duchess is,' the second lady added, gulping down her champagne. 'There has been so much wrangling about her title and precedence! It will be most amusing to see what happens when she gets to England. Who will prevail in the end, Victoria or Marie?'

The first lady gave her a disapproving glance at such informality and Violet was rather glad she wasn't the only one who needed to mind her *p*'s and *q*'s. Maybe it was only a sham engagement, but she found she had no desire to embarrass William, just as Lily wanted Aidan to be proud. She, Violet, who had never minded for one moment what anyone thought of her, except her sisters!

Was this what it felt like, then, she wondered, to be a real, grown-up lady like Lily? It was very strange and not altogether unpleasant.

The musicians high up in a hidden gallery struck up a lively tune and couples began forming for the dance. William reached her side at last, looking not the least bit ruffled for his long, much-interrupted passage, because of all the people who wanted to talk to him. To be near him. Just as Violet did. She smiled up at him in answer to his nod.

'Hello, *Will*,' she teased. Despite all the formality around them, she felt so strangely light. Happy.

A dull red blush touched his sharply etched cheekbones. 'You've been talking to Princess Vicky.'

'Yes, she is very kind. She tells me she used to boil eggs for you. I hope you don't expect that from me. I fear I'm not quite sure how to make water boil.'

'Yet you mix up all those chemicals for your photographs.'

'That's quite different. Cooking is a vast mystery. Like alchemy, really. Turning a pile of flour into bread.'

'I doubt Vicky has any idea how to cook an egg now, either. That was a very long time ago, when she and her siblings had a little Swiss chalet at Osborne, where they would make tea and grow vegetables to sell to their father. It was meant to teach them about the wider world.'

Violet studied the ballroom, all gold and velvet and diamonds and gardenias. 'Oh, yes, I can see that,' she said wryly.

William laughed. 'Yes, I'm not sure it worked out as their father planned. It didn't with Prince Bertie, certainly.'

'But with you? The Princess said you were one of their few playmates.' She thought of her own childhood, climbing trees and running on the beach at Newport until their mother decided they had to be fine ladies. Her friends had been her sisters and sometimes the gardeners' children, not princesses. And yet he talked to his people, spent time with them, cared about what they wanted and was prepared to help them attain it. 'Maybe it took rather well with you.'

His eyebrow arched. 'I hope so. Shall we dance? It might help warm up this draughty old place.'

'Yes, thank you.' Violet took his offered arm and let him lead her to the dance floor. Thankfully, the slow, stately, elaborate opening pavane, led by Princess Vicky and her brother Prince Bertie, had finished and the piece was a pretty waltz. Violet at least knew how to waltz and always enjoyed the spins and twirls every minute when William held her close. It *was* warmer when he touched her, his gloved hand on her back, guiding her into the swooping opening, as light as a feather on a breeze. How easily they moved together! She felt like a top set free on a summer sunbeam.

'How very astonishing your world is, Will,' she said. And how delightful that name sounded on her lips! She tried it again. A *Will* could not be as fearsome as she had once imagined him. A Will could have fun. 'Royalty cooking for you, palaces open before you…'

'It's a world like any other, surely. A place where we must learn to exist. To fit into our place.'

'Where you have obligations.'

'Of course. Privilege brings duties. And mine are not as onerous as poor Vicky's.'

'Did you learn that from your mother, along with the value of charity?'

'Yes. She was thought almost a saint at Bourne.'

A saint. Violet thought then that it was good she would never really be Duchess of Charteris. She could never, ever be a saint. But the Duchess had certainly passed some fine qualities on to her son, like duty and kindness. Maybe even those green eyes?

He suddenly spun her around in a wide arc, making her laugh as her skirts belled around them. He twirled her again and again, until they found themselves alone in a small corridor, having danced away from the crowd.

Violet couldn't quite catch her breath. She tilted her face up to his in the dim light, watching the glow of his eyes as if she was mesmerised. His head bent and his lips brushed against the pulse that beat frantically at her temple, leaving tiny touches of fire that made her tingle all the way to her toes. She shivered with the overpowering force of emotion that rushed through her. This was what she had longed for all evening and hadn't even realised it.

She went up on tiptoe and met his lips with her own, and the flame within her roared into burning life. She moaned softly against him and that small sound ignited something in him, too. He groaned and dragged her so close that there was nothing between them at all. Her lips instinctively parted under his kiss and his tongue lightly touched the tip of hers, as if seeking, questing, before he deepened their touch.

She wound her arms around his neck, her fingers twining in his hair, as if she could hold him with her forever. But he didn't seem to want to leave her. The kiss slid down, down, into a need she hadn't even known was in her. Something so raw, so fiery, so deep-down necessary.

She swayed, as if she would fall, and he lifted her up to press her against the wall. His lips trailed from hers, over the arch of her throat, to touch the tiny hollow where her pulse pounded with raw need for him.

'Violet…' he whispered heavily, his breath ragged against her.

'I—I know,' she answered, and something in those words frightened her. She pulled away and ran, running from him— or maybe from herself and the feelings she never wanted to acknowledge.

Chapter Eleven

Those ladies-in-waiting had been quite right, Violet thought as she stared up at the Winter Palace as their sleigh drew up in the cobbled courtyard below the towering, carved front doors. The Neues Palais was nothing compared to the overpowering splendour of St Petersburg.

She had been in awe and uncharacteristically quiet ever since they had left the train and even as they were driven through the icy streets. They rode past bridges that arced in lacy patterns over the river and canals, past pastel-coloured mansions and glittering shop windows.

But this palace—no, she could not believe it was real. It was a giant, blue and white and gold chocolate box, glittering with hundreds of windows.

Yet it *was* real. Footmen with powdered hair and gold-encrusted livery, the Tsar's cipher on their coats, reached up to help her and Lily from their sleigh, and the stones were quite solid and un-dreamlike under her feet. She was actually there.

She took a deep breath and smelled pine and woodsmoke on the icy breeze. She shivered and tucked her hands deeper into her sable muff.

An impossibly stately butler in black came forward with a low bow. 'Your Grace, la Duchesse?' he said in accented English. 'Your rooms are quite prepared. Her Highness the Grand Duchess asks if you will join her for tea after you have rested? There shall be a small dinner this evening.'

'Small?' Violet squeaked. She couldn't imagine that.

He gave her a slightly disapproving glance and another bow. 'Only one hundred and fifty, I believe. You are Mademoiselle Wilkins?'

Violet nodded, astonished that he could know that. Did he know everyone's name who visited the palace? She was sure he must. She felt so small next to all—that. William, though, she was sure was right at home. He seemed at home wherever he went.

'If you will follow me. Your luggage will be waiting.'

He led them through the doors and up a flight of stairs lined with yet more footmen. Violet hurried after her sister, trying to emulate Lily's serene smile and not stare at everything. They went through a long gallery, their footsteps muffled by a thick carpet woven with flowers and ribbons, a Rastrelli fresco high above their heads, and passed under an arch to face a staircase. It was the famous Ambassador's Stairs, all pink and white marble. Violet stumbled slightly on the low steps and quickly righted herself, pretending nothing had happened.

At the top of the stairs, a row of blue marble columns stretched off to the right, like a gleaming forest, and tall windows draped in blue velvet looked down to the frozen river on the left. Ahead, open doors guarded by more footmen revealed an enfilade of staterooms spilling like a pirate's treasure chest, all elaborate parquet floors, green malachite, silver standing candelabras, crystal and silver, Venetian glass chandeliers, brocade and satin. Endless halls of it.

At the end of yet another corridor, he opened a set of doors and led them into a sitting room. Though 'sitting room' seemed like a paltry thing to call such a space. It glowed with light from the windows, pastel satins and alabaster tables dotted over a pink-and-white carpet, landscapes and flower scenes on the pink walls.

Three more doors opened off the sitting room and Violet glimpsed a small army of maids hurrying about, unpacking their trunks. The bedchambers were just as pretty, all done up in pink and blue and pale green like candies, warm and cosy with crackling fires in all the marble grates. A silver tea tray sat on a malachite table next to one of the brocade-draped windows, looking down at the courtyard.

'Please ring if you require anything else at all, Your Grace...*mademoiselle*,' the butler said, bowing his way out.

'Good heavens! I shall get quite spoiled here,' Lily cried, throwing herself into a deep, satin armchair. 'I must redecorate as soon as we return to London! Look at that ceiling.'

Violet looked up to find a fresco high above their heads, gods and cupids peering down at them from blue and white billows of clouds. 'Amazing.' She wandered around the room as if on a cloud herself, looking at the paintings on the pale blue walls, the tiny silver snuff-boxes and alabaster vases on every table, the view of the river beyond the courtyard. She popped a salmon sandwich from the silver tray into her mouth. 'What must the Tsar's rooms look like, if this is just a little guest suite? How many chambers do you think there are altogether?'

'Fifteen hundred,' Aidan said, bursting into the room eagerly, his handsome face glowing with delight to see his wife. 'And one thousand, seven hundred and eighty-six doors.'

'Aidan, my darling,' Lily cried, leaping up to throw her arms around him. As they held on to each other, it looked as if they were all alone in that one perfect moment, just the two of them. Violet looked away with her cheeks turning warm, leaving them to their greetings as she reached for another sandwich.

She stopped chewing for an instant as she noticed a familiar figure hurrying across the courtyard, his coat very dark against the icy cobbles. *William.* She raised her hand to wave, then felt very silly, for surely he couldn't see her. Wouldn't be looking for her.

'And Violet,' Aidan said, kissing her cheek. 'I'm so overjoyed you're both here now. How was your journey? How dull Berlin must have been.'

'It was a long journey,' Lily said. She rested her head on his shoulder with a happy sigh and he pressed a tender kiss to her hair. Violet wondered if anyone would ever be so happy to just be with her? To just sit with her like that? 'But I did find Princess Vicky and her home so interesting. Violet was a great success with the royals! The Princess expressly asked to see some of her photographs while we were on the train.'

'Of course she was a success.' Aidan laughed. 'No one can resist a Wilkins girl! Charteris is very lucky.'

Violet smiled, but a touch of icy discomfort made her look away. They didn't know this was all unreal; she worried she was begin-

ning to forget that herself. That she was becoming rather enamoured of her play-fiancé.
The more she discovered about him, the more
intrigued she was, and that was dangerous.

'But this place! How very, very grand,'
Lily said. 'I've never seen anything like it.
It makes Buckingham Palace seem positively
shabby.'

'And wait until you see the staterooms,'
Aidan said. 'The Gold Drawing Room, the
Nicholas Chamber, the Malachite Room...'

'All fifteen hundred of them!' Violet said.

'I doubt you'll be expected to see them all.
It would take a decade,' Aidan answered.
'But, tell me, Lily my darling—how are you
really feeling?'

Violet smiled and went into her bedchamber to leave them alone.

So this is how a duchess could live, she
thought, gazing around the room filled to the
brim with brocade and gilt and ivory; her life
would be visiting royalty, bathing in marble
tubs, beauty all around for inspiration. She
trailed her fingertips over the satin cushion
of a chair, wondering what that would be like.
Would she ever fit in amid such things?

She turned away to sit on the edge of the towering, velvet-draped bed, which was so high she had to climb a set of carpeted steps. She leaned back on the cool silk of the embroidered comforter. It was very beautiful. She had to admit that. Yet she thought of the little Swiss chalet playhouse cottage, where princesses boiled eggs. That would be the really extraordinary place, a quiet, pretty little house to be alone with William. Just the two of them, Will and Vi, sipping tea by their little fireplace, laughing over simple jokes.

But that was *not* how it was. He was a duke, with obligations and duties. He had to live his life in places like this. She ran her fingers over the ocean of blue silk and stared up at yet another fresco, this time of rather disappointed-looking goddesses in their chariots on clouds that she wished could carry her and William away…

Violet sipped from her cup of tea, a wonderfully smoky lapsang, and studied the scene over the gilded rim of the translucent china. They'd been told this was a 'small family drawing room', not one of the staterooms, but she wasn't sure she believed that. The soaring, frescoed ceiling, the malachite-panelled walls, the green-and-white-striped satin chairs, it all seemed too fancy for family life. Even the cup in her hand was a work of art, porcelain so pale the light shone through it, delicate as a moonbeam to touch.

It would make such a lovely photograph, she thought, with the bright white sunshine streaming from the tall windows making all that splendour glow. All the Grand Dukes, sons and brothers of the Tsar, were gathered around their parents, Tsar Alexander with his jowly face and elaborate, white-dusted moustache, the Tsarina pale and small in white and blue lace ruffles, a sad little smile on her colourless lips. Princess Alexandra whispered with her sister, the Tsarevna Marie—called Minnie, Violet had heard—while Prince Bertie twirled a cigar nearby.

And then there was the bride, who was sitting beside her mother and father in a dark green gown that frothed with pleated ruffles and bows. Prince Alfred had been right; she was not beautiful, with her round face. But she fairly vibrated with interest and animation and energy. She looked as if she could jump up and fly off at any moment, unable to sit still any longer. Yes, she would make a very interesting portrait study.

William left Princess Vicky and came to sit next to Violet at the edge of the floral and beribboned sea of Aubusson carpet. He gave her that smile she loved so much, that small, secret smile that said they were in some intimate moment, just the two of them. 'Well, Violet, what do you think of it all?'

'It's terribly elaborate. I feel quite shrunken next to it all,' she admitted. 'If this is their small family parlour, I shudder to think how I'll feel in a dining room or state hall. I'm bound to forget all my proper manners. Does one even *know* the proper manners for a place like this?'

William laughed. 'I don't see how that's possible. Manners are the same everywhere, aren't they? But maybe if you slid down the banister of the Ambassador's Stairs it would lighten the mood a bit. Trying to converse here is a bit like pulling teeth, if a person can even hear us. The acoustics of such high ceilings and so much marble are dreadful.'

Violet studied the royal party gathered on the brocade chairs and chaises and hassocks a little more closely. 'Hmm. The bride and groom look happy enough, I think, if not exactly set afire with joy. And Princess Alexandra is definitely glad to be with her sister. But everyone else does look a bit as if they're on their way to a funeral rather than a wedding. Prince Bertie is trying to jolly them along, though.'

'I'm not sure even his famous charm will do the trick.' William leaned closer, so close his sleeve brushed her arm, making her shiver through the thin muslin of her dress. He whispered, 'The Tsarina is not well and she and the Tsar don't often find themselves in the same room any longer. This seems to have stretched their acting skills to the limit, entertaining so many important guests, saying goodbye to their only daughter. And she was a German princess, you know. Their acting ability is not great at the best of times.'

Violet tilted her head, studying the Tsarina's sad, pale face and noting the way she held on to her daughter's hand as if she would not let it go. 'But why are they never together now? Surely so many royal couples are not exactly lovebirds, but they muddle along.' In exactly the way her own parents did—and the way she never wanted to do with any husband of hers.

His dark brow arched. 'I fear a certain countess lives in apartments above the Tsarina's, with her three little children. The Tsar's children.'

Violet felt her cheeks burn. 'Oh. I see.' No, she definitely did *not* want a grand marriage like that. She thought of her dreams of the little cottage, the man next to her by her side, and felt them disintegrate like clouds.

'It's the way of some of these royal marriages, I suppose, but one does feel sorry for her,' he said quietly and his eyes did indeed look dark and rather sad as he looked at the Tsarina. 'She usually escapes by going to German spas with her daughter, but for this time she's trapped here.'

'And soon her daughter will be far away in England,' Violet murmured. 'Do arranged *ducal* marriages go the same way, then?'

His lips compressed slightly, the only hint of emotion behind his handsome face. 'They can. My own parents were often apart. They didn't have much in common besides their estate and me. My father enjoyed London life and my mother preferred the quiet of Bourne.'

'But they married anyway?'

'She was an earl's daughter and her dowry included a large tract of land right next to Bourne that allowed the home farm to expand considerably.'

Violet felt so very sorry for William, for the child he had been, to have such distant parents on a huge estate. At least her own parents had once loved each other, and she'd always had her sisters. 'And is that what they wanted for you, when it was time for you to marry?'

He smiled ruefully. 'Maybe once, but times have changed. Even royals can expect a bit of romance along with their practicality. I dare say the Grand Duchess and the Prince will be happier than her parents.'

'I do hope so.' She looked at the engaged couple over the edge of her cup again, watching as they smiled together. She remembered that they had been wanting to become engaged for years, and now the wedding day was near. Maybe there could be a bit of happiness in gilded halls after all. 'Did everyone in your family marry for land? Before the romantic times, that is.'

He looked away. 'No, not all. There was my wild uncle Edward.'

'Ooh, a wild uncle!' she said in delight. 'What happened to him?'

'He had been engaged twice in his younger years, once to a goddaughter of the Queen, but the marriages never came off. Everyone imagined he loved all ladies too much to settle on one. As perhaps Prince Bertie would have been, given his preference. But then my uncle eloped with a young lady in her first Season, almost thirty years younger than him.'

'Did he really?' she gasped. 'Good heavens! Struck by Cupid's arrow?'

'He must have been. It was the scandal of the year.'

'Was it? But why? I mean, it sounds quite surprising, and, yes, maybe not the done thing, but men marry younger ladies all the time.' She thought of Mr Rogers, who was her father's age, and shuddered.

'That is very true. But before she eloped with my uncle, Miss Dennison was engaged to me.'

Violet's mouth fell open in shock. She put her teacup down on an alabaster table with a sharp click and turned to face William. He still looked just the same, his cool, ducal mask in place. 'You—were engaged?'

'I was young and foolish, I admit. Oh, don't look like that, Violet. Yes—even I was young once. And Daisy was very beautiful and sweet, the deb of the Season. A great prize.'

'And your uncle snatched her away?'

His brow arched again, making her wish that the mask would fall away, that she could see how he had really felt about it all. That he would let her in. 'Cupid's dart, right?'

'Did you love her a great deal?' Violet asked. She didn't think she really wanted to know the answer.

'Perhaps I thought I did. She seemed to care for me. But not as much as she did for my uncle.'

'So you never wanted to wed again.'

'You needn't look at me with your beautiful eyes like a sad rainstorm. As I said, I was young. I had a romantic streak back then. I saw Daisy with dazzled hopes.'

'And you have no romantic streak now?'

He firmly shook his head. 'None. It would be of no use.'

'Oh, William,' she said quietly. She did indeed feel rather like a sad rainstorm to hear of the crushing of his youthful hopes, the closing of his heart. 'What happened to them? Do you still see them?'

He reached for a fresh cup of tea and took a long sip. 'No. They died of a fever in Naples, where they went to live. It was all a long time ago.' He gave her a small smile. 'So, you see, Violet, a practical marriage may not be so bad after all. Everyone goes in knowing the truth, able to make their own decisions.'

'Perhaps. But what a dull business it sounds!'

'Life is often dull, I fear. But not when you're near, Violet Wilkins.'

She laughed. 'Do you think so?'

'You are like—life itself. Like the sun. All warmth and change.'

She studied him carefully, half wondering if he was teasing her, half hoping he truly meant what he said. But he looked at her with such seriousness. Such steadiness. She glanced away, blushing. 'But some people think I just burn.'

'And so you do, sometimes.' He looked at her solemnly, carefully. So closely. 'But if a man is freezing—'

He broke off and turned away from her as the drawing room doors opened and more guests arrived in a flurry of laughter. Violet tried to smile, to pretend that nothing had changed, that nothing had shifted between them. She would need all those acting skills the Tsarina did not possess. She longed so much to pull him close to her again, to tell him that he made *her* feel as if she burned, too. But she knew she couldn't say any of that, not ever.

Chapter Twelve

William appeared promptly as the palace clocks were chiming to escort Violet to dinner, looking quite heart-achingly handsome in his perfectly cut black evening coat and snowy-white cravat, with his cream satin waistcoat. The vivid blue ribbon across his chest, fastened with a diamond-and-ruby badge of the Order of the Garter, made him look terribly important as well as gorgeous. But his green eyes were as dark as a winter forest, solemn and watchful as he took her hand.

Violet feared she couldn't nearly match him, not in beauty or dignity. She was so nervous she was sure she would go running down the endless corridors shrieking and throw herself into a snow bank. She glanced quickly in the mirror and smoothed her gown, a pretty confection of red-and-white-striped taffeta trimmed with red velvet bows along the low edge of the bodice and the ruffled hem. She wore her double strand of pearls and a diamond laurel wreath borrowed from Lily in her curled and plaited hair. She fidgeted with her gloves and with the pearl drops in her ears, until William's hand on hers stilled her.

'Don't be so nervous, silly goose,' she whispered to herself. She had been in royal castles before! Even aboard a royal train. But those places were nothing like the Winter Palace. She'd never seen anything so overwhelmingly rich and lavish before, with layers and layers of pearls on gold, everywhere she turned. She couldn't picture a cottage anywhere near the place.

And yet she was meant to belong there now. To be an almost-duchess. She took a deep breath and tried to smile carelessly, to be like Lily. Her sister sat calmly on a satin sofa, her apple green silk and white lace skirts around her like delicate petals, slowly turning the pages of a fashion paper as if she hadn't a care in the world.

'As soon as the gong sounds we will go down,' William said softly. 'Just like in any house.'

Violet nodded, wondering at how careless he seemed, how almost bored he and Aidan and Lily looked. She felt so worried and that was not like her. She didn't care for the sensation.

She made herself laugh merrily and spun around in her delicate skirts. 'Well, what do you think? I fear I am not quite up to royal standards...'

'You would grace any palace you ever chose,' he said with an answering laugh.

'Just don't climb any trees in your new gown,' Lily warned teasingly.

Violet glanced out of the window and saw that it was snowing again, a thick white blanket against the gold of the palace. 'As if I could. They're all covered with ice. How do they stand it, closed up in these stuffy rooms for months and months?'

William joined her at the window, watching the snow, his arm against hers, steadying her. 'I doubt they are always closed in.

There is sledding and skating, trips to the country...'

'Yes, we're invited to go skating tomorrow! I'm so looking forward to it. If I remember how—it's been ages since I tried skating,' she said eagerly. 'Will you be there, too, Will?'

He frowned. 'I have a great deal of business correspondence...'

'Oh, not that much, surely,' Violet protested. 'I'm afraid I'll fall down right in front of the Grand Duchess and make a cake of myself. I need you there to preserve my dignity. No one would dare laugh at me with a duke at my side. And it will be fun, I promise.'

He laughed and she loved the sound of it, the way she could make him laugh. 'Well, if a lady's dignity is at stake, how can I say no?'

'You won't regret it! I will be very careful not to embarrass you.'

'You never could,' he answered, though she thought he was probably just being gallant. She could and all too often did.

They watched a line of troops in the royal red uniform march past in the courtyard below and William leaned closer to whisper, 'Are you sure you're quite all right? You look a bit pale.'

Violet swallowed hard and nodded. She couldn't tell him she had been unable to sleep almost all night, thinking about him and his lost love, his once broken heart. 'Just so overwhelmed by it all, I think.'

'Ah,' he said teasingly. 'What you need is someone to distract you.'

That didn't sound so bad to Violet. 'How so?'

'Oh, like this, maybe.' He took her hand and pressed a light, tickling kiss to her gloved fingers, making her giggle. 'Or this…'

He gently brushed away a loose curl that had fallen from her tiara and laid it against her neck. She shivered at the sensation.

'Or this,' she said, and went up on tiptoe to kiss his cheek. His face was lightly rough under her lips, his scent of sandalwood soap delicious. He turned and kissed her cheek, too, his lips soft on her skin.

The gong sounded, low and stentorian, not to be dismissed, and Violet reluctantly stepped away from William. She couldn't quite look at him, she feared she was blushing so much.

'Come along, you lovebirds,' Lily said merrily, putting aside her magazine and going to take her husband's arm. 'I am proving to be a terrible chaperone, aren't I?'

Violet laughed and took William's offered arm. To her amazement, her nervousness was gone, as was her wariness over what life held in store for her. She felt only a low, fizzy excitement for the evening ahead. With William beside her, suddenly everything seemed possible!

They joined a long line of lavishly bejewelled people moving along the corridors towards the Ambassador's Staircase. The ladies' tiaras and necklaces sparkled blindingly in the gaslight, moving past all the tall silver vases of exotic lilies, the paintings and crystal and porcelain.

'Is Bourne Abbey anything like this?' she whispered to William.

'Not at all, though I suppose we have two or three nice paintings. And a Canova sculpture of my grandmother. Not like that one, though.' He nodded towards a trio of marble goddesses, embracing amid floating carved draperies. 'But I suppose it could be redone à la Russe, if a duchess had a mind to it.'

Violet looked at the soaring ceilings, painted gilded panelling beneath twisted malachite columns. 'It's all very impressive, to be sure. But how can they live like this all the time? It must feel a bit like being strangled with marble.'

'They have smaller summer palaces to retreat to, out at Tsarskoe Selo. I imagine this is all just meant to awe us mere mortals into silence.'

Violet had a hard time imagining William as a 'mere mortal', or awed in any way. 'Good luck getting *me* to shut up, especially when they give us so much to talk about. Oh, look at that! Is it a real Rembrandt?'

William laughed. 'Would the Tsar have a fake one?'

'No, I suppose not, unless the real one was in hock.' At the turning of the staircase, where they all joined the royal receiving line, was a large mosaic-topped table that held a silver vase overflowing with flowers. White roses, red gerbera daisies, as large as dinner plates, blooming in winter.

She remembered his story of his lost love, Daisy. Did he ever wish she was there, holding on to his arm? Was she a lady who could never be replaced? Maybe he hid a broken heart beneath his calm demeanour, his ducal dignity.

He did seem to stare at the flowers rather wistfully, or perhaps Violet just imagined it. Her instinct was to distract him, make him laugh. She tugged him away to the stairs, facing the long line of royals, shining like Christmas trees laden with diamonds and medals.

'Goodness, who is that lady on the end? The one with the emeralds the size of eggs perched on all that grey hair? She looks as if she will shoot off into the sky like a firework! She's so bright, I cannot look at her. How paltry my little tiara is. I could never be a *real* duchess, could I?'

She was rewarded for her silly chatter when he chuckled, a low, rough, sweet, dark sound, and she felt a warm glow.

'I think you would make a fine duchess,' he said.

She glanced around her at the sparkling company and wondered what it would be like to really belong there. To have a real part to play. She'd never felt certain of herself in such a way before and the thought that he might be…

It was rather overwhelming.

They reached the end of the line ahead of Lily and Aidan, and Violet had to prepare her curtsying knees. She could never have imagined such a vast array of royals before.

Prince Alfred and Grand Duchess Maria stood at the end. The bride was nearly buried in lace ruffles, diamonds and pearls, her brown curls crowned with a tall tiara. Maria smiled stiffly as an elderly countess offered her very prolonged congratulations, and Violet remembered how the Prince said his fiancée preferred to be noisy and active. She resolved to try not to babble.

The voluble Countess at last moved on and it was William and Violet's turn to bow and curtsy.

'Ah, Miss Wilkins, our photographer!'

Prince Alfred said happily. 'My dear, you will not believe it, but this young lady takes photographs, much better than my own, I dare say.'

'Indeed?' A touch of interest brightened Maria's bored face, and she smiled. That smile was brilliant, sweet, and quite transformed her. Violet thought how much she wished she could capture that fleeting light. 'How fascinating. I have never tried it myself, though I would enjoy it. My father is rather old-fashioned, he always thinks paintings are best. I'd like anything that doesn't make me look like a pug dog!'

Violet laughed. 'I'm going to be photographing my sister at the skating tomorrow, Your Highness, if you'd like to come and take a look at my camera. I'm always very happy to give lessons on my interests!'

The Grand Duchess's smile widened. 'I would enjoy that, Miss Wilkins.'

'Miss Wilkins is also engaged to the Duke of Charteris here,' Prince Alfred said.

'Are you going to gain inspiration from our nuptials here, then, Miss Wilkins?' the Grand Duchess asked, glancing around again. She seemed to find weddings much less interesting than cameras. 'I'm afraid it will be rather dull and long! I quite fell asleep when my brother married Minnie.'

Violet shook her head, pushing away the pang that came whenever someone asked about her 'wedding'.

'Ours will be a small wedding, Your Highness.'

'You are very fortunate, Miss Wilkins. Give up the nonsense and just be married, I say,' the Grand Duchess said heartily.

William bowed and took Violet's arm and they made their way through the towering white-and-gold doors into the Pompeian Dining Room. It was an elaborate recreation of ancient villas, with red-, white- and gold-painted walls, a blue-and-gold ceiling with mosaics of toga-wrapped singers and musicians. The long table and rows of chairs were also decorated with Roman scenes, each one different, and mythological creatures were carved on the legs of the stools and tables and buffets, painted in dark bronze. Red velvet cushions were placed on the woven seats of the chairs and Violet noticed that the china even matched, painted with scenes of the lost city.

'What a photograph this would make,' she whispered to William. 'I wish I could just go from room to room, capturing images.'

'The staff might notice you dragging your camera all around.'

She studied the lines and lines of footmen in the Tsar's sparkling livery, standing behind each velvet chair as the guests found their places. Violet was seated next to William and sighed with relief to know she wouldn't be left alone in the long evening ahead.

'I do wish cameras were tiny, so I could hide it in my skirt folds and just whip it out to catch people unaware,' she said with a sigh. 'Instead I must persuade them to sit very still for minutes!'

The royals filed in with a fanfare of trumpets, taking their throne-like chairs at the high table. Once they were all seated, the first course was served. Fruit presented on gold platters and soup ladled into shallow bronze-edged bowls were set before them while a rich, ruby-red wine was poured into the fine crystal glasses.

'I fear I could get used to this sort of thing,' she said with a happy sigh, sipping the expensive wine. 'They even say there will be fireworks afterwards! I could run such a home, I think.'

'And no one would grace it better,' William teased, making her laugh. The evening didn't seem at all intimidating any more. It was so strange. The very man who most unsettled her making her feel the most at ease she had ever been, even in a palace.

Soon, the fireworks did start, a great, crackling explosion, and the glow of glittering white and green and blue through the windows sparkled against the snow. A few braver souls ventured out on to a terrace, watching the show above their heads. Violet wandered to the edge of the marble floor, her head tilted back, staring up at the night that suddenly seemed like brightest day. She felt awestruck, drifting through an infinite space, untethered.

'How wondrous,' she whispered.

'Wondrous indeed,' William said, his voice rough, low. He took her hand in his and she felt the warm steadiness of his touch envelop her until she didn't feel alone at all, flying through the cold Russian night. She knew she was safe there in that moment, with him.

She glanced up at him and saw that he did not laugh, that his face was serious, intent, cast in shadows, and she couldn't quite breathe. He drew her closer to him, into those outside shadows, away from everyone else. His hands were tight at her waist and that feeling of warm safety sparked into—something more. Much more, shimmering and irresistible as those lights above their heads. It was nothing like everyday life, but more like watching a photograph develop before her, life but so much more. So much better. She found she didn't want to let it go, didn't want *him* to let her go.

She swayed closer to him and wound her arms around his neck so this dream couldn't fly away and leave her alone. She wanted to stay there in his embrace, quiet, not needing to say anything at all, just feeling, all night. Forever.

She stared up at him as a starburst of golden fireworks lit up his face, those sharp, beautiful angles. 'How gorgeous you are,' she whispered.

He gave a startled laugh. 'Me? I am ordinary.'

Ordinary? She shook her head in astonishment. He was the least *ordinary* person she had ever known. But she had no words left to tell him that, her head fuzzy with champagne and fireworks and glamour. She pressed her lips to his in a swift, sweet kiss, then another, longer, deeper, and another. She thought she could never have her fill of his intoxicating taste.

He groaned and pulled her closer, so close there was not even a breath of the cold night between them. He leaned into the kiss, his tongue seeking the touch of hers, and she was lost completely, falling down and down. Lost in that wild need to be so close to him. To draw all that he was into her until they were inseparable.

He pressed tiny, fleeting, alluring kisses to her cheek, her temple, that tiny, sensitive spot behind her ear. She shivered at the sensations that rushed through her.

'Oh, Violet,' he whispered hoarsely. 'How can we go on like this?'

She pressed her face into his shoulder. She tried to take a deep breath, but that only seemed to bring him, his scent, his essence, even closer. He was all around her. She shivered, and he drew back.

'It's too cold to stay out here,' he said, and she nodded. Too cold to stay where she was—but how could she move ahead? How could anything be the same, now that she knew him?

Chapter Thirteen

The day was cold but crystal clear. The snow had stopped, the sky shimmering like a sapphire set amid tiny, fluffy white clouds. Violet's breath came out in cold puffs and her fur-lined boots slipped beneath her as she followed Lily down alongside the Neva. The palaces beside the embankments shimmered gold and red, and laughter rang out on the wind. It didn't look real, more like a vision in a dream.

Or maybe she was still caught in the dream of last night. William kissing her, holding her, just the two of them wrapped in the snowy silence of the night.

She shook her head and paused to adjust her camera tripod on her shoulder, letting the memory, the sensations, wash over her again. Carry her up and up into that endless blue sky.

'Hurry up, Vi!' Lily called merrily and Violet waved and rushed to follow her. She couldn't let impossible romantic daydreams distract her from her work, not now. They didn't have a lot of time in Russia.

Not a lot of time left with William. Not a lot of time to dream that he could be hers forever.

The skating pathways were lined with tall fir trees in silver pots to show where was safe. Tables lined the riverbanks, laid with steaming cider and cocoa, platters of cakes and meat pies. The royals and their attendants were already there, Princess Alexandra and her sister Tsarevna 'Minnie' holding hands and giggling as they spun in wide circles, dressed alike in chocolate-brown velvet and sables. Prince Alfred and Grand Duchess Maria skated arm in arm, smiling up at each other as her mother watched from a chair nearby.

Lily sat down on a bench to strap on her skates, laughing as her husband spun an elaborate figure of eight to show off for her.

'Are you coming out on to the ice, Vi?' she asked. She stood up and took a small, tentative glide, her rose-pink-and-silver fox skirts belling out.

'Soon. I want to take some images first, of those palaces along the embankments,' Violet answered. 'Do be careful, Lily!'

'Don't worry, I have her,' Aidan said, catching Lily gently around the waist. 'Nothing can happen to you and our wee princess in there.'

Lily gave him a tender smile and they slowly slid away, a sweetly graceful romantic scene. Once again it made Violet feel strangely wistful, almost longing.

She knew the figures would be blurry, but it gave the scene a romantic, wintry charm, a sense of motion, like she had seen in Mrs Cameron's images at the exhibition. Or at least she hoped it would.

'How fascinating! You are truly a photographer, then,' a woman said, her low voice touched with a musical accent as she pronounced the English words.

Violet glanced back to see the Grand Duchess herself watching her. 'Your Highness,' she gasped, and dropped a hasty curtsy. She had been so wrapped up in her work, she hadn't heard anything else.

'My Alfred does enjoy these machines and I admit I am curious. It looks very complicated! How clever you must be.'

'Once you learn all the different parts, it's not so very complicated. It's just a process,' Violet said. This had been the opportunity she had hoped for ever since setting out for Russia! Now it was here, she felt quite unaccountably nervous and she wished William was with her. 'Would you like me to show you, Your Highness?'

'Oh, yes, please.'

As she showed the Grand Duchess how the plates worked, how to frame a scene in the viewfinder, Prince Alfred joined them, swaying on the blades of his skates as he took his fiancée's hand. 'Oh, you are lucky, Marie, getting a close look at such work! They're quite the latest thing now, those little tripods.'

'I do wish I had a camera like yours, sir,' Violet said.

'But it is quite amazing, Affie. I see why you enjoy it so,' Maria said, peering into the viewfinder of the camera. 'Imagine, images of right this moment preserved on these little plates. We can see this very afternoon forever!'

'Perhaps once we're settled in England, Miss Wilkins can give us lessons, and some day we can take photos of our children together,' he said with an indulgent smile.

Maria scoffed. 'I do hope they won't look like me, these poor children! Maybe like little English bulldogs.'

'It's all a matter of light and angles, Your Highness,' Violet said. 'Here, let me show you.' She quickly gave the Grand Duchess a small 'tour' of the workings of her camera, how the plates captured the images, how they were later transformed in the darkroom to indeed capture any moment forever.

'Amazing indeed,' the Grand Duchess said.

'Perhaps I could take a photograph now of you and the Prince? I won't show it to anyone else when it's finished, just the two of you,' Violet suggested. The light did look just right, beaming down softly on the icy scene. Cold and clear and bright.

Maria glanced at her fiancé. 'I don't know…'

'Come, my dear, it will be fun.' Prince Alfred playfully drew her close, his arm looped around her waist. She laughed and teased him, and her round face beneath her fur hat glowed in that perfect light.

Violet hurried to set her plates and release the brass lens cover, and took the image as they beamed at each other. She knew it wouldn't be sharp enough for an official portrait, but it was sweet and filled with a hopeful feeling she sincerely wished would come true for them. With the way the light slanted through the trees, and the curve of the Grand Duchess's lips on a laugh, she didn't think the lady looked in the slightest bit doglike.

'I'll develop them fully this afternoon, Your Highness, if I can find a proper darkroom.'

'I'll make sure you have all you need,' she promised.

'Ah, look, here comes your own sweetheart, Miss Wilkins,' Prince Alfred teased. 'We shan't monopolise you any longer! Come, Marie, let's skate a little longer and leave the lovebirds alone.'

As the royal pair glided away, Violet saw William coming towards her along the riverbank, his own gleaming silver skates slung over his shoulder, his hands in his overcoat pockets in a way that was positively jaunty for her usually formal duke. He smiled, his eyes bright in the cold, his cheekbones flushed.

'I see you've made friends with their Royal Highnesses,' he said.

'Friends? Not at all. But they *were* friendly. They let me take their photograph. Shall I take yours, too?' She peered into her viewfinder, as if she could just snap one off, but he stepped sharply back, his hand raised, making her laugh.

'You must let me take it one day,' she said.

'One day, maybe,' he answered. 'But right now we should skate. I doubt we'll get many more such clear days here.'

Violet nodded and sat down next to him to strap on her skates. He knelt down to knot her ribbons when her gloved fingers faltered. His touch was warm on her foot, his sandalwood scent clean on the breeze. She longed to reach out to touch the gleaming, windswept wave of his hair, to caress his cheek.

He looked up at her, his smile darkening as if he'd read her thoughts, and she glanced away.

Without a word, he helped her up and looped his arm around her waist, launching them off at the edge of the crowd. The hard strength of his arm against her thrilled her and made her feel safe at the same time. He spun her into a loop, making her laugh as the river blurred around her, the trees and people and palaces as one.

'Oh, look at you, Vi, you are good at skating! And you said you were not at all.' Lily laughed as she and Aidan swept past. 'Come, figure of eight with me.' She grabbed Violet's hand, making her laugh even more, and spun them together until Violet was quite giddy with all the delight. Everything in that moment—her sister and Aidan, William and his smile, the glorious sky, the cold wind, the beauty of that strange city—it was all absolutely perfect. She wished it could go on for-ever, the laughter and fun and beauty. That she could live in this moment with them al-ways.

Aidan joined hands with her and Lily and they spun in a star, laughing and teasing. Violet glanced over her shoulder at William, who had dropped back. To her shock, he looked rather…sad. Not hard, not angry, not contemptuous of their high jinks, just wistful. She felt a cold pang deep inside. Did he think of his lost love?

'Will, what is it?' she said. 'Come, join us!'

He shook his head wonderingly. 'You— you're a family. A real family.'

'And so are you.' Lily laughed. 'You are quite stuck with us Wilkins now, I fear.'

And Lily, with that sweet open-heartedness Violet loved so much about her, reached out and grabbed his hand, drawing him into their ring. Violet took his other hand and he was a part of their perfect circle.

'When I was a boy, my mother taught me how to make chains on the ice, like this.' Aidan demonstrated an intricate step, back, toe, glide, while Lily and Violet laughed to imagine the very dignified Duchess doing such a thing. Or skating at all.

'Come on, then,' Aidan said. 'You all try it! Hold on to me to make a line.'

Lily held on to her husband and Violet held on to Lily. She felt William's hands close around her waist, tight and warm and safe. She heard him laugh and the glow came back into the day.

They dashed across the ice, lashing around, snapping back together, faster and faster. Violet laughed until she was hoarse, until she felt entirely giddy. It was wonderful! Lily and Aidan broke away to glide off hand in hand with Aidan insisting she had to rest even as she protested.

'I feel more well than I ever have!' Lily said, but she sat down next to her husband on one of the cushioned benches. The Tsarevna and Princess Alexandra, mothers many times over now, fussed around her with warm cider and iced apple cakes, sending for blankets, as Aidan hovered close.

A brass band dressed in the red-and-gold imperial uniforms launched into a waltz and Prince Alfred and his fiancée swooped and twirled around the ice, followed by other young couples.

'Shall we?' William asked, offering Violet his hand. He smiled at the dancers, but he still seemed rather wistful, distant as he watched Aidan and Lily.

But Violet still felt that fizzing energy inside of her, that strange up-and-down exhilaration that being near him always brought. She didn't want to give that up just yet, didn't want to lose the lovely day. 'Thank you, yes.'

His arm came close around her back, the other stretched out to clasp her gloved hand in his. He drew her much closer than they would be in any ballroom and, even through their heavy furs and velvets and woollens, she felt the length of his body against hers. Strong and warm, fitting against hers as if they had always been just like that.

They spun slowly at first, finding their footing under themselves, gentle, lazy circles that seemed to lift her higher and higher off the ice, made her float in his arms.

His touch tightened and then he did actually lift her, spinning her around and around until she laughed. The swirling snow, the dazzling bright white sunlight, the Easter-egg-coloured palaces, all blended into a rainbow around her. She held on to him, her one still point in the crazy world. Her one reality.

'Oh, bravo, Vi!' Lily applauded. 'You could join the Imperial Ballet while you're here.'

'You're just jealous at my grace and skill, Lily darling,' Violet answered with mock haughtiness that gave way to helpless laughter.

'Oh, yes. I shall never know grace and elegance again, ungainly cow that I am now.' Lily sighed, patting her barely-there stomach under her furs.

William slowly lowered Violet to her feet, holding on to her a moment until she was steady on her skates, and the bright blue sky still whirled above her. She held on tightly to his shoulders.

She glanced up into his face, shadowed by the brim of his hat, the dark fur of his collar blown by the breeze against his jaw. He was giving her that solemn, all-penetrating look again, the one where she was sure he saw everything about her, every secret she had ever held, and she could see nothing of him.

'What is it?' she whispered. 'Have I made a fool of myself again?'

'Not at all. I just—you do have a nice family,' he said quietly, roughly.

Puzzled, Violet glanced at Lily, who was sipping her cider and happily gossiping with the Princesses. Aidan skated nearby in lazy loops. She thought of Rose, so far away, possibly in some kind of trouble, and she longed to have her twin close, as the others were.

'Yes,' she said slowly. 'They often drive me insane, but I am glad to have them. My sisters are always on my side, no matter what.'

'It must be nice to have someone to rely on so absolutely. Someone to do battle for you, confide in you. Be happy for you.'

Violet suddenly realised with a cold shock that William had nothing. Oh, he had hundreds of people depending on him and a few friends like Aidan who understood what responsibilities came with being a duke, but, apart from his sister, William was actually quite alone in the world. The thought made her heart ache for him, made her want to put her arms around him and hold him close. Yet he held himself so stiffly, so far apart even though he hadn't moved, that she didn't dare do anything. She just laid her fingertips against his sleeve and he flinched. But she refused to let go.

'My sisters were often great trouble, I promise you,' she said. 'They steal your gowns and ruin your parasols and push you into the sea. Well, I'm sure *your* sibling would never have done such things to you. You have no parasols.'

He laughed finally and she beamed at him. 'My mother would have liked more children than two, I think, but she was of a sickly disposition.'

The sainted Duchess, renowned for her duty even as she was ill. Maybe that was all she had needed, one perfect son and daughter and her duty. 'And I think my parents would have liked a son, but my mother declared three children was enough. And it was not a problem, my father's fortune is not entailed.'

'But to have people around you who know you so well, who are always on your side—it must be useful.'

'I suppose it is. They can tease and be dreadful, but heaven help anyone else who is mean to one of us! Listen, Will, you are perfectly welcome to come be a part of our family any time you like. If you can bear it. We quarrel and shout a lot, but there's a lot of fun, too.'

'That is kind of you to include me.'

Violet laughed. 'Not at all. When some-one else is nearby, there isn't as much name-calling or things thrown about. And Mother wouldn't be able to push unwanted suitors my way.'

He gave her an unreadable smile. 'We can-not have that.'

'No,' she said, quite captured as she looked up into his eyes. 'No, we can't.'

A bell rang out and the skaters glided off the ice to start taking off their skates and gather their noisy children and fur rugs and picnic baskets. It was time to dress for dinner, no doubt another eighty-course feast on gold and silver plates off brocade cloths, sparkling under massive Venetian glass chandeliers.

'Will you ride in the carriage with me back to the palace?' William said.

Violet glanced at Lily and Aidan, who was helping his wife remove her skates as she ca-ressed his hair, the two of them wrapped in their own world. 'Yes, thank you. I should like a moment's quiet!' She bent down to remove her own skates and found the laces were hopelessly tangled. 'Oh, drat this knot!'

'Here, let me help.' He knelt beside her and

took her foot carefully on to his thigh. He drew off his glove to work at the knotted strap with his bare fingers, his touch brushing over her ankle lightly. Violet found her breath tight in her throat as she looked down at him.

He laid aside the first skate and straightened the buttons on her kid boots. 'All better?'

'Yes,' she whispered. 'All better.'

Even though the palace was not far from the river, it was a slow journey back, with the long line of carriages and waggons bearing courtiers, chairs, skates, rugs and blankets, and the army of servants. Armed outriders rode alongside, and several of the fur-wrapped skaters had gone quiet, as if remembering the threats that always lingered around them in St Petersburg.

But William didn't mind the long ride with Violet. They were so seldom alone in a place like the dim quiet of a carriage, and he could watch her face, observe the light dusting of freckles on her nose, enjoy her bright eyes as she looked out of the window and receive her sudden smiles. He could listen to her soft breath, smell her flowery perfume, watch the play of sunlight over her cheeks. She was strangely quiet for her, as if the day had worn her out, or her own thoughts preoccupied her.

He wanted to snatch her attention back to him, to 'tire her out' in another way, see her long legs amid the rumpled sheets of his bed, taste her lips against his again. He shook his head, trying to push away those thoughts, push away his burning need for this woman.

'You are quiet,' she said, almost as if she could read his thoughts. He certainly hoped she could *not*. 'Did we Wilkins girls shock you with our silliness?'

He smiled at her. 'Not at all. Your family is charming, despite that ridiculous feather in your hat.'

Violet laughed and blew at the rather bedraggled red feather, which brushed against her cheek. She impatiently tugged her hat off, loosening some of her curls from their pins, and tossed it out the window. 'Better?'

'Much.' He reached out and gently smoothed her hair back, his fingers brushing against her soft skin. 'I was just thinking of something a friend told me once.'

A frown flickered over her brow. 'Daisy?'

He was rather surprised she had even remembered that sad tale. 'No, someone quite different, an old friend. He told me I should be less serious all the time because life passes too fast. There are so many things to miss. Perhaps he was right. Maybe the world won't smash to bits if I laugh at it once in a while. You've certainly shown me that. But I fear I don't know how to be any other way.'

Violet's lips parted, as if his words startled her, and she leaned forward to take his hands between hers. Her touch was light, delicate, yet it seemed to reach through to his very heart. 'Perhaps we should take this fun business slowly? Learning new lessons is never easy.'

He smiled at her. How sweet she looked, peeking up at him earnestly from beneath her lashes as she proposed teaching him to have fun, but slowly. 'Indeed, it is not.'

She slid to the edge of the carriage seat until their knees brushed, and she looked into his eyes. They both sat very still, very straight-backed, and he nodded at her, as if waiting for a lesson. Yet he was mesmerised by her face, her parted lips, her wide eyes.

'Yes, having fun is never as easy as it seems,' she said.

'It seems easy enough for you and for Aidan and your sister.'

'Lily and I have always known each other and it seems as if Aidan has always been there, too. Teasing comes easily to us. Sometimes, I do wish...'

'Wish what?' he asked, curious.

'That I could confide in them seriously, just as easily. They do love me, I know, and would listen to anything I wanted to tell them. But I am sometimes afraid to let my real hopes and fears see the light. I'm afraid to be teased about them. So I often keep them locked away.'

'Oh, Violet,' he said quietly. 'I wish you would tell them to me, then. I would not tease, and once I am told a secret, by anyone, it is locked away forever in the Bourne oubliette.'

Violet squealed. 'You have an oubliette?'

He laughed. 'Not yet. But I can build one, if you like.'

'How wonderful. Would you store your own secrets there?'

He shrugged. 'I have few of them.'

'Oh, but you must have some secrets! Everyone does.'

'Is that one of your lessons in fun?'

'Life surely isn't much fun if we don't do something once in a while that we must keep secret.'

They turned on to a narrow, darker lane, the gold dazzle of the palaces on their wide boulevards momentarily dimmed. The horses' hooves were muffled, the slim walkways empty above drifts of snow.

He slowly reached for her hands and leaned towards her, unable to resist any longer. 'Perhaps we could have one of our own, then. A secret. Another one, I mean.'

She went very still, her breath caught. He hardly dared to breathe himself. She squeezed her eyes shut and swayed towards him. His lips brushed hers, once, twice, like butterflies' wings, before claiming them in a firm caress. Her hands clung to his forearms as she sighed, her lips parting beneath his.

'See? You can teach me this, if I can teach you to have more fun,' she whispered, and he smiled against her lips. The softness of her as she melted against him, the smell of her sweet perfume all around him—how could such things knock him so much off his feet, make him question everything he had lived by until that moment? He wanted her, needed her, more and more every time he saw her. Her laughter and energy and creativity, the very difference of her, the burning life within her. His unique Violet.

After Daisy all those years ago, his heart was not broken as much as frozen. He had been infatuated with her, her giggles, her golden curls. He had imagined the life they could have together. But his Daisy hadn't been real. The real Daisy had wanted glamour and excitement, and while he could give her a title, his uncle could give her those other things.

Maybe Violet wanted excitement, too, in her own way. But she was not Daisy. Her work was very important to her, as his was to him. They would see their inconvenient suitors off and then go their own ways, make their own lives.

But for now, for this moment, they were entirely alone.

His lips slid from hers, pressing a gentle kiss to her cheek, before he forced his arms to fall away from her and he sat back on the seat. She stared at him, wide-eyed, silent, her lips reddened.

He stretched out his long legs across the carriage, trying to pretend nonchalance, but his heart was pounding.

'I don't think you need very many lessons in fun,' she whispered.

'Oh, I don't know. I am far behind.' He smiled at her. 'Now, why don't *you* kiss *me*?'

She laughed, startled. 'Me?'

'You. I have a feeling you don't need many lessons in that, either.'

Violet bit her lip, looking as if she was trying to hold back a giggle. He did love that about her—how easily every small moment with her became an adventure. She placed herself next to him on the narrow seat. Then she closed her eyes tightly, a tiny line of concentration forming on her brow. A red curl bounced over her eyebrow and he gently swept it back, making her shiver. Her gloved hands floated, landing lightly on his shoulders, and a soft sigh escaped her lips as she kissed him at last.

He was right—she was better at this than she knew. Her lips were soft on his, then firm, seeking, becoming hazy, tasting of cider. Her arms wrapped around his neck and she held him close as he eased her on to his lap. They fitted so perfectly together, their lips and arms and bodies just so.

He never wanted to let her go.

The carriage jolted to a halt and William blinked the warm haze of desire out of his eyes to see they had returned to the palace courtyard. The footman outside coughed softly and waited a moment before opening the door. Perhaps this sort of thing happened quite often at the Russian Court, then.

Violet slid off his lap and straightened her jacket and gloves, as he smoothed his hair, which was rumpled from her fingertips. She studied him carefully, her eyes narrowed.

'You *must* let me photograph you, Will,' she said. 'It would be my masterpiece!'

Before he could answer, the carriage door opened and a footman helped her alight. 'Prince Alfred has arranged a darkroom for you, Mademoiselle Wilkins, if you would care to see it,' the footman said with a bow. Another servant carried her camera ahead.

Violet glanced back into the carriage with a wistful little smile. 'You see, Will! A new royal darkroom, just for me—I must take advantage of it. Do say you'll be my first real subject outside my family!'

He feared he was her subject already.

She walked away with a laugh that floated back to him like a sunlit cloud, leaving him alone with his bemusement, his own laughter and a raging desire to kiss his red-headed sprite all over again.

Chapter Fourteen

Violet stared, wide-eyed, into the windows of the Fabergé shop on Bolshaya Morskaya Street. Mother-of-pearl and ruby opera glasses had been among the dinner party favours at the Winter Palace and she had thought them so pretty she had wanted to see what else Fabergé created. So she had slipped away into the cold day by herself, to study the glittering shop windows, the bell-ringing sleighs zipping through the snowy streets past the fur-and-velvet-clad shoppers.

She hadn't imagined anything quite like this, though. The large windows were filled with cascades of beautiful objects, spilling from white satin-draped shelves. Vases and frames, snuff bottles, perfume flagons, brooches and hair ornaments, sparkling and glittering like sun on new-fallen snow. The workmanship and detail were astonishing.

A reflection suddenly appeared in the window glass, just to her left, and for a moment she was sure she'd imagined it. William— a dark fur collar outlining his chiselled jaw, his eyes bright in the snowy day. A smile on his lips. He seemed to just *belong* there amid the elegant riches.

But when she glanced back, he was really there. He lifted his hat, his smile widening. 'Good day, Violet. Imagine seeing you here.'

'Did you follow me, then?' she teased.

'Not at all. I thought I would look for a few gifts to take back to England, since I doubt we will have a quiet moment again before the wedding.'

Violet looked back at the jewels on display, the bracelets and brooches and tiaras. 'A gift for—a certain lady?' she choked out. She felt like such a fool; he was a wealthy, handsome duke. Why had she never considered he might have a *chère amie* before, like the Tsar?

William laughed. 'Not at all. Just some

cousins and my sister, Honoria. And my old nanny, who is retired to a cottage at Bourne.'

'Oh.' Violet laughed, too, feeling even *more* foolish. He was nice to his old nanny! It made him even more attractive, blast him. 'Yes. I should find something for Rose and Mother, too, since they couldn't be here.'

'The trouble is, I have no idea what they might like. Perhaps you would help me? I am sure an engaged couple can be allowed to shop together for an afternoon.'

An engaged couple. Violet was shocked at how lovely that sounded. How—how real. Did she *want* it all to be real, this strange dream? She turned away to stare unseeingly into the window, flustered and unsure and too warm. 'I'm not sure I could be of much help. I think you should buy one of everything.'

'Then that is what we will do.' He offered her his arm. 'Shall we?'

Violet nodded and took his arm, letting him lead her into that hushed, glorious wonderland. A man in a black coat hurried forward to offer his assistance and quickly led them to the glass cases at the far end of the velvet-and-satin room.

Violet examined a small picture frame of deep green enamel, edged by scalloped gold and trimmed with small diamonds in a sunburst pattern. She wondered if she would ever be talented enough to create images that would look just right in such a creation. 'You should get this for your nanny, William. Perhaps put a photo of yourself in it. Surely she would like that.'

He studied it carefully. 'Perhaps you are right. I'm coming round to the idea. If *you* would take the photo.'

'Oh, no.' Why had he had a change of heart? Suddenly she was doubting her ability, as much as she still wanted to take his portrait. 'Not until I have had more practice.'

'Nonsense. Every time I've had my image taken, I've looked horribly stern and quite old. You make people look—well, like themselves. Only better.' He picked up a pink enamel frame, edged in topazes. 'You should put that photo you took of Lily in this one, as a gift for your sister Rose.'

'Do you really think so?'

'Of course. It was a beautiful image. You

have talent, you know, and it's no good to deny it.'

Violet laughed, blushing at the compliment, but she nodded. She chose a frame for Lily, and a few small, jewelled flowers, while William picked out great bouquets of pink and white and diamond roses in vases of crystal 'water' for his cousins. Shopping with William was far more fun than she could have imagined; he had exquisite taste and was very generous. And everything in the shop was absolute perfection. She always appreciated artistic excellence when she saw it.

'Shall I have your maid take the packages to the palace for you, *mademoiselle*, once they are wrapped?' the attendant asked.

'Oh, no, she didn't come with me,' Violet answered. 'I can carry them.'

He looked quite shocked and Violet imagined all the diamond-draped Russian ladies probably shopped with armies of servants. 'I shall have a messenger take them to the palace for you, *mademoiselle.*'

Violet laughed as she strolled with William along a glass case filled with pearls and sapphires. 'Did I shock him?'

William gave her a crooked smile. 'Most ladies do shop with their maids.'

'I wasn't really planning to come in, just to stare through the windows. It didn't seem worth the trouble to find a maid.' She sighed. 'I am terrible at being "prudent and proper", I fear!'

'But you are very good at finding adventure in the world,' he said. 'I think I have been *too* prudent at times.'

She peeked up at him and wondered if he had really just admitted that. If he was beginning to see the value of 'fun' after all. Wonders truly never ceased.

'Tell me, Violet, what is your favourite thing here?' he asked, gesturing at the treasure cave of the store.

'Oh,' she said, flustered. 'I couldn't choose, I'm sure! But my eye was caught by these. Such intricate craftsmanship.' She gestured at a pair of platinum filigree hair combs in the case, set with pink and white pearls, like something a Spanish infanta might have worn in another time. 'So exquisite.'

He nodded solemnly. 'A good eye, as usual.'

* * *

An hour later, when Violet went to her bed-chamber to find her Fabergé packages wait-ing for her, the pearl combs were resting in their blue velvet box on her dressing table.

Violet tried not to stare like a country peas-ant girl as she followed Lily and Aidan into the palace's Nicholas Hall for the grand ball the night before the wedding. She'd thought the other staterooms were very grand, but this vast room put them all to shame. It seemed to be made of white and silver ice, with sharp, shimmering crystal chandeliers overhead hanging from the gold-inlaid ceiling. The only colour was the red velvet throne on a dais at one end.

She smoothed the Chantilly lace of her sleeves, glad she had let Lily buy her a Worth wardrobe after all, and especially glad of the new pearl hair ornaments William had given her on their shopping excursion. The shimmery, changeable pale green silk of her gown, trimmed with rich swaths of lace and clusters of pearl-dotted satin carnations, was not as grand as some of the other ladies' outfits, but it was certainly no disgrace.

The room was crowded with courtiers, scarlet and white and black uniforms pinned with medals, gowns of amethyst and garnet and pearl white, and so many jewels she was surprised there were any left in a shop in the world. They all stood to one side of the still-empty dance floor, clustered between the pink-veined marble of the columns, which were reflected endlessly in the silver-framed mirrors. An orchestra played somewhere, a quiet medley of Strauss, almost drowned out by the hum of chatter.

Lily glanced over her shoulder to Violet with a smile. 'All right, Vi darling?'

'Oh, yes, of course! It's all very astonishing. I thought I'd be used to it all by now, but I doubt I will ever be! Surely we won't see anything like this again.'

Aidan laughed. 'Of course you will, when you're a duchess. But it doesn't mean we can't laugh at it all.'

'I'll be so happy to have someone to gossip about everything with, someone who really understands,' Lily said.

When she was a duchess. Violet sighed. It was getting harder and harder to lie, especially to Lily. Harder and harder to lie to herself. To tell herself she did not really want William. Did not crave his kiss, his touch, his rare smiles. His reassuring, strong, quiet presence that told her it would all be well. That she was not alone.

She glanced around, trying to be surreptitious about seeking him out, but she didn't see him in that thick crowd. She frowned in cold disappointment and immediately berated herself for it. Soon she wouldn't see him at all, wherever she went. He would be at Court or Parliament, and she would be— somewhere else. Who knew where?

She thought of their merry shopping excursion, when time had seemed not to matter. It had been just him and her, talking and laughing, strolling arm in arm down the glowing, beautiful streets and through the glittering shops. How she had wished it would never end, that they never had to go back to their real lives!

That he was not a duke at all.

They neared the head of the line to make

their bows to Prince Bertie and Princess Alexandra and the Tsarevna, Prince Alfred, the Tsar, the delicate and tired-looking Tsarina in her lavender satin and pearls, and at last to the bride. Grand Duchess Maria wore an unflattering, very elaborate gown of dark green satin, frilled and ruffled and tied with velvet bows, her dark curls piled high and crowned with a tall diamond tiara.

But her rather bored pout brightened as she saw Violet. 'It's our American photographer! Miss Wilkins, how lovely to see you. Did you enjoy the skating? Seeing our city?'

'It's very beautiful indeed, Your Highness.' Shyly, uncertainly, quite aware of everyone nearby watching, and with Lily's encouraging little nudge, Violet slipped the small photograph from her reticule. 'I hope you'll accept this little wedding gift, ma'am.' She looked at all the lavish gifts on display…the jewels and silver and ivory, the lengths of satin and lace, and thought the image so small. She wished she'd bought a proper frame for it. But it was more important for the Grand Duchess to see it.

Maria took it eagerly and her smile widened. 'But I do not look pug-like at all! Affie, do see this, aren't we lovely?'

'You never look pug-like, my dearest.' The Prince laughed, peering down at the black-and-white image. 'But we do look rather happy, don't we? Not at all stiff, like photographs too often are. Well done, Miss Wilkins. You must tell me some of your darkroom techniques.'

'Perhaps you'd like to take my photo in my wedding gown tomorrow,' Maria said, exactly what Violet had hoped for so very much. 'After the vows, perhaps? I fear it's terribly elaborate, it takes all day just to put it together. And there won't be much time before.'

'I would be honoured, Your Highness. I will be there at any time you desire,' Violet said, trying not to shout in joy. She curtsied and moved ahead with Lily.

'Oh, Vi, how brilliant you are!' her sister whispered, squeezing her arm as they found a spot between the columns to watch the Tsar lead his daughter into a stately polonaise to open the ball.

'You look happy this evening, Violet,' she

heard William say, as he slid into the spot beside her.

She beamed up at him, delighted he was there to share this little moment with her. 'The Grand Duchess liked my skating photo,' she whispered jubilantly. 'She said I could take an image of her in her wedding gown!'

His watchful, sharply carved face broke into a wide smile. 'Of course she did. The photograph you showed me is a lovely image, and you are exceedingly talented. Much more so than Mrs Cameron.'

'Do you—do you really think so?'

He glanced down at her, his brow arched as if he was surprised at her doubtful tone. 'Of course. I admit I am not an expert on photography, but I like how your work seems to peer deeply into your subjects, showing them as themselves. You can surely do anything you set your stubborn Wilkins mind to.'

In his voice, 'stubborn' sounded like the rarest of compliments, and she found herself blushing with delight.

The polonaise ended and a waltz struck up. 'Shall we?' William said, offering his arm, and Violet nodded. She felt as if she was walking on a cloud as he led her on to the parquet floor.

He held her a bit closer than the dance called for, closer than she knew was strictly proper. His hands were warm and strong, as he swirled her around the floor, his scent heady around her. His eyes gleamed like emeralds as he smiled down at her. She tried not to look directly at him, as one would with the sun itself, tried to keep smiling politely, to watch the room around them instead. There were plenty of people she *could* watch. She even glimpsed Lily dancing with Prince Alfred, her pale blue gown flashing in and out of view like a cloud. But she knew only William in that moment.

When the music changed again, she went reluctantly to dance with her next partner, one of the royal Russian cousins. She found she hated to relinquish William's hand, even as she spun around and around, laughing at the dizzy whirl. By the end of the dance, she was light-headed, giddy, and she shook her head when other partners sought her out, tiptoeing out of the crowded ballroom to find somewhere quieter for a moment.

But peace was the last thing she found, as the small chamber she stumbled into was already occupied. By William.

He rose in the shadows, putting out his cheroot. He watched her, not moving, the moment frozen, just the two of them. And Violet found she could suddenly breathe again, a deep breath, knowing he was there.

'Violet?' he said, his voice rich and deep, like a velvet blanket wrapped around her in the cold night. 'Are you unwell?'

'No, not at all,' she answered, feeling the door at her back as she leaned on it. 'It's just all the dancing—I couldn't catch my breath.'

'I felt the same way myself,' he said, and took a step, then another, towards her.

'But we are safe here,' she whispered.

'I'm not sure about that,' he said, and reached her at last. His arms came out to catch her as she swayed. He drew her close and she knew well what he meant—she suddenly didn't feel safe at all. She felt her heart pound so much harder than it had in the dance, racing within her, making her feel reckless and light and—and joyful. With William! It was amazing, wonderful.

She rested her forehead against his chest, the soft wool of his evening coat warm on her skin. She closed her eyes and concentrated on the sound of his heartbeat, moving in time to her own.

In her life, she always seemed to be rushing ahead to the next moment, the next thing. With him, in that moment, she could just *be*. She knew she shouldn't be alone there with him, that it wasn't so good for her own peace of mind, but she couldn't let it go yet. She slid her arms around his waist, feeling how strong he was.

He pressed a kiss to the top of her head and she tilted her face up to his. His brilliant eyes glowed in the shadows. His lips touched her brow, the pulse that beat in her temple, her cheek, leaving tiny flames that made her tingle all the way to her toes. She shook with the emotion that flowed through her, like a fire.

She stretched up, holding him even closer, and at last his lips met hers. A small, questioning, sweet kiss, but it made that flame burn higher. He groaned and dragged her so close there was nothing between them at all.

They seemed to fit together so perfectly, as if they had always been just like that.

Her lips instinctively parted under his kiss and his tongue lightly touched the tip of hers before he deepened their kiss. She wound her arms around his neck, her fingers twisting into his hair, as if she could hold on to him forever. But he wasn't leaving her, not yet. Their kiss slid deeper, into a desperate need she hadn't even known was within her until she found him. She felt so hot, so—so soaring high—and she swayed, sure she would fall.

He pressed her back against the wall and his lips trailed over hers, away from hers, along her throat, touching the tiny hollow where her pulse beat with such need.

'Violet, I…' he gasped roughly. She opened her eyes to see that he rested his forehead against the wall beside her, breathing as heavily as she did, as if they had run a mile. That breath was ragged in her ear, his tall body shuddering as if he, too, struggled with the force of that sudden longing. She feared that if she stayed so close to him she wouldn't be able to think at all. She slid to one side, dizzy, trying to stand on her own.

'Violet,' he said softly.

She looked up at him, at the reassuring glow of his eyes in the shadows, his rueful smile.

'Oh, Violet. Vi. You've turned my life upside down.'

She'd never heard such a tone in his voice before, a crack in her careful, controlled William. Her duke. 'As you have mine, Will.' And he had. She'd been so sure of what she wanted before—her work, her freedom. Now she didn't know anything at all.

She kissed his cheek, feeling the light prickle of his stubble against her lips. It tickled and made her laugh, made her close her arms around him to hold on to him as tightly as she could. As long as she could. He would be gone from her all too soon. But he drew her closer, his lips finding hers again one more time.

William waited until Violet was gone from their hiding place and he was alone in the silence, his fists braced on an ivory-topped table, trying to resist the powerful urge to knock the vase of white roses to the parquet floor. But he knew that wouldn't get rid of the longing that poured hot through his veins. Longing for *her*.

Being a duke was filled with responsibility, true, but it had its recompenses. Its powers. Violet might only be William's fake fiancée, but he had come to care for her—more than he had realised until that moment. He cared for her, craved her presence, needed her laughter. And he would not see her hurt by silly gossip.

He pushed back from the table and the icy windows and turned towards his own chamber. He could hear the music from the ballroom, the laughter of hundreds of people, the merriment against the cold night, but it didn't call to him. He only wanted to be with Violet.

Chapter Fifteen

The day of the royal wedding dawned cold and pearl-grey, lacy snowflakes drifting from the sky to land on the icy river below. Long lines of carriages and sleighs, forming since dawn, made their slow progress to the court-yard of the Winter Palace, depositing ladies in Russian court gowns of brocade and vel-vet and gold embroidery, jewelled *kokoshniks* on their curled hair, and men in satin knee breeches and fur-lined mantles. But Violet hardly saw them even as she stared down on the sparkling parade, her breakfast tea and toast growing cold on the table next to her.

She had barely slept at all. She had lain awake remembering every detail of the ball, of William's kiss, his touch. She had never felt so discomforted, so *excited* in her life. She didn't know at all what to do with it.

'Violet! You'll never be ready in time,' Lily called. 'We have to be in our place at the church before the Grand Duchess arrives, or it will be quite the scandal.'

Violet glanced back at Lily, who looked as gloriously beautiful as always in a gown of pale blue satin and deep blue velvet, edged with silver fox and blazing with diamonds. The maid was laying out Violet's own gown of pink and silver brocade, and the coiffeur waited to dress her hair.

No matter what William did now, she knew Lily was right. This day was so important. It was why she was in Russia, to try to advance her art. It was vital for Lily and Aidan, too, if Lily wanted to be a lady-in-waiting. Violet couldn't let them, or herself, be disappointed now.

'Of course,' she said. She gulped down her cold tea and hurried over to let the maid help her into her heavy gown.

It seemed to take forever to put the whole thing together, as she tried not to fidget while the gown was put into place and her hair was dressed with her borrowed tiara. But once she faced the gilded mirror, she could hardly believe it was her, Violet Wilkins, who stared back at her. This was a perfect, gleaming creature, all pink and white and silver, a work of art. If only she could keep from moving.

'Is this—me?' she whispered.

Lily laughed, and carefully kissed her cheek. 'Not bad for the little Wilkins sisters, eh? Wait until William sees you! You look positively regal.'

Would he think her beautiful? she wondered. Like a—a duchess? Violet ran an uncertain hand lightly over her lace-edged sleeve, and half hoped, half feared.

The ormolu clock in the corner tolled the hour, and Aidan promptly knocked on the door to fetch them. 'I shall be the envy of the whole Court,' he declared. 'Two such lovely ladies beside me!'

'You don't look so bad yourself,' Lily said, examining her husband's breeches and brocade coat, his velvet Garter robes. It was true, he hardly looked like Violet's laughing, silly brother-in-law, just as they did not look like the 'Wilkins sisters'. It seemed like a fairy tale.

Each of them took one of Aidan's arms and

he led them down the labyrinth of corridors and staterooms into the palace church. It really felt like suddenly landing in a different world, on a higher plane, Violet thought as she studied the light, sparkling church. It was all golden with marble columns, red carpet underfoot, an elaborate altar of painted and gilded icons with candles lined up around it, incense misty in the air. It was hushed and reverent despite the crowd pressed around them.

Violet went up on tiptoe in her velvet shoes, looking for William. She saw Princess Vicky, the Prince and the Princess of Wales, so elegant in crimson velvet embroidered with gold, pearls wound around her throat. All those tall grand dukes in their uniforms. At last she glimpsed William, standing near the altar, his distinctive dark hair gleaming in the candlelight. He caught her eye and smiled.

She turned away, her cheeks heating with one of those ridiculous blushes he always inspired.

'What are you looking at?' Lily whispered. She followed Violet's glance and laughed happily. 'Oh, your true love! Of course. It *is* a wedding.'

There was a sudden hush, just as Violet feared she would start to fidget like a child at the long wait, and then a swell of chanting from an invisible choir, which seemed to float all around them. The procession appeared, led by rows of ladies-in-waiting in their white satin gowns, their velvet court trains edged with sable and the blue sash of the Order of St Andrew pinned with their diamond badges that matched their *kokoshnik* headdresses.

The Tsarevich and Tsarevna were next, he a burly giant in his uniform, she tiny like a porcelain doll in blue and silver velvet and a blaze of sapphires. The bridegroom with his brother and the elderly Duke of Saxe-Coburg came behind them. Even the full panoply of their dress uniforms, medals and orders, were outshone by the Metropolitan in gold brocade vestments and a tall, jewelled mitre, carrying an icon high. How Violet wished she could take a photo of it all, but she tried to memorise it to sketch later, so she could always remember it.

Then came the bride on her father's arm, moving very slowly as if weighed down, which she probably was. The small Grand Duchess, with her face surrounded by dark hair curled into two long ringlets on her shoulders, wore a gown of white satin covered by a robe of cloth-of-silver lined with ermine and another mantle of red velvet held in place with a large diamond clasp. Her sleeves, trimmed with more ermine, reached the floor. Diamonds looped around her neck and wrists, and cherry-shaped diamond earrings dusted her shoulders. On her head were not one but two tiaras, a *kokoshnik* with a massive centred pink diamond and a small crown. Maria did not look very happy, despite the pages who scurried behind her to try to carry it all.

'That is—quite the bridal costume,' Violet gasped.

'It's tradition,' Lily whispered. 'Every royal Russian bride has to wear it. Poor things.'

'Good thing you were just an English duchess, then, with your shabby Worth gown and lace veil,' Violet whispered back. She remembered how lovely and sweet Lily had looked on her wedding day and for just an instant she had an image of herself in white with orange blossoms, clutching a bouquet. She shook it away before she could imagine the groom who waited for her.

But all the harsh glitter of the massive church, the elaborate costumes, the jewels and incense, seemed to vanish just for a moment as the Grand Duchess took her prince's hand and they smiled shyly at each other, a sweet, secret little smile. They were handed lit candles and knelt together before the altar, the six pages scrambling to arrange the long train before it pulled the bride over.

Violet peeked across the church at William, only to find him watching her. She felt her cheeks turn warm and glanced away, but she couldn't help smiling to herself.

Chapter Sixteen

'Very well, Your Highness, if you will just look towards the window,' Violet said. 'Just so…'

Grand Duchess Maria gazed in the direction of the window, the waning light, pink and orange and amber where it reflected off the snow, falling over her face and her wedding finery. The chamber was one of the smaller palace drawing rooms, but it was filled with a soaring, frescoed ceiling, velvet draperies, tapestries, silver and amber decorations and lots of flowers. It was a magnificent backdrop for the bride while her new husband stood nearby, giving her encouraging smiles.

It should all be very beautiful, very regal, yet something was not quite right as Violet peeked through her viewfinder. Prince Alfred had been correct when he said his wife didn't ever look quite like herself when she posed for photographs. It needed to be quick and informal, as it had been at the skating.

Violet examined the scene, trying to decipher a new arrangement. Their time grew short, for the couple needed to make their way to their banquet. 'What about a book?' she said, remembering that the Prince had said the Grand Duchess was a great reader.

Maria laughed. 'Why would I read on my wedding day? My head aches too much from these infernal crowns!'

Violet could definitely see why. It was *two* crowns after all, perched on her curled hair.

'Just for a moment, then, and then we can go change for the banquet,' Violet said. 'We'll just try it.' She found a small volume, bound in red leather and stamped in gold, on the table, and put it into the bride's jewelled hands.

'Oh,' she said, suddenly distracted as she turned the pages. 'I do love Keats!'

'Read your favourite poem, then, Your Highness, and turn towards the window again. Just so. Tilt your chin a bit to the right and down. Hold the book up...' Yes, that was it. Maria looked lovely with that half-smile, the light carving angles into her face, sparkling on her jewels. Violet slowly counted down until the image was taken.

'You look lovely, my dear,' the Prince said with a gentle smile.

Violet glanced into her viewfinder. 'Now, sir, if you will stand beside her, perhaps put your hand on her shoulder, as if she is reading to you? And smile at her, just as you were.' She thought of the stiff poses of their engagement images, the two of them looking wide-eyed and frightened, as if they would run away. She didn't want that now.

Their time ran out too quickly, the light sliding away towards the endless Russian night, but she had what she needed. 'Wonderful!' Violet cried. 'I'll just hurry off to my darkroom now.'

'Oh, Miss Wilkins, if only you could stay here in St Petersburg!' Grand Duchess Maria said. 'You are not at all like the stuffy, serious old photographers Mama finds.'

'Now, my dearest, we will be in England soon enough, as will Miss Wilkins,' the

Prince said. 'She can take our first child's photograph!'

'I would be honoured, Your Highness,' Violet said. She removed her plates and turned away to go and develop them, leaving the two newlyweds to laugh together. In the corridor, on her way to her borrowed darkroom, she found William waiting for her, leaning lazily against the silk-papered wall.

'William,' she said. 'I was just—the Grand Duchess's photograph…'

His smile was bright with delight, not at all like his old, small, secret smiles. 'So you fulfilled your great wish here!'

She laughed shyly. 'Well—we shall see. Once it's developed. It might look quite awful.'

'I'm sure it will not.' He stepped closer, his expression turning serious.

She suddenly felt a bit shy. 'Will you—that is, maybe you would like to see how a photograph is developed?'

'I would be fascinated to see that.'

'Then come with me,' she said, and led him to her borrowed darkroom, a small closet behind the grand corridors, outfitted with a fireplace and all the chemicals she needed to see her creations come to life.

She showed him how she used the new-fangled dry-plate method to treat her plates, how it offered her greater light sensitivity and was much easier and faster than the old, elaborate wet-plate method she had learned from originally. 'See, then we pop it into its bath, in order to fix it, and we—wait.'

She was very aware of him close to her in the dim light, his soft breath, the warmth and clean scent of him, and she could hardly breathe. Together they watched as the bridal couple appeared before them, caught forever in a moment of happiness.

'It's beautiful, Violet,' he said quietly. 'I know little about such an art, but you can see *them* in that image, their true, human selves. Their affection for each other.'

'Yes, it came out rather well. Almost as good as these.' She showed him more of the skating photos on a nearby table, waiting to be framed. Lily and Aidan, the bridal couple, William himself giving an embarrassed, adorable laugh. 'Maybe you *would* let me take your formal portrait? I know you offered before. You surely know how handsome you are?'

His lips quirked. 'You find me handsome? Do tell me more.'

She laughed. 'Don't be conceited. I know you must look in the mirror sometimes.' She glanced away, suddenly aware how close they really were to each other. All alone in the warm darkness. It seemed only right to kiss him, to press her lips to his and hold on to him in the shadows. He answered her with a groan, pulling her even closer, kissing her as if he really meant it. As if he would never let her go. She looped her arms around his neck and closed her eyes, knowing that this moment would always live in her memory.

'I wish—I wish…' she whispered, but her words were lost as he claimed her lips again. She put all she had into that kiss. It wasn't a gentle kiss, but one filled with all they couldn't say, all the desperation she felt as she sensed their time there slipping away.

Chapter Seventeen

A crowd was already gathered in the palace courtyard when Violet hurried to join them the next morning. She was running late, finding that she was rather tired after all that had happened that previous day, and her feet felt tied to the snowy ground. But there was also a wonderful, fizzing energy, a light that seemed to dance around her with every step. The world seemed brighter, lighter, more beautiful. Sleighs and carts waited, piled high with fur blankets, picnic baskets, sleds and skates.

The bridal couple were already there, returned from their wedding night at Tsarskoe Selo, laughing and holding hands, bright-eyed despite the long wedding day, banquets, balls.

Violet started towards Lily, but someone

caught her hand and turned her away from the crowd. When she spun around, startled, she saw it was William and the day suddenly became even brighter. Here was her beautiful Will, his eyes brilliant in the snowlight, an uncertain smile on his lips. Her fear turned to delight in an instant and she impulsively kissed his cheek, making him give a startled laugh.

'I do believe there's a seat here,' he said, leading her to a nearby sleigh. His smile widened, became freer, and she suddenly realised how often he'd done that in the past few days. His old stiffness and caution seemed to drop away, like a mask he no longer needed. He looked so much younger in the sunlight.

How she had once misjudged him! Much to the peril of her heart. Yet he made her feel things she had only imagined before. He *saw* her, the real her, deep down, and he never turned away from that true her. She knew she should run, but instead she took his hand and let him help her up on to the narrow seat. He tucked the fur rug carefully around her against the cold wind.

'I hope you slept well enough, after all the wedding excitement,' he said.

She swallowed hard, remembering that it was his kisses that had truly kept her awake. 'Not really,' she admitted. 'I've never seen anything so lavish, so filled with tradition, and…and…'

'So dull?' he said with one of those teasing smiles that made her heart flip.

She laughed. 'Maybe a bit. I don't think my feet will ever stop aching. But the photographs will be lovely. Tell me, Will, have you been sledding before? You were quite a good skater.'

'Never. There's usually not quite so much snow where I grew up. But I'm sure you'll help me. You seem an expert.'

'Do I?' she said, puzzled.

'The tea tray on the stairs.'

'Oh. Yes. Erm…that.' She looked away, remembering too well how she had felt when she tumbled at his feet. How silly he must have thought her. 'But there was no snow there. I'm sure this will be very different from the sledding I used to do on the hills back home.'

'And I am quite sure you're equal to the occasion. You always are.'

'Am I?' Violet said doubtfully. She hadn't felt 'equal' to much in this lavish royal world. She hoped William could see something that she could not.

The caravan had left the city by then and the glittering palaces and canals fell behind as they crossed the frozen river. The snow had turned the winter forest stark and icy so that it glittered, like strangely beautiful and mysterious stars. Their sleigh shot around a corner, gaining speed. Violet wasn't braced for the sudden motion and she fell against William's shoulder. He caught her close, holding on to her, a warm haven against the cold day, and she smiled up at him.

'You're always there to catch me,' she said breathlessly.

'I do try,' he answered, his voice low, quiet.

She wanted to hold him, to wrap herself up in him, but they arrived all too soon at a hilltop, near the others, and she had to let him go. He jumped down and held out his hand to help her alight. He still held her hand, clasped in his, and she felt so wonderfully safe. So filled with quiet pleasure. Everything else seemed far away.

'Thank you, Your Grace. Will,' she whispered, curling her gloved fingers around his.

'My pleasure, Miss Wilkins, I assure you.'

Everyone else scattered through the trees as the footmen laid out the sleds and maidservants set tables for the picnic later and built up the bonfires. Lily and Aidan went towards the larger sleds at the front of the line, leaving the small, two-person one at the back for Violet and William. She was sure her sister gave her a sly little smile as she left.

'I think you're right. How different can it be from a tea tray?' she said. She tugged his hand hard, making him laugh as he followed her to their sled.

She perched at the front, clutching at the steering, praying she wouldn't pitch them into a snow bank. William sat close behind her, his hands around her waist, and she shivered at the feeling of him through the wool and velvet. The delight of being so near.

'Ready?' she cried and he pushed them off. They went faster and faster, flying across the hard-packed snow, Violet laughing as she never had before. How wonderfully free it felt, soaring over the earth with him! How perfect as the wind whistled around them, wrapping them in their own world, just the two of them.

William laughed, too, and she had never heard him like that before. As if freedom had got inside of him just as it had her. Until they landed hard in one of those snow banks, rolling over and over, holding on to each other. They slid to a stop, Violet on top of him. He looked up at her, laughing, looking so carefree and young, so unlike his usual self.

She couldn't help it. She bent her head and pressed her lips to his, catching that laughter, tasting snow and cold and the wonderful, dark essence of *William*. It was the merest brush, but she felt the warmth of their breath meeting and mingling, binding them close together.

He groaned and deepened the kiss, giving her what she craved so much. The kiss slid over some precipice into something wild and frantic with need, something she longed for even as it frightened her. He held her close, so close that not even the cold wind could come between them. There was no past or future, not in that one instant. It made the day absolutely perfect for her, the finest she had ever known.

William watched Violet as she laughed with Aidan and her sister, sipping spiced wine near the roaring bonfire, her hair vivid against the grey light of the day. She waved her hand exuberantly as she told some wild tale, spilling a bit of the wine, which made her laugh all the more.

How wonderfully *alive* she was, like the burning summer sun on a cold day, warming everything around her, turning all that was bad and dark into good. All that was dour and dull into adventure.

He was shocked to realise that he could barely remember his life before her. It had been a monotonous trial of work and duty, never changing. He had never been dissatisfied with any of it; he had been born to it, and it was what he knew.

But ever since Violet had burst into his life, it had all looked brand new. Like living in a cave and emerging to see the ocean, the woods, the blue, blue sky. Suddenly feeling the laughter erupting out of him, as if it had been imprisoned for too long. He longed to taste her lips, smell her perfume, watch the intensity on her face as she took her photographs.

He felt insane. He *was* insane! Where was his old self? It had vanished when he touched her hand. He felt drunk with her.

Yet soon she would be gone. To America, or Paris, or Egypt, or Outer Mongolia for all he knew. She could do anything, be anything. Why would she want to be a duchess?

And he found that he wanted, more than he had ever wanted anything, for her to be his duchess. Not a fake one, not a temporary bargain where they would one day go their separate ways. For real. His duchess, his wife.

Because he *loved* her. Loved Violet Wilkins. Who would ever have thought it! But he felt alive when she was near. He felt like his old self. And he would do anything to see her happy.

'William?' he heard Aidan say, his tone a bit puzzled. William shook his head, trying to free himself of such fancies, to bring himself back into the real world. It didn't quite work. 'You look as if you've just been struck by lightning.'

And so he had been. William turned to his old friend and found Aidan watching him with a quizzical smile. How odd, the way the world had just vanished for a moment.

'I'm quite well,' he said.

Aidan glanced at his wife and at Violet, who were joining in a song by the fire, laughing with their arms around each other. 'The Wilkins spell? I know the feeling well.'

'Violet—she is—' William broke off, not knowing what to say. 'I just want to make her happy.'

'Nothing easier. You just let them be themselves.' He smiled at his wife and sister-in-law, who were singing with Princess Alexandra then, making her giggle. 'We are lucky men indeed.'

Aidan was lucky. William only hoped he could be half so. How, how could he persuade Violet to make this betrothal real?

Chapter Eighteen

Violet followed Lily and Aidan into their box at the Mariinsky Theatre. Just as at the royal wedding, she felt like the veriest bumpkin… an American milkmaid pushed into some unreal fairyland. She sat down on her white velvet and gold seat next to Lily and carefully arranged her frothy, creamy tulle skirts, trying not to stare at everything. But her attention kept getting caught by the sparkle of the boxes, the swagged gold-and-blue curtain across the vast stage, the icicle-sharp crystal chandeliers overhead and the sound of music as the orchestra tuned their instruments. And then there was the royal box with its Romanov crest and rich drapes of blue velvet.

Lily perused the programme with a laugh. 'I see Verinskaya is dancing! She quite scandalised the theatre last year with how short her skirt was. I wonder what she'll wear to-night.'

'What is the ballet?' Aidan asked.

'Giselle,' Lily answered. 'The man she loves betrays her, so she dies and becomes a Wili, one of the undead spirits of women who were treated badly by their men. They capture the evildoers in the cemetery and dance them to death in revenge. But Giselle takes pity on her former love and saves him. It's quite lovely.'

'Sounds quite dour.' Aidan laughed. 'If I fall asleep, you must nudge me, darling.'

Lily playfully smacked his shoulder. 'You have no romance in your soul!'

'Of course I do. I married you, didn't I?' Aidan said. 'I just prefer my romances to end happily, rather than in despair and parting and death.'

Violet bit her lip, pushing away a pang at the thought of romances ending in parting. She glanced at the empty seat beside her, waiting for William. She remembered their snowy kiss, and then the strange way he had acted as they made their way back to the palace, the quiet distance after a day filled with laughter and fun. She wished she could read him, but she feared he was beyond her forever.

'Shall I fetch you some lemonade, ladies? Or perhaps some champagne,' Aidan asked.

'No, thank you, I am quite all right for the moment, brother dear.' Violet raised her new Fabergé opera glasses to study the crowd. A few of the royals were in their box now, Princess Vicky and Prince Bertie, who avidly studied the ladies, but no Princess Alexandra or the newlyweds.

Then suddenly the door to the box opened, and William finally appeared there, silhouetted by the lights in the corridor. He looked like the austere Duke again, after their rumpled, laughter-filled day, impeccable in his dark evening clothes, watchful and unsmiling.

And yet now she knew what was underneath, the real William.

'I do apologise for my tardiness,' he said, taking his seat beside her. She could smell his sandalwood soap as he reached out to touch her kid-gloved hand. 'I had a bit of shopping to finish.'

'You went shopping?' she said, trying to stay light, teasing. 'What does a duke need that he could not send a servant to procure?'

He flashed her a quick smile. 'Oh, you'd be surprised. St Petersburg is filled with temptations.'

Violet studied him, so handsome in his black-and-white evening dress, his dark hair slightly tousled from the icy wind outside, a smile quirking his lips, and she knew he was quite right. The city was full of delicious temptation.

For an instant, as the chandelier lowered again and the lights grew brighter, Violet blinked, hardly aware of where she really was. As so often since coming to Russia, she felt like everything was not real, that the world of the stage was like one of Mrs Cameron's fanciful photographs, drawing her deeper and deeper into an imaginary spot. The gauzy colours and graceful movements of the dancers, the sadness of their emotions, had quite gripped her.

Then she heard her sister sigh. 'How very glorious! I wish I had been taught to dance like that.' And Violet was back in St Petersburg, in the lavish, overheated theatre, with her family. She glanced at William, who was watching her curiously, and gave him a watery smile.

'I shall just go for a breath of air, I think,' she whispered, wanting a moment to absorb what she had seen.

'Let me ring for the footman to go with you,' Lily said.

'No, I'll go. It won't take very long and I won't go far,' Violet said quickly, gathering her Indian shawl around her. She rushed away before anyone could stop her, making her way down the blue-carpeted corridor to the grand, gilded staircase that went down to the foyer and the champagne bar.

'Why, Miss Wilkins,' a lady called. Violet turned to see one of the young royal ladies-in-waiting, a Miss Priddy, sauntering across the lobby. She was quite surprised, since most of the ladies didn't really speak to her unless she was with William, then she remembered Miss Priddy was a friend of Thelma's. 'How grand to see you here! I have not glimpsed you since the wedding. And what an—astonishing gown. How clever New York dress-makers must be. Shall we walk a bit? We've had no chance for a real chat in so long! My dear Miss Parker-Parks says we should be good friends.'

Before Violet could stop her, Miss Priddy grabbed her arm and led her towards a crim-son velvet sofa in a small, curtained alcove. She sat down, her pink skirts billowing around her, her smile bright and her back as straight as a queen's.

'Now, my dear Miss Wilkins,' Miss Priddy said with a giggle, 'how remiss I have been in not offering my best wishes on your en-gagement! Charteris is such a prize. A hand-some young duke, so rare! And you, lucky girl, quite snapped him up. None of us had any idea he needed American dollars.'

Violet bit back a smile. Charteris was one of the richest men in England, everyone knew that quite well. She couldn't lure him with her dollars if she tried. 'I hardly snapped...'

Miss Priddy trilled a laugh. 'Of course not! But, my dear—you *are* American. Love is hardly what is required in an English ducal marriage. A duchess has an important job to do and she must do it perfectly. I am sure your sister has told you all that.'

Violet stiffened. 'Lily is perfect in all that she does.'

'Of course. But there are so many missteps that can be made. A duchess can't afford any mistakes. Ancient family names depend on her. She must know all the courtly etiquette, how to charm crusty old politicians, how to take care of tenants and servants. English ladies learn such things from birth, it is like second nature.'

Violet thought of Miss Priddy's friend Thelma's entrapment scheme. 'And honesty? Do they learn that?'

Her expression hardened. 'Charteris has ambitions, as I'm sure you know. Hundreds of lives depend on him. I am sure you care for him. I am sure you care for his title. How could any lady not? Yet how can you help him when you were not brought up knowing what is proper behaviour in his world, or understanding the many duties?'

Violet's first instinct, as it so often was, was to argue, protest, quarrel. But she *did* care about William. More than she could ever have imagined. She wanted nothing more than for him to be happy, to have all his hopes come true. He was not what she had once imagined, the Duke of Bore. He wasn't boring at all. He was kind and strong and thoughtful. And gloriously handsome, of course.

And this lady, and those like her, were right. Violet was not duchess material. She was too loud, too opinionated, too bold, too independent. And William deserved nothing but the best.

She rose to her feet. 'Thank you, Miss Priddy. You have given me much to think about.'

She smiled sweetly. 'I knew we would understand one another, Miss Wilkins. I shall tell Thelma we had this little chat.'

'Indeed.'

After Miss Priddy left, Violet sat in the alcove for a long moment, her thoughts whirling around and around in her head. Was it time to free William from their bargain now, so that he could find his real duchess? Was she ready to let him go? She knew she was not, but she couldn't see another way. She must not be like Thelma; she had to think of him first.

At last, she rose and hurried to the long, polished bar where refreshments were being served. Ignoring the rather scandalised glances that a lady would dare to be there alone, she ordered a glass of champagne. She gulped it down and asked for another. The fizzy, cool liquid soothed her hot rush of blood, slowed her racing thoughts.

Thelma and her friends like Miss Priddy were silly women, it was true. It was ridiculous to scheme to spend your whole life with a man you had to trap like that. Thelma would have ruined her own life as well as his. Thelma's own life was hers to tear down, of course. But not William's.

He deserved so much more.

She had once thought this a mere plan to achieve her own ends, just as Thelma had in her own way. And she couldn't bear the thought of it now. Now that she really knew William, really cared about him. But did she really want to let him go?

She drank down one more glass of champagne and made her way slowly back through the sparkling crowd to find a quiet corner where she could be alone and think. Where she could try to envisage her future alone once again.

The great velvet curtains swished up and a flank of ladies floated under spheres of moonlight in their clouds of white tulle. They seemed to hover perfectly still for a long moment, silent. Even the crowded audience ceased fluttering their fans and whispering, as if caught in a magical moment of ghosts and thwarted love. William thought it amusing at how wide-eyed the ladies looked, how discomfited the men.

He turned to see if Violet had noticed, if she would laugh at it, too. It had become too much of a habit of his, looking to see Violet enjoying a joke or sharing a moment of wonder at something beautiful. To see how she took in the world in her own unique Violet way. He had never known anyone quite like her, so very much her own self, filled with the joy and beauty of all around her. Beauty he'd never even seen before, not without her.

Such joy, such audacity—he'd missed that in his world before he met Violet.

Yet Violet wasn't there. Her chair was empty, only her fur-edged stole draped on its seat.

'Has Violet not yet returned?' he quietly asked Lily.

She glanced at her sister's seat, but did not seem very concerned. 'She did say she needed a breath of air. I'm sure she will soon return.'

'Or she's studying the staircase, trying to work out how to photograph it all,' Aidan said.

Lily laughed affectionately. 'She does get distracted by pretty things so easily.'

William nodded. How often he had seen her go stock-still staring at a frosty tree or a beautiful roofline. Still, as poor Hilarion was being danced to death on stage and the Wilis turned to Albrecht, Violet still hadn't returned. He felt a bit worried to think she might have become *so* distracted by the vast, gorgeous theatre she was lost. He slipped out of the box and made his way down the corridors and the flower-bedecked staircase towards the lobby. Most of the crowd had returned to their seats, but a few people milled about still, sipping champagne, whispering, laughing, watching the glittering snow drift past the windows. One of Miss Parker-Parks's silly friends, a Miss Priddy, nodded and simpered at him, and he wondered if she would report back his engagement's progress to London.

William nodded at her and quickly turned away. He saw an alcove of windows looking down the snow-dusted street towards the dancing school, the vista of pale green and blue and cream buildings gilded in moonlight, hazy in snowflakes, framed by dark blue velvet draperies.

Violet stood there alone, staring into the night as if she could float out into the sky, just like the Wilis. The flowers and jewels in her extraordinary hair glittered and her profile looked like that of an ancient goddess, pale and powerful, self-possessed. Free. How William longed to know her in that moment, know all of her, share all her thoughts and secrets, but he feared that for all Violet's laughter and sense of fun she could never *really* be known. Not deep inside.

'There you are,' he said, and joined her in her little window refuge. It was cold there, the glass streaked with frost, and her shoulders were bare since she had left her stole behind. Yet she hardly seemed to notice. Her face was filled with awe as she studied the snowy scene.

'Did Lily send you to find me?' she asked. 'I didn't mean to dawdle so long. I just got so caught up in—things.'

'Aidan did say you were probably planning to photograph the staircase,' William tried to tease, but he was rather worried. She seemed so quiet, so pensive, not at all her usual exuberant self. She slowly reached out and traced a flowery pattern in the frosty glass with her gloved fingertip.

'Caught up in St Petersburg's beauty?' he asked.

'Of course. Who could not be? Just look at those buildings, like gilded bonbons frosted in crystal! But it must seem all old and dull and usual to you, William! You have seen so very much. Even Egypt!'

'Egypt was astonishing indeed, as is Russia. They are amazing even to an old stick-in-the-mud like me. But it is difficult to think of two such different places as St Petersburg and Cairo.'

'How so? One is sun and the other snow, I suppose?'

'Of course, there is that. More that—they are two different worlds. In thinking, in practices, in their joys and sorrows.'

She glanced up at him, her eyes wide. 'Tell me more.'

William tried to recall all he could of Egypt, of its hot suns and bright blue skies, green Nile waters, spicy scents, the cries of prayers, the silks and jingling bells and perfumes and flowery drinks and spicy food. He wished he had paid more attention to it all, every detail, just to be able to tell it to her. He could only try to convey what he *did* remember, which he was sure wouldn't be enough for her artistic heart.

Violet sighed. 'How much I would love to see it! Think of the images I could photograph there. Like Mrs Cameron does in Ceylon.' She looked back to the night, the pastel walls and golden onion domes in the black-and-white night, the fat, diamond flakes of snow drifting down on the sleighs and carriages hurrying past in a jingle of bells. And William saw how easy it would be to love that whole world, with her beside him, seeing it with him. It was all new with Violet.

'Not that I don't have a plethora of subjects right here,' she said. 'I must learn to capture them before we leave.'

'The Grand Duchess loves the photographs you took. She shows them to everyone. You will have more commissions than you can handle and a fine patron once she is settled in England as Duchess of Edinburgh!'

Violet laughed. 'Crowned heads? I can't say I'd mind a few royal portraits for my portfolio, especially one as unusual as the Grand Duchess, or as beautiful as Princess Alexandra. If an artist wants attention, such patrons are vital. Yet I don't want to *just* do portraits.'

Of course, Violet wouldn't want to just photograph finely dressed ladies and vases of flowers. She would never want to do anything the usual way. 'What would you *want* to do, then? To add to your portfolio?'

Violet tapped her gloved fingertip at her chin. 'I want to join the Photographic Society and the Solar Club! That sounds wild, I know, they take so few ladies, and I have so much to learn. But to be acknowledged as a talent, to meet and learn from such artists...' She gave a little shiver. 'It would be glorious. I could learn so very much from them.'

'As I've already confessed, I know very little about the art form, but your photos look like *art* to me. They look—well, somehow they look exactly how you see the world.'

She glanced up at him with a radiant smile. How very much he would give, just to make her smile like that all the time. He would give everything. She laid her hand, the glove cool with the frost, on his wrist. 'Your words mean so much to me, Will, truly. You are the most honest man I know and I know that I can trust you. Yet to be a part of such a group of artists...'

'I understand,' he said.

A frown flickered between her eyes. 'Do

you? A duke *always* belongs, wherever he goes. Even the eccentric ones.'

He smiled at her. 'Do they? I once had a great-great-uncle of sorts, he was said to be so strange he was locked in the attic at Bourne for life. He thought he was a cat, you see, and only wanted to chase the mice. A terrible look in front of guests.'

Violet gave a startled laugh. 'My heavens. My own family can boast no mousers in their ranks, I admit. But if a lady even wants to have an ordinary career, let alone one chasing mice, if she even wants to venture out of her house alone, she is considered a great menace. Yet I've never been able to sit still.'

'No,' he said gently. 'Then you would not be Violet and that would be terrible.'

She stared up at him in the diamond-edged moonlight for a long moment, nodding finally as if she might have decided something. 'It's true I only know how to be myself. With my sisters, being myself has always been easy, the only thing that mattered. With my parents, though, with higher society—it's never good enough. If I was good enough for the

Solar Club, the Little Holland House set, if I could belong *there...*'

'Then take my portrait,' he said impulsively. Possibly the most impulsive thing he had ever done.

Violet's mouth opened on a startled 'o'. 'Yours? Do you really mean it?'

'Yes. Tomorrow. If you take an image you like, it could be another one for your portfolio. *Stuffy English Duke.*'

She shook her head. 'But—why?' she said with a puzzled little laugh. 'You've pretty much refused to sit for me before.'

'Well, that was *before*. You have convinced me that your camera contraption is not going to explode in my face. That your work will never make me look ridiculous. What about tomorrow morning? I have no meetings until the afternoon. It might not give you very much time...'

'Oh, no, it's perfect!' Violet cried, her face filled with its usual bright life and enthusiasm again. 'You won't be disappointed! You shall look so gloriously handsome. *The Duke of Dukes*!'

He laughed. 'Not my usual gargoyle mien, then?'

She chuffed him on the shoulder. 'You are very good-looking and you know it. You need no flash powder for that.'

'We could do a scene like at the gallery? Nude gods swimming? Only not in the Neva, I fear.'

That made her stammer and blush, a wondrous pink he wanted to see again and again. 'Certainly not. If I want to show off the image, it must be *ducal*, not scandalous! I cannot wait.'

'Shall we meet somewhere quiet after breakfast?' he said. 'If there is a truly quiet place in all of the Winter Palace.'

'Grand Duchess Maria said I could use her small sitting room at any time, as she and the Prince are to return for a few days to Tsarskoe Selo before they go to England. It has a great many windows, perfect light. Nine thirty, then?'

'Of course.'

Violet looked as if she wanted to say something else, but she just gasped, 'Lily will be wondering where I am! Surely the Wilis are almost done murdering by now. Until tomorrow!' She dashed away in a flurry of ribbons and silks and auburn curls. 'I'll see you then, Your Grace!'

Once her footsteps faded away and all was silent again, William felt quite alone in the hush of the falling snow. Her perfume wafted around him like one of the ghostly Wilis.

Only Violet was much too alive to be a spirit of any sort. Too full of adventure and audacity and confidence, and if he could help it at all, she would stay just that way. Just like Violet. *His* Violet. Who could never really be his.

Will couldn't quite bring himself to return to the busy theatre yet, to sit quietly beside Violet and pretend nothing had changed for him. That something profound and freeing hadn't shifted deep inside of him, just from one glance from those eyes, one smile, one touch. One chance at a photo that would hold all their lives in it, his and hers both.

He took a cheroot from his pocket and lit it, inhaling the cherry smoke against the chilly night, thinking of Violet, her enthusiasm, her happiness, her moods, her way of looking at the world. Her energy and kindness. Everyone said she would make a terrible duchess; even she said that herself. But *why* would she be terrible? It seemed to him a good duchess needed all those qualities. *He* needed all those qualities in his own life. Plus her kisses...

Why should he *not* marry Violet for real? He knew of only one real, formidable obstacle. Violet herself.

Chapter Nineteen

Violet hurried from one chair to another, to a footstool covered in gold fringe, to an alabaster table piled with books, unsure what to do. The Grand Duchess had said she must arrange things just as she liked, just as was needed, but it felt very strange, just moving someone else's furniture about.

The Grand Duchess was correct that there were many windows on all sides and the early light was exquisite. It fell in silvery, diffuse rays through the east- and west-facing windows, turning the pastel colours of the chamber to a jewel box, creating intriguing shadows. And the room was much smaller than any other Violet had seen in the palace, perfect for intimate portraits.

Yet it was clearly *not* an English duke's room. It was all gilded and swagged and silked, filled with figurines and flower paintings and French sofas. And she wanted William to look absolutely in his right place. But where was that?

She closed her eyes for a moment and tried to imagine him in his proper place, his real home. An English manor? A ballroom? On top of his horse surveying his land? No. Working. William sounded as if he was always working for his people.

She opened her eyes and found a desk, a bit smaller and plainer than the others in carved English oak. She dragged it close to the window, with a wide drape of velvet behind it casting shadows, and placed a pile of books and papers at the edge of the desk. She shooed one of the Grand Duchess's Pomeranians from under the table, as the lapdog did not exactly convey the 'hard at work on estate business' atmosphere. She added a potted fern to the background and nodded. Perfect.

She glanced at the ormolu clock on the alabaster mantel and gasped. Nearly nine thirty! He would be there at any moment. She rubbed her chilly palms against her apron and went to work setting up her camera to keep from being nervous. She wanted this image to be perfect.

At last, there was a knock at the door and William appeared. He wore his usual dark morning suit, pale waistcoat, cravat, his dark hair smooth and glossy, waved back from his face. He carefully smoothed his lapels, looking uncharacteristically unsure. 'Is this all right? I wasn't sure what to wear?'

Violet laughed. 'Perhaps you were afraid I would want you to dress like a Roman centurion? A Byzantine emperor?'

'I wouldn't be surprised at anything with you.'

'Perhaps later. Today, I need an image of *The English Duke*. Here, sit down beside this desk, make yourself comfortable, as if this was your office and you are merely working. Ignore the Pomeranian.'

As he sat down in the chair, settling his coat around him, his legs casually crossed, Violet finished setting up her camera tripod, the bowls of water nearby, the fixed plates waiting. She opened the windows partway, despite the frigid day, to let out some of the chemical smell of the prepared plates. As she fussed with the plates and the lenses, arranged and rearranged William in his seat to be best in the light, she felt herself fall deep into that other world. That world of images and stories and ideas, where that was all that mattered.

'When did you take your first photographs?' William asked quietly, letting her arrange his arm along the edge of the desk.

'Oh, ages ago! I persuaded my father to buy me a camera, a heavy old thing. One of our neighbours was an amateur photographer and showed me the basics of it all, and then I read about it and studied whenever I could. I ruined so many plates at first! But then, once I got better, I made albums for my mother and sisters one Christmas and they quite liked them. They showed them off to their friends and everyone wanted a photo of themselves. It was the first thing I ever felt good at.'

'I'm sure that can't be true.'

'Oh, it is! I can't play the piano, can't speak German, can't embroider worth a fig. I can sketch and paint all right, but I like this better.'

'And why is that?'

Violet considered this for a moment. 'Because it's one moment that lasts forever. The subject and photographer, all mixed up together in this instant. It feels like magic, but *I* am in charge of it all, where to place the camera, how to focus and frame the image, who and what to photograph. Using scientific skills to make sure it all comes out just right. I love it and I know I am good at it. I must just keep fighting until everyone else sees it, too.'

'Fighting for what we want through every adversity, because it is a part of ourselves, that must feel good,' he murmured.

'Yes,' she said, surprised he, a man, a duke, could see that. She glanced at him to find him watching her intently, and quickly turned away to adjust her camera. 'Now, Will, just turn your chin slightly to the left and down, towards the light. Rest your hand on the books, as if you are working. Oh, you blasted dog, quit growling! Now, just one tiny smile. You enjoy the work, but you are serious about it! And keep very still. One. Two. Three.'

She ducked behind the camera to release the plate, holding her breath as she always did until it seemed as if all would come out, the image would hold. And she could tell by peeking through the viewfinder that it would be a fine portrait indeed, every handsome angle of William's face there forever. And she had made it so.

'And—done,' she said finally, letting that breath out. She took out the plate, ready for it to go into a bath of pyrogallic acid and fixed with hyposulphite.

William rose from his chair and hurried towards her. 'Can I see?'

Violet laughed. 'So impatient! No, I have a great deal of developing to do now. I will show it to you as soon as I can.'

She tucked it away and he pretended to grab for it, making her laugh. 'I did hear all dukes were spoiled and impetuous! They must have everything now.'

'You should have gone with the Byzantine emperor costume, then,' he said with a wry smile. He was very close to her. His hand reached up, as if he could not help it, just as she could not move away, and his finger-tips toyed with the lace of her sleeve. A light touch, yet it burned as if with the glow of life itself.

'You should push me away, Violet,' he whispered. 'For both of us.'

'I...' she whispered. 'I can't do that.'

'Heaven help me, but neither can I.' His hand trailed over her arm to her waist, his touch warm and gentle through her velvet skirt, her muslin blouse. It made her want so much more, to feel the intimacy of taking a photograph come to life, of bare skin on bare skin, that deep connection.

She pressed her hand over his and held him closer. His other hand, cool with the winter's day, reached up to caress her cheek, and she kissed his palm. He smelled of smoke and tea and snow, and it made her head whirl. There was only here and William, there in their eternal photograph.

She closed the small space between them, touching his lips with hers. The merest brush, but she felt the whisper and heat of their breath meeting and mingling, holding them close.

William groaned and deepened the kiss, giving her what she craved so much. His tongue tasted the curve of her lower lip, light, teasing, until she parted her lips in eager welcome and leaned hard into him. And her ghosts fell free, tumbling down over some precipice, wild with need.

She broke away from him, suddenly frightened. Of him, herself, she didn't know. 'I—I have to go and develop this or it shall be ruined,' she gasped. Before she whirled away, she saw him run his hand through his hair, leaving the dark strands ragged, and she glimpsed her own uncertainty deep in his eyes.

Chapter Twenty

Violet stared unseeingly into the mirror as the maid finished curling her hair, pinning it up carefully and fastening it with diamond stars, a sparkling array that matched the gold constellations embroidered on her white satin skirts. It was to be another lavish night, a dinner for three hundred people in the Hermitage wing of the palace. She would usually be jumping about with excitement to see such art close up. But now she felt only distracted, confused—and sad.

She fiddled with the silver-topped perfume bottles on the tulle-draped dressing table, remembering William at the theatre, William's photo. That morning had felt so right, so perfect, but like an image itself it was only fleeting. It wasn't the truth. She knew what a man like William needed in a wife. In a duchess.

And it wasn't Violet. Her fist curled tightly around the handle of a silver hairbrush. This plan had begun so easily, so carelessly, as a way to avoid her future as long as possible. Maybe even a way to spend time with William, though she would never have admitted it at the start. Now it was suddenly so very different.

She loved him, truly and deeply. He was a good man who had been hurt in the past and had not let it harden him. A caring, strong man. She couldn't waste his time a moment longer. Their farce had gone on too long already.

'What do you think, *mademoiselle*?' the maid asked, stabbing one last pin deep into Violet's hair.

She glanced back at the mirror, at her startled, wounded eyes, her pale cheeks. 'It's lovely, thank you.'

The maid beamed and went to fetch Violet's gloves and painted silk fan. Lily rushed in, pulling on her own gloves, glowing with love and motherhood and a contented life. Violet felt a tug of envy again, as well as happiness for Lily. Would she ever find such a thing in her own life? A real place to belong?

'Oh, Vi, how pretty you look!' Lily said. 'William is sure to be even more infatuated than he already is.'

And there was that twist again, that tug of terrible remorse. Violet took her gloves from the maid and waved her away. 'Lily, darling, I must—must tell you something.'

Violet's quiet tone must have alarmed Lily, for her happy smile faded. She drew a chair up close to Violet and carefully sat down. 'Anything, my dear. You can tell me anything.'

Violet took her sister's hand tightly in her own and swallowed hard before she began. 'I—I can't marry William. I never could.'

Lily shook her head in confusion. 'But why? Did he hurt you in some way? Say something you found cruel? These Englishmen can be so blunt sometimes. Oh, I will kill him!'

Her sweet, gentle sister looked so fierce that Violet had to smile. Whatever else happened, however her heart broke, she had her sisters, always. 'Not at all. He is perfect.

Which is why I can't marry him.' Before she could carefully choose her words, the whole tale came pouring out. The false betrothal, the days together in Russia. She couldn't bear to look up at Lily, to see her dear sister be disgusted or, worse, laughing. Laughing at Violet's foolishness.

But when Lily answered, her voice was only sad and full of sympathy. Her hands tightened on Violet's. 'Oh, Vi. My darling. Do you know why I first married my Aidan?'

Violet glanced up at Lily, at her sister's steady, knowing gaze. 'Because you loved him?'

'I do. I did. I just didn't know it then. I only knew that he was a good man and that, if I was a duchess, I could always protect you and Rose. You could do whatever, be whoever, you wanted, without Mother and Papa's interference.'

Lily had married to protect them? Violet shook her head. 'You did that for us?'

'I would do anything for you and Rose. I wish you *did* love William, then we could be near each other forever. But mostly I just want you to be happy. Stay with Aidan and me, and the children. Take your photographs. Do whatever you like. I will look after you. I love you, no matter what.'

Violet burst into sobs and hugged her sister hard. Lily held her close, smoothing her hair carefully, soothing her with soft hushes. Violet knew then she was not alone; she was never alone. She had her sisters. And that would have to see her through the heartbreak of not being able to have William. Not being able to have her love.

And she did love him. Too, too much.

The gala dinner that evening was to be a very special one, at long, damask-draped tables in the Hermitage wing among the Tsar's greatest treasures. As champagne was served before the meal, Violet strolled away from the music and laughter to examine the wondrous art, to try to lose herself in the beauty as she usually could. She examined the Vermeers, the Rembrandts and El Grecos, and found herself in a quiet corner with a Raphael Madonna. She stared at it in wonder, caught by the ineffable sadness in the mother's blue eyes, the tender touch of her baby on her shoulder. It made her want to cry and she wasn't even sure why.

She didn't see William come to stand by her, but she knew he was there. No one felt like him, smelled like him. No one made her feel as he did.

'It's beautiful, isn't it?' he said, gesturing to the painting.

'Very beautiful indeed,' she whispered. She curled her fists tightly around the handle of her fan, bracing herself for what she knew she had to do. If she loved him, she had to do what was best for him. But, oh, how it ached! As if a cord that bound them together was about to snap away.

'Yet sad. It looks rather like you tonight, Violet.'

'Me?' She glanced up at him in surprise. He watched her steadily, that all-seeing glow in his eyes, her solemn, serious Will. She always felt that he could see deep into her soul, could read all her secrets, see her true self. She turned away, twisting her fan between her hands.

'What's amiss tonight?' he said. 'You are always so full of laughter.'

She tried to laugh now, but even to her own ears it came out all wrong, strangled and bitter. 'I'm just tired, I think. What a constant whirlwind life is here! I don't know how they can bear it.'

'We will return to England very soon. It's much quieter there in winter. You can work on your new photography album.'

'Of course. Yes. That will be good.' The photographs. They had been all she'd wanted, all she'd longed for. And she still loved her work, it could still be an escape. But now something else filled her heart. William. Her handsome, kind, solemn duke. She longed for him, but she knew he didn't really want her. Couldn't want her. Not in a forever way. It had to be forgotten, their silly bargain. At least she had a few precious memories that would always be there, jewels she could take out and smile over when everything was cold. Sledding, skating, dancing. Kissing. Oh, yes, she would always remember his kisses.

He cleared his throat, and she was shocked to see that her calm and collected William looked a bit—was it *nervous*? 'That is what

I wanted to speak to you about. The return to England.'

'England?'

'Yes. You see, Violet, I have been considering things very carefully and I believe we should become engaged. In truth.'

Violet had never been more shocked in her life. Her stomach seemed to drop to her feet, the same way it had felt when she had been a child and leapt off a conservatory roof. For an instant, she was launched into space, untethered, unsure, full of exhilarated hope. Could he possibly feel as she did? Was there a way out of her fear that she was entirely unsuited to be a duchess?

Yet his next words plunged her to the hard, cold earth again.

'I do have need of a duchess and you have need of a home away from your parents. It is only sensible for us to make this engagement real, I think,' he said straightforwardly. He was so matter of fact. So—chilly. 'We get along and I think we understand each other. We could follow our own pursuits. I would only ask for a hostess at political dinners once in a while.'

'Sensible,' she whispered, turning completely numb. So he did not love *her*. Did not want her for herself. Just a duchess at his dinner table. They would lead separate lives. And she was here, she was convenient and he wouldn't have to look any further. It sounded desperately lonely. She did want him—but it was only good if he loved her, too.

'Yes. I have always lived my life by good sense. We could forge a successful partnership.'

'But I fear I have always led my life by lack of good sense,' she said, finally finding her voice in the face of heartbreak. 'I would be a terrible duchess. You know it's true.'

He looked surprised. 'I know no such thing. You are beautiful and intelligent. You've charmed everyone here.'

'I am loud and full of opinions and pranks,' she said. 'I can't change. Neither can you, William. I want—so much more. And you certainly deserve more. We should end all this now.'

He frowned. 'End it?'

'Yes. You are surely safe now from Miss Parker-Parks. And Lily says I can live with her and Aidan as long as I like, away from my parents. I think our bargain has served its purpose.' She held out her hand, hoping he didn't see how it trembled. 'Thank you so much, William. I will send your photograph as soon as it's ready. And goodbye.'

He slowly shook her hand, holding on to it for an instant too long before she turned away. She couldn't bear the thought that it was the last time she would touch him. The last time she would be alone with him. She would surely see him in England because he was Lily's neighbour, but it would always be in crowds or at a distance.

She made herself walk away, slowly, as if nothing had changed at all. As if her heart wasn't shattered inside of her.

She was gone. He had lost her.

William stared out over the city from the marble balcony, not even feeling the freezing wind, not hearing the music and laughter from the party. He only saw Violet, walking away from him. Just as he had realised he never wanted to be without her. *Couldn't* be without her.

Where had he gone wrong? He lit a cheroot and inhaled its cherrywood smoke as he remembered her hand slipping out of his. He had proposed to a lady once before, to Daisy, when he was young and silly and full of clumsy ardour, but he barely remembered what he had said then. He didn't know how to be romantic, how to tell Violet his real feelings. He didn't even really know how to sort through them himself. Perhaps he had been too awkward, yet he hadn't wanted to frighten her with the force of his desire.

Perhaps he should read more poetry. Maybe that would help him find the words to tell her how the light only seemed to shine in his life when she appeared. She was all energy and laughter and fun, and he craved her as a person craves the summer sun after a long winter.

He glanced back through the tall windows at the lavish, sparkling, candlelit scene. Violet still sat at the table, a crystal goblet of wine in her hand, a faraway smile on her lips as she listened to a damnably handsome young grand duke speak close to her ear. Perhaps she wanted someone like that now, a prince rather than a mere English duke, someone to give her a lavish palace and Fabergé every day.

But William wanted to give her so much more! A home, a life, a place where she could practise her art and be her full self. He could not quite imagine a royal life was what she wanted. His lovely, creative, fiery Violet. He wanted to stride into the crowded party, snatch her into his arms and carry her away from everyone else. Something told him, though, that as dramatic as Violet could be, a big scene now was not the way to win her forever. And he would be terrible at big scenes, anyway.

But he would not give up. He would find a way to show her how he truly felt, how he would work so hard to be a good husband to her. Violet couldn't be completely lost to him, not yet. He just had to believe that.

Chapter Twenty-One

Violet hurried away from the palace in the pale light of the early morning, clutching her skates. She'd had another restless night, tossing and turning as she remembered walking away from William. Walking away from happiness, she saw that now. She felt like such a fool, but she also knew that true love meant doing what was best for William. And what was best for him was surely not marrying her.

She glanced back at the gates and thought she saw someone at one of the windows, a face. Was it him? For an instant, her heart leapt, but then she realised she had to be imagining things. He wasn't there watching her, yearning for her as she was for him. She was alone.

She whirled around and hurried towards

the bridge that would lead her to the skating area of the river. She passed a small cottage that usually held a guard, but it was empty now and she was alone in the freezing cold. It was a perfect time for clearing her head and steeling her resolve. She strapped on her skates and launched herself on to the ice, moving faster and faster, as if she could out-run everything.

But the trees that had marked the perimeter when she had skated with the crowd were not there today and as she neared the centre of the river she heard a sickening crack and felt the ice give way beneath her. She tried to scream, yet nothing came out as she was plunged into the icy water. She barely even realised what was happening.

For an instant, she felt nothing at all, then a thousand freezing knives drove into her body. She gasped and took in a mouthful of rancid water.

Is this how I die?

The thought flashed through her mind and she realised she only wanted to live. She only wanted to see William again.

She struggled up, only to be dragged down

by the shackles of her sodden skirt. She broke through the ice at one point and sucked in a breath. The light was piercing, brilliant, and she kicked towards it again with all her strength.

'Violet! Violet, where are you?' she heard William shout. For an instant, she thought she *was* dying, that he was her last hallucination. But, no, it *was* him, really him, who appeared before her, his face above her, lined with fear and determination. His green, green eyes.

She saw his arms stretch towards her and she caught on to him. He lifted her out of the freezing water and wrapped her in his heavy, fur-lined coat, holding her close.

'Thank heavens your sister told me you were coming this way, that I saw you fall,' he whispered fiercely. 'I thought I'd lost you!'

Violet feared she would start to cry as William gently held her in his arms and she knew that she was truly no longer alone in the world. That she was safe *and* free with him. She rested her head on his shoulder and closed her eyes. Everything had gone suddenly still and quiet, as if the world had ceased but for the one shining point that was him.

How could she ever bring herself to give him up, to walk away, again? She clung to him, unwilling to let that moment slip away.

She felt his lips press against her cheek. 'You're safe now, Violet. Let me get you somewhere warm. You're safe, you're safe.'

'I know. Only because of *you*. You always keep me safe.'

He carried her back to that guard's cottage she had noticed as she had made her way to the river, and she saw inside it was small but comfortable, furnished with a cushioned iron chaise and a few chairs as well as a stove for tea. William quickly built up a fire and found some towels, rubbing her hair until it was drying, holding her close. He then loosened her dress so that she could step out of the sodden garment. Carefully wrapping her in some blankets he'd found in the cottage.

'Why did you turn away from me there at the Hermitage?' he asked.

'Because you deserve more than a convenience as a wife. You deserve—everything.'

'Oh, Violet. My darling girl.' He kissed her cheek again, his lips lingering, so warm and sweet against her skin. 'You are all I want, even though you are not *convenient* at all. You are so funny and creative, and sweet and strong. You bring *life* to my life, which has been as cold as this river for too long. I've never known happiness except when I'm with you. I never even thought such a thing could be real. Please, don't send me back to that dark state. I won't let you leave me again. Not unless you can truly say you do not love me.'

'I do love you,' she whispered. It was the hardest, and the easiest, thing she had ever said. 'I love you so much. You are not boring at all, are you? You are complicated and kind, and the most handsome man I have ever seen.'

'Oh, Violet. I do hope I don't bore you.' He drew her even closer, so close they were like one being. 'Then it's settled. We're staying together. Because we love each other.'

'Yes. Because we will always take care of each other.' Violet reached up and caressed his rough cheek, marvelling that this man was hers, just as she was his. That everything had ended in this sweet way.

'And you will marry me? I know I can do anything at all with you beside me.'

And she knew she could do anything with him. That he made her life complete. 'Yes. I will marry you.'

She fell back on the old iron chaise nearby, drawing him with her. He wrapped his arms around her, holding her so close, so very close.

She clumsily, eagerly, unwrapped his scarf and let it fall to the floor at their feet. Something hidden deep inside of her, something urgent and instinctive, guided her as she pushed back his coat, his shirt, as she shyly touched his bare, warm skin and marvelled at the raw, heated life of him. The glorious reality of this moment. He warmed her, healed her, as nothing else could.

Clinging to each other, they tumbled down together, the beamed ceiling whirling over her head. She rolled on top of him, unable to breathe as she studied him in the faint light.

His body seemed gilded, glorious, as if he truly was a god.

Her trembling fingertips traced the coarse sprinkling of dark hair over his chest, the thin line that led tantalisingly to the band of his breeches. His stomach muscles tightened, his breath turning ragged as her touch brushed against him.

'Vi, my darling, be careful,' he gasped. She gloried in ruffling his famous reserve, knowing he felt just as she did in that moment. Overcome with emotion.

'I think this is the very best moment *not* to be careful,' she said, and knew it was true. This moment, being with him—it was the most *right* thing she had ever done.

She fell back into his arms, their lips meeting, heartbeats melding. There was nothing careful or practised about that kiss; it was as hot as summer sun, full of need, like those fireworks bursting in the black St Petersburg sky. She felt the slide of his hands over her back as he removed her damp chemise. The winter air was cold on her skin, but she barely noticed it. Clothing only held her back from what she really wanted, his bare touch on her. She shrugged out of her remaining clothes.

'Violet,' he groaned. 'How beautiful you are.'

She hoped she was, for him. She kissed him again and he rolled her body beneath his. She laughed as her damp hair tumbled from its last pins, spilling around them, binding them together. She *did* feel beautiful as he looked at her, felt free at last, completely herself. He had given her that gift. There was only now, that one moment, fully theirs. Her heart was his and she had been foolish to think she could ever take it back, that she could ever walk away from him. He kissed her again and all thought vanished.

She closed her eyes and let herself revel in the feelings his touch created and in his kiss. Her palm slid over his back, so strong and warm, sheltering her with his strength. Her legs parted and she felt his weight lower between them, a delicious sensation she had never even imagined.

She had read naughty French novels and listened to her sisters' married friends giggling, but she had never known it could feel like this. This heady, dizzy sensation of falling, falling, being caught up by another person and soaring with them into the sky.

'I don't—want to hurt you, Violet,' he said tightly. 'Never.'

She smiled up at him, into the glow of his eyes. 'You never could, Will. Never.'

She spread her legs wider in invitation and he slid into her, making them one. It did hurt a bit, a quick, burning sensation, but it was nothing to the joy of being with him. She arched her back, wrapping her arms and legs around him so tightly he couldn't escape her.

'You see?' she whispered. 'I feel completely perfect.'

'My beautiful Violet,' he gasped roughly. Slowly, so slowly, he moved again within her, drawing back, edging forward, more intimate with each second. She closed her eyes, feeling all that ache ebb away until there was only pleasure. A tingling delight that grew and expanded inside of her, warming her heart like the sun. She'd never imagined anything like it.

She cried out at the wonder of it all, at the

bursts of light she saw behind her eyes, all blue and white and gold, the heat that was almost too much. Would she be consumed by it?

Above her and around her, she felt his body tense and his back arch under her touch. 'Violet!' he shouted out.

She flew apart, clinging to him, and let herself fall down into the fire, surrendering to her feelings for him.

After long moments, she blinked open her eyes, wondering if she really had fallen into a different world. But it was just the rough cottage, warm now from the stove, and his arms around her, keeping her safe.

But the world was *not* the same. That wondrous sparkle followed her, transforming everything forever.

Beside her, collapsed on to the chaise with his arms around her, was her William. She wondered if he was asleep. His eyes were closed, his breath slow, his limbs sprawled in exhaustion, as if, like her, he hadn't been able to rest until this moment.

She smiled at the glorious sight of him, and closed her eyes, letting herself float back down to earth. Nothing else mattered now, only this moment out of time, when she had become someone else in his arms, someone free and beautiful. A real duchess. *His* duchess.

Epilogue

London

'It's here! Look, Vi!' Lily cried as she rushed into the bedchamber.

Violet tried to twist to look at her, but Rose said, 'Don't you dare move, Vi! Or I will never get this straight.'

Violet obediently sat still as Rose arranged the Valenciennes lace veil on her hair, held in place by the diamond-and-pearl Charteris tiara. But she glimpsed a bit of red morocco leather, stamped with gold, in Lily's hand, and she ached to see it. To know it was what she thought it was, that it was real.

'All right, now you can move,' Rose said. 'I think we have done rather a fine job here.'

Violet glanced at herself in the mirror and could hardly believe that was *her*. Her Worth

gown, ice blue silk edged with lace ruffles
and heavy with pearl beadwork, the veil, the
blue velvet train, the sapphire earrings William had given her as a wedding gift, the
bouquet of white roses and deep purple violets—it whispered of such splendour. Such
dignity. In it she would be very much a duchess. No, that could not be her.

But the eager sparkle in her eyes and her
pink cheeks as she imagined seeing her William at the venerable altar of Westminster
Abbey—that was all her. Even with all the
ducal panoply, it would be her and Will, together for the rest of their lives.

'You are indeed a miracle worker, Rose,'
Violet said. 'Now, show me what you have
there, Lily!'

'It just arrived from the publisher. An early
copy,' Lily said. She laid it carefully on the
dressing table.

Violet stared down at it in wonder. *'A Photographic Album of the Royal Wedding*, by
the Duchess of Charteris.' She read the words
the gold letters spelled out. 'They're a bit
early on the name,' she whispered.

'Only for another hour! Look how beautiful it is, Vi.' Lily turned the gilt-edged pages revealing the images Violet had created of St Petersburg, the bridges and palaces, the dancers and skaters, the bride and groom. Grand Duchess Maria certainly did not look like a pug, Violet thought happily, which should please her. She knew the Grand Duchess and her prince, now the Duke and Duchess of Edinburgh, would be among the guests at the Abbey, along with Prince Bertie and his beautiful Alexandra, dukes and duchesses, marquesses and their marchionesses, and American millionaires that her mother had insisted on inviting. She wished she could toss the book to Maria like a bouquet.

But that wouldn't befit the dignity of a duchess.

'It is truly the happiest day of my life,' she gasped. Her true love, her work, a real home—everything was within her grasp now. Perhaps even membership of the Solar Club! The whole world belonged to her. She could barely believe it was true.

'Oh, my darling,' Rose said, and hugged her carefully through the silk and lace and jewels. She was still far too thin in her amethyst taffeta gown, too pale. Violet couldn't understand why Rose wouldn't confide in her if something was amiss. At least they would always be near each other now. 'No one deserves this more than you.'

'Except you and Lily,' Violet said.

Their mother appeared in the doorway, every inch the mother of duchesses, in an amber brocade gown trimmed with sable, a velvet toque pinned with topazes and diamonds on her golden hair. 'The carriage has arrived, girls! Come along, now, we can't be late.'

'Of course,' Violet said, her stomach seizing with nerves. It was really, truly happening. She helped Rose pin on her feathered hat and reached for the bouquet.

Stella straightened Violet's already perfect veil and clucked. 'Oh, my dears, you will never guess what I just heard! The most delicious bit of gossip. Your father's friend Mr Rogers just eloped with Miss Thelma Parker-Parks. Her family was beside themselves! And what do you think, he is not nearly as rich as he said he was, not once your father got him out of the business.'

Violet glanced at her sisters, all of them wide-eyed with amazement. It seemed the perfect touch of absurdity to add to the day. Rogers and Thelma, bound together forever!

There was no time to dwell on it, though. Violet was hurried down to the carriage with her father and, before she could even take a breath, they had arrived at the Abbey, amid the cheers and congratulations of a crowd gathered across from those ancient doors, flower petals showering down on her in blessing.

'I know this wasn't quite what you expected, Papa,' she whispered as he led her into the shadowed church, the beginning of the vast aisle.

He gave a rueful smile. 'Of course not. It's much better. Your mother was right about that. I just hope you'll be happy here, as Lily is.'

She squeezed his arm. 'I know I will be.'

The organ and trumpets sounded out a great fanfare and she started down the aisle, her train held up by a bevy of white-clad bridesmaids, guiding her on a slow march between the soaring stone columns, the shadows and flowers and memorials of that ancient, hallowed place. The place where royalty, and now Violet Wilkins, took their vows. It was awe-inspiring.

But Violet could see only the man who waited for her at the altar, the man who would share everything in her life from that day forward. Her Duke of Bore no longer! Just her love. Her true love, her William.

He smiled at her and took her hand, and every doubt was banished, every fear forgotten. She had every happiness at last.

* * * * *

Author Note

When I started writing Violet's story, I was so excited to combine two of my old passionate interests into one book—the history of the British royal family and nineteenth-century Russia!

I also got to bring in another interest of mine, which might not really seem to fit into the eighteen-seventies—nineteen-thirties screwball comedies! I love it when strait-laced Cary Grant begins to enjoy life, thanks to Katharine Hepburn or Irene Dunne, and learns to have fun at last. I also got to learn about something quite new to me: Victorian photography.

Much like Prince Charles and Lady Diana in the nineteen-eighties, Prince Alfred—the second son of Queen Victoria, and a career naval officer—and Grand Duchess Maria—

the only daughter of Tsar Alexander II, who had many, many sons!—had the wedding of the decade.

They met in 1868, but neither family approved of the match and they didn't marry until January 1874. It was a very lavish wedding, at the Winter Palace—an Orthodox ceremony followed by an Anglican blessing, then a banquet for seven hundred and a ball for three thousand until the early hours of the morning. It was the sensation of the newspapers, with a *Who's Who* guest list of people like the Prince and Princess of Wales, the Princess Royal Vicky and her husband Prince Frederick, and the elderly Ernst, Duke of Saxe-Coburg—who had no legitimate children, so Alfred eventually was his heir.

For more wedding details, I love the sadly now-defunct blog *Order of Sartorial Splendor*, whose archives are a gold mine!

The couple had five children—one son and four daughters, including the famous Marie of Romania—but it was not a happy union in the end. They had little in common and the Prince was often away on his naval assignments. They moved often, including to

Malta and Coburg, and came to be titled the Duke and Duchess of Edinburgh. Maria did not like English life and was a Russian Orthodox grand duchess all her life. She died in 1920 in Switzerland, long after her husband, in reduced circumstances.

I am sure Violet and William are *much* happier in their life together!

One quick note on the photographic exhibition Violet visits: it's based on a famous display in 1864, a 'Bazaar for the Benefit of Female Artists' at the Horticultural Gardens in Chiswick. The photographers Julia Margaret Cameron, Clementina Hawarden, Lewis Carroll and Oscar Rejlander are, of course, real figures—as are the royal family.

If you're curious about the time period, I loved these sources, which you might read for further study!

And do visit me at ammandamccabe.com for more info.

Bibliography

Baird, Julia (2016) *Victoria: The Queen: An Intimate Biography of the Woman who Ruled an Empire* Blackfriars.

Bennett, Daphne (1971) *Vicky: Princess Royal of England and German Empress* Collins and Harvill Press.

Bernard, Bruce (1980) *Photodiscovery: Masterworks of Photography 1840-1940* Harry N. Abrams.

Davenport, Alma (1999) *The History of Photography: An Overview* University of New Mexico Press.

de Guitaut, Caroline and Patterson, Stephen (2018) *Russia: Art, Royalty and the Romanovs* Royal Collection Trust.

Gustavson, Todd (2009) *Camera: A History of Photography from Daguerreotype to Digital* Sterling Publishing Co., Inc.

Hough, Richard Alexander (1993) *Edward and Alexandra: Their Private and Public Lives* St Martin's Press.

Howarth-Loomes, B.E.C. (1974) *Victorian Photography* Ward Lock.

Kschessinska, Mathilde (2019) *Dancing in Petersburg: The Memoirs of Kschessinska—Prima Ballerina of the Russian Imperial Theatre, and Mistress of the Future Tsar Nicholas II* Pantianos Classics.

Marie, Queen of Roumania (2019) *The Story of My Life* Independently published.

McCaffray, Susan (2018) *The Winter Palace and the People: Staging and Consuming Russia's Monarchy, 1754–1917* Cornell University Press.

Olsen, Victoria C. (2018) *From Life: Julia Margaret Cameron and Victorian Photog-*

raphy National Portrait Gallery exhibition catalogue.

Papi, Stefano (2013) *The Jewels of the Romanovs: Family & Court* Thames & Hudson Ltd.

Ridley, Jane (2014) *The Heir Apparent: A Life of Edward VII, the Playboy Prince* Random House.

Tinniswood, Adrian (2018) *Behind the Throne: A Domestic History of the British Royal Household* Jonathan Cape.

Van der Kiste, John (2013) *Alfred: Queen Victoria's Second Son* Fonthill Media.

Vorres, Ian (2002) *The Last Grand Duchess: Her Imperial Highness Grand Duchess Olga Alexandrovna, 1 June 1882-24 November 1960* Key Porter Books Ltd.

LET'S TALK
Romance

For exclusive extracts, competitions
and special offers, find us online:

 facebook.com/millsandboon

 @millsandboonuk

 @millsandboon

Or get in touch on 0844 844 1351*

For all the latest titles coming soon,
visit millsandboon.co.uk/nextmonth

*Calls cost 7p per minute plus your phone company's price per
minute access charge

Want even more
ROMANCE?

Join our bookclub today!